THE CRITICS RAVE ABOUT ED GORMAN AND *COLD BLUE MIDNIGHT!*

"A wonderfully pulpish, greased-lightning homage to Robert Bloch."

—*Kirkus Reviews*

"A darkly humorous Hitchcockian journey, flawlessly conceived and stylishly written."

—*The Mystery and Thriller Guild*

"In this pacy, polished novel nothing is as it seems . . . A riveting read written with insight and skill."

—*Manchester Evening News*

"All the cliches of reviewing come true. You will *not* be able to put his books down. You *will* keep turning the pages. You *will* jump at sudden noises. Gorman's going to be seriously big in a Dean Koontz, Thomas Harris manner. Ed Gorman's coming to get you!"

—*Crime Line*

MORE PRAISE FOR *COLD BLUE MIDNIGHT!*

"Neat twists and Hitchcock-style suspense . . . I strongly urge you to read it."

—*Beyond*

"*Cold Blue Midnight* has everything . . . suspense, dark humor, romance and one of the best murder scenes in contemporary mystery fiction."

—*Mysteries & More*

"One of the best, most under-recognized writers working today."

—*Afraid*

"The modern master of the lean and mean thriller."

—*Rocky Mountain News*

"A master storyteller."

—*Dallas Morning News*

MORE RAVES FOR ED GORMAN!

"The poet of dark suspense." —*Bloomsbury Review*

"One of suspense fiction's best storytellers."
—*Ellery Queen*

"One of our best writers." —*Mystery News*

"Gorman has a wonderful writing style that allows him to say things of substance in an entertaining way."
—*San Francisco Examiner*

Other *Leisure* books by Ed Gorman:
BLACK RIVER FALLS

Cold Blue Midnight

Ed Gorman

LEISURE BOOKS  NEW YORK CITY

I'd like to thank Max Allan Collins for telling me the Leopold-Loeb story, upon which this novel is based.

A LEISURE BOOK®

August 1998

Published by

Dorchester Publishing Co., Inc.
276 Fifth Avenue
New York, NY 10001

ISBN 0-8439-4417-X

Printed in the United States of America.

To two of our favorite people
the Knights—Sue and Tracyl

Prologue

A sunny day in May, 1954. Nothing especially noteworthy – not at the moment, anyway. But watch. Listen. Because what happens in the next hour or so will leave people talking for long years afterward . . .

Evelyn Daye Tappley was just about the best mother of her generation. At least, that's the impression you got if you talked to any of her Junior League friends. If poor seven-month-old David had so much as a sniffle, Evelyn would cancel all her social engagements, even those including any senators or governors her well-connected husband might have invited to the mansion that night. And as for know-how about raising her one and only child . . . Evelyn could quote you chapter and verse from Dr Benjamin Spock's bestseller, *Baby and Child Care*.

Wealthy as her background was – her Ohio family made one of the early fortunes in steel, just about the time Mrs Woodrow Wilson was secretly taking over the White House – Evelyn had seen both her younger brother and sister die from influenza in the terrible epidemic of 1931. She was not about to let a similar fate befall her own child.

On that sunny day in 1954 Evelyn hired two extra workmen to help her seed and plant her half-acre garden on the eastern sweep of the grounds. She left David in the capable care of his nanny, a stout Irishwoman named Margaret Connally. Margaret had been David's nanny since he was brought home from the hospital. Of all the threats to young David, Margaret was perhaps most afraid of kidnappers. No wealthy person in the United States had ever forgotten the sad fate of the Lindbergh baby . . . But thus far in his life, the only thing young David had had to contend with was a predisposition to diaper rash, which often left him irritable late at night after he'd soaked himself while sleeping.

The morning of 5 May went just fine . . .

Early in the afternoon, Margaret Connally decided to bring The Little One, as she inevitably referred to him, outside to enjoy the sun. She herself would sit several feet away in a rocking chair enjoying lemonade and a few pages of the new Agatha Christie paperback she was reading. Evelyn approved of this. Margaret deserved a midday break, and this way she could relax while still keeping an eye on David in his playpen.

Scamper the tabby kitten swatted at the netting of the playpen as David sat in his sailor suit, playing with a gray rubber mouse that squeaked when he pressed it between thumb and forefinger. Scamper always resented being kept outside the playpen.

After her afternoon *Our Father*, *Hail Mary* and *Glory Be* (her Dublin mother having taught her to pray hard even when things were going well; that way God would be even more kindly when things suddenly went badly), Margaret then settled into *The Body in the Library*. She was pleased to find that this was set in a small English village, village mysteries being her favorite kind.

At the same time Margaret began reading, another creature, unseen at this moment, entered the grounds. It had spent the morning in the rocky wooded slopes to the west of the estate. At dawn it had sated itself with a fieldmouse. It was not hungry now, it was merely exploring. The heavy rains of the past few weeks had caused many animals to seek lower lands.

The afternoon wore on . . .

Margaret was very much intrigued with her new Agatha Christie. It was perhaps the best Miss Marple story she'd ever read, especially the daring (for Christie) portrait of the immoral dance-hall girl, for whom Margaret felt great pity.

Scamper hissed and cried as soon as he saw the timber rattler that had eased itself through the netting of the playpen on the far side.

The snake, coiled directly in front of David now, was the color of urine, with dark blotches over its scaly, glistening skin.

That was when, having belatedly recognized Scamper's cry Margaret looked up from her book and saw the serpent in the playpen just as it uncoiled and lashed out at The Little One, its fangs striking him in the chest.

Margaret screamed—

Evelyn had just started working on her tomato plants when she heard the scream. She had no doubt what it signified – that something horrible had happened to David.

Years later she would remember the expression on the face of the workman who swung around to look at her. The scream seemed to have chilled him deeply. He appeared to be paralyzed.

Evelyn took off running.

She saw all this in the next few moments: Margaret hurling her paperback at a huge slithering rattlesnake that was hurrying to escape the playpen—

David falling over on his face, sobbing—

Scamper jumping up perhaps half a foot in the air as the frantic timber rattler hurried past him—

Then Evelyn was reaching into the playpen and lifting her wailing infant into her arms.

And then she was running for the house as a gray-uniformed maid appeared in the back door.

'Call an ambulance! Hurry! Hurry!' Evelyn shrieked.

It was one of those ironies that only the darkest gods in the universe could take any pleasure in.

The ambulance arrived within minutes. The passage to the closest hospital was untroubled. One of the doctors on hand knew, from his Army training at Fort Hood in Texas, exactly how to treat young David.

The injection was given.

The Little One, calmed now, seemed fine. He was put in a private room, assigned round-the-clock nurses.

The doctor, pleased with himself and rightly so, smiled a great deal and invited Evelyn and her husband down to the cafeteria for some coffee. The importance of the Tappley family was not lost on him.

They were three steps from the cafeteria when the doctor's name was called, in a rather frantic way, over the public-address system.

He took off at a trot back the way he'd come.

The Tappleys were only a few steps behind him.

The doctor was joined by two others and they worked without pause for the next hour and a half.

Uselessly.

David had survived the snakebite itself just fine. But he was one of those rare humans to have a violent – and in his case, fatal – reaction to the vaccine . . .

STATEMENT

of Peter Tappley

By the Tuesday of that week I was in pretty bad shape. I didn't even go home. I just kept thinking about the previous Friday night, wondering what had happened exactly. If anything had.

I looked through the ads and found a place in a tranquil old Chicago neighborhood called Edgebrook. It reminded me of how my mother always described her upbringing, where you had a backyard that met a wooded area filled with wildlife. But in Edgebrook you didn't need to be rich. I took a small apartment on a three-month lease, which the landlady was adamant about. 'I run a respectable apartment house,' she said. 'Not a motel.'

I was still counting the hours it had been since I'd taken a drink. A hundred and four. The crying jags were pretty bad by now, as were the shakes. But I wasn't hallucinating, which was a very good sign. No delirium tremens. I ran a low-grade fever and had severe headaches. I was having prostate pain, too, a lot of it sometimes, as if somebody were jabbing me with an ice-pick every few minutes. Sometimes emptying it helped. But I couldn't get an erection. That was a sure sign of the panic state I was in.

Late in the afternoon, as I lay on my bed looking out the

window, I saw a fawn come to the edge of the woods. She was so thin and frail and spindly of gait that I wanted to run out and pick her up the way you would an infant. And then disappear into the woods with her. She would teach me the ways of the shadowy forest, and there I would live for ever, not quite man, not quite beast, and then Friday night would not matter to me anymore.

I stayed three days in the room without eating. Mostly I sweated and slept. On the second day I was able to masturbate but the prostate relief was only temporary. There wasn't even any pleasure in it. Sex was not something I cared to think about at the moment.

I'm not sure when the idea came to me. But I knew right away that it was the only idea that could get me out of my predicament.

In those days, 1979, back before the police were as strict about handguns as they would later become, finding a pawnshop willing to sell you a weapon on the spot was not very difficult. I went down to Maxwell Street, that little hymn to the Third World that the good citizens of Chicago never care to acknowledge, an open-air market of scabrous disease and harsh and myriad foreign languages, and the quick sad cunning of people who live out their lives utterly without joy. I found a gun inside of twenty minutes – a .221 Remington Fireball, a weapon far more powerful than I needed.

I went through the phone book looking for delivery services: there was one just a few miles away. I drove over, parked two blocks past the large cinderblock warehouse, then walked back. The place was laid out simply enough – a small office up front, a huge receiving and dispatching facility in back, with perhaps half a dozen bays for truck repair. This was 8:30 in the morning. Some drivers were just getting started for the day. I walked to a far door and then hurried inside and over to a truck that had just been loaded. I stayed in the deep morning shadows, looking around to see if anybody in the big echoing warehouse had seen me. Apparently not. I snuck aboard the truck and hid in the back.

Fifteen minutes later, the truck driver climbed in, heavy enough that the truck tilted to the right when he did.

I let him get a couple of miles from the warehouse and stop at a light before I hit him. I got him with the butt of the Remington right on the crown of the head. He slumped over immediately. He hadn't seen me at all. I dragged him into the back of the truck and hit him again to make sure he stayed out. I took his place in the seat and drove to an alley four blocks away. I went in the back and bound, gagged and blindfolded him with stuff I'd brought along. He was still out. I took his uniform off and put it on. The sleeves were too long so I rolled them up. Same with the trouser legs. I then drove back to Maxwell Street where I bought a large steamer trunk with a sticker that said WORLD'S FAIR 1939. The interior of the trunk smelled like 1939, too.

The address I wanted was over in Montclare. By now it was raining, which would be helpful. A guy in a service uniform was anonymous enough; a guy in a service uniform in the rain was virtually invisible. Nobody would pay any attention.

I was still hoping that nothing had happened, that it was all just panic and fantasy.

By the time I pulled up behind the two-story white apartment building, the truck driver had come awake and started muttering beneath his tape. I went back and hit him once more and once more he was blessedly silent.

I opened the rear doors of the truck and took down a dolly. Then I reached up and pulled down the steamer trunk, using the dolly to transport it inside the building and up the dusty carpeted stairs to apartment 6B. The hall smelled of cigarette smoke and long-dead sunlight – a scent that had traveled millions and millions of miles.

I knocked and there was no answer but then I hadn't really been expecting any.

I snugged my leather gloves even tighter and then went to work with two of the picks a felonious friend of mine had once given me to hold as collateral on a two-hundred-dollar loan. The picks never failed me, but the friend had: I never saw him again. Within thirty seconds I was opening the door and pushing dolly and trunk inside.

There is something almost sexually intimate about being in somebody's residence when you're not supposed to. You are walking around in the echoes of their secrets, the things – beliefs, desires, longings – they whisper only to themselves, that nobody else will ever know.

For a long and almost giddy time, I sensed that the apartment was empty and that I had therefore been worried about nothing.

No, I hadn't actually come back from a tavern with a woman and then, just as we were making love, cut her throat. No, it had all been a terrible nightmare. Yes, I'd been here but I'd gone home and nothing bad had happened. She hadn't answered her phone in the following days simply because she'd been called out of town. Simple explanation. Sane and Simple. Unlike the shadowy fantasies of my imagination.

I followed the smell to the bedroom, the odor redolent of the sickly-sweet smell of pigpens on the hot summer days when we used to visit my uncle's farm.

She was sprawled naked across the bed. There was red from her blood and yellow from her urine and brown from her feces on the otherwise white chenille spread. Her skin was the blue of deep and abiding bruises, and a curious buff-blue film covered the whites of her brown eyes. Her legs were spread and her sex looked lonely and vulnerable, exposed that way. Blood had sprayed across the white wall behind her.

Getting her in the trunk took twenty-five minutes and in order to do it, to fit her inside properly, I had to break both of her arms and one of her legs. Thunder rumbled across the gray mid-morning sky as I worked, and rain slid down the dusty windows, sealing me into a melancholy I didn't need.

When I was all finished, when I'd made certain that every inch of the trunk's exterior was clean of her fluids, I hefted it onto the dolly and exited the apartment, locking the door behind me. Then I took the trunk down to the truck. I had to give our friend the driver another slam across the back of the head. He was going to have one terrible headache later on.

There was a point on the river, twenty miles to the east, where a stand of second-growth trees gave a man some protection from curious eyes.

I got her to the river's edge, the chill filthy water lapping as far up as my knees, and then I took hold of the trunk-handle and dragged her as far out as I could, careful not to step off into some unseen hole on the murky bottom and drown.

The current was fast. The water was murky all the way down. In moments, the trunk sank without trace. Perfect.

I drove the truck back to the city, dressed the driver in his clothes once more then left him in the blind and empty alley. Probably wouldn't be found for awhile.

Back in my room, I slept for the next two days. I awoke feeling pretty good. I took a long and steamy shower, put on fresh clothes, packed up all my stuff into the leather briefcase I carried, and left the key behind on the dresser along with a note that said: I've decided to patch things up with my wife. I've enjoyed my stay here. Thank you.

Everybody likes a happy ending, even crabby landladies.

There was going to be an execution and it was going to be a good one. The prisoner was rich, handsome and only thirty-two years old. You couldn't ask for more excitement than that.

The morning of the execution, a long, expensive mobile van pulled up to the prison gates. It was a gray and rainy day.

The gates swung open but the van remained still.

Two armed guards in black rain ponchos appeared and began walking around the van, checking every inch of it. Finished with the exterior, one of the guards knocked on the side door and went inside. He reappeared five minutes later. Presumably, he had checked the inside as assiduously as he had checked the outside.

More than one hundred reporters watched the guards do their job, though exactly what that job was, the reporters didn't understand.

To whom did the van belong?

What were the guards looking for?

Would the van ultimately be allowed inside the high gray walls of the institution?

The last question was answered soon. The guards, apparently satisfied that the van was not carrying any kind of contraband, waved it inward. The gates closed immediately. All this was overseen by two other poncho-clad guards toting shotguns.

The reporters went back to their own vans and trucks and cars to wait out the rest of the long day.

Only the protestors were dutiful. They had been marching with their picket signs since just after dawn.

ONLY GOD SHOULD
TAKE A LIFE

was typical of the placards they carried. For some reason, all the protestors, at least half of whom were clergy of one kind or another, were fat. And that gave them a certain pathetic, almost comic look as they strode up and down the parking lot adjacent to the institution in their dark, bulky rainclothes. They looked like a species of animal that had been neither clever enough nor strong enough to survive.

The printing on their placards began to run with rainwater. One of them read:

ONL G D CA
JUDG A SOUL

Many of the reporters had taken to betting. A thirty-two-year-old rich boy like Peter Emerson Tappley was probably going to get a reprieve. True, all the lower courts had ruled against Tappley. And true, the Supreme Court had decided just this morning *not* to grant a stay. But Governor Edmonds – even given the tight race he was in against a very tough law-and-order candidate – owed the Tappley family a lot. Some said he even owed them the Governor's mansion. So the bets were that he'd draw it out as long as possible and then say, at the very last moment, that he'd wrestled with his soul (the Governor actually said things like that) and concluded that there was enough evidence to grant a stay.

Maybe Peter Emerson Tappley really hadn't raped and cut up those three women seven years ago.

An hour after the van entered the prison grounds, a pool was started. People bet on various times that the Governor would order the stay.

The ritual for execution was unvarying, even for a prominent inmate like Peter Tappley. He was given the breakfast of his choice (oatmeal and wheat toast with strawberry jam and a large glass of orange juice and two cups of coffee) served to him in the privacy of his death row cell.

Then he was moved down the hall to a special visiting room where he began receiving a succession of guests, all emerging from the expensive van that belonged to his mother.

First came his sister Doris, who spent half an hour with him; and then his beloved mother. White-haired, handsome and matriarchal as ever, Evelyn Daye Tappley spent three hours alone with her son. She even shared a few bites of the club steak he was brought for his lunch. It was quite good, actually.

In the afternoon, Doris came back, joining her mother and brother. There was a great deal of tension, as one might expect, but there were more than a few smiles and laughs as they all remembered long-ago days when (or so it seemed) the sun had always beamed, the sky was a beautiful cornflower blue, and life was filled with puppy dogs and croquet games on the lawn and dips in the family pool. Tears merged with laughter, and Evelyn and Doris seemed to be constantly hugging Peter.

All this stopped at 3:07 p.m., when Jill Coffey was let into the room by a guard.

Jill, dark-haired, blue-eyed, pretty in a casual and freckled way, was Peter's wife. Or had been up until the divorce two years ago, just at the time Peter began exhausting the last rounds of his appeals.

The Tappley family ceased talking.

They all stared at Jill.

'It wasn't necessary for you to be here,' Evelyn said.

'I wanted to be,' Jill told her.

She knew how much they despised her, and always had. For one thing, while her father had been a prominent banker in a small downstate Illinois town, Jill had hardly been the social equal of the Tappley family. For another, she had not hesitated to tell Peter how much she disapproved of his family.

'I don't want you here,' Evelyn said.

'Mother,' Doris said, embarrassed. 'She has a right to be here if she wants to be.'

Jill had always felt that Doris was her secret friend. Doris could never be demonstrative about this because her mother would get angry, but during the roughest spots in Jill's marriage, Doris had always been there to comfort her. Jill and Peter had lived in the family mansion ninety miles due west of Chicago. Doris was an inmate in the same prison. She still lived there, though her nervous little husband had moved out long ago.

Evelyn was too angry to control herself. 'If she'd been a decent wife to my son, he wouldn't be here today. I blame that damned job of hers—'

Doris blushed, her angular but pretty face touched by tiny red spots on her cheeks. Even for Evelyn, this was an irrational outburst. Both Peter and Doris had fought Jill's determination to keep taking photography assignments in

Chicago. To satisfy them – Evelyn felt that a woman who worked was unseemly, overlooking the fact that she herself commanded an empire, and frequently put in twelve-hour days six days a week – Jill had quit for nearly a year but she missed the work too much to stay away from it any longer. And as soon as she'd started taking assignments again, driving in from the mansion to Chicago a few days a week, her marriage had gone into a steep decline. Peter had been so threatened by her job that he became impotent.

And apparently, about the same time, he also began stalking and murdering women.

'I don't want you here,' Evelyn hissed. 'You wait out in the hall till Doris and I are finished.'

Jill looked at Peter and Doris. As usual, they were clearly intimidated by their mother.

Peter especially seemed resentful of Evelyn. But he nodded quietly, a somewhat frail man now, the old handsomeness gaunted out of him, in a prison uniform as gray and cold as the rainy sky outside.

'I'll be back,' Jill said to Peter.

She waited forty-five minutes in the hall. A guard brought her bitter black coffee. The assistant warden showed up once and asked her if she wouldn't be more comfortable in the lounge. She thanked him but said no.

The prison was an echo chamber of hard harsh noises, gates slamming shut, prisoners shouting at each other, footsteps marching down vast hollow corridors. In some ways, the noises frightened Jill as much as the walls themselves, as much as the armed guards in the towers. In prison, there would be no true silence in which to think and be alone. Ever.

Evelyn made a point of ignoring Jill as the assistant warden led the two women from the visiting room.

A guard took Jill in, shutting the door behind her.

Peter stood at a barred window, staring out.

'It's a good day for it, anyway,' he said, turning back to her and smiling. 'I mean, I'd be really pissed off if the sun was shining and everybody was outdoors having a good time. If I have to suffer, they should suffer, too.'

She said nothing. Just watched him.

The room was small. Dusty. It contained an overstuffed couch and two overstuffed chairs. Two empty Diet Coca-Cola cans sat on the floor next to the couch. The floor had been waxed, but more than anything the room smelled of strong disinfectant. She was sure this would be the dominant smell of the prison.

'Any particular reason you came to see me?' Peter enquired, his grin making him suddenly handsome again. She remembered what it had been like to be in love with him. He'd been a lot of fun, he really had. God, she'd loved him so deeply and truly it had been almost painful. And it had certainly been scary. Neither before nor since, had she been able to give herself to a man with such abandon. 'You didn't bring me a cake with a file in it or anything, did you?' he went on.

She smiled. 'Afraid not.'

His grin faded. 'Evelyn still thinks there's going to be a reprieve.'

He'd always called her Evelyn as a way of proving to himself that he had some distance on her.

'But there isn't,' he said. 'The public likes the idea that a rich guy is going to get fried. They think it proves that this is a democratic country, after all.' The smile again, sad this time. 'What a way to prove it, huh?'

He hadn't mentioned the women he'd killed. He never did. That was how she'd known, in the days following the police first coming to the mansion and questioning him, that he was a sociopath. He felt no guilt for what he'd done, merely a kind of ironic anger that he'd been caught. Ted Bundy had been very much like that.

'Why have you come, Jill?'

She'd known he would ask this. She wished she had an answer. 'Oh, I suppose because we were in love once, and had such high fine dreams together for our future, and because you'll always be a part of me – even after everything that happened.'

'The women, you mean?'

She nodded. Could he just once say how sorry he was for what he'd done?

He said, 'You know, I never would've killed them if you hadn't gone back to work.'

She waited for the grin. He had always been good at mocking his mother. Wasn't he mocking her now, her absurd notion of somehow blaming Jill for the murders?

'You went bitch on me, Jill. Just like a woman.'

They were standing barely inches apart. He took his finger and jabbed it angrily at her breastbone. 'You had to have a job. Had to get back into the Chicago thing. How many of those guys were you screwing on the side, anyway?'

She didn't know what to say. But that was all right, because he wasn't done.

His face was a mask of rage, of dark frantic eyes that bulged, of lips frothy with spittle, of cheeks flushed with crimson.

'When I was cutting those women up, I was thinking of you, Jill. I really was.'

The grin again, but this time she saw the insanity in it.

She started backing toward the door.

Preparing herself to call out for the guard in case he wasn't looking through the observation window.

'I could've saved myself a lot of hassle, couldn't I? I should've just killed you. You were the one I wanted: you and all the guys in Chicago you used to shack up with.'

She'd always known he was jealous. *But not like this*.

He sprang.

She was shocked by both his speed and strength as his hands took her throat and he slammed her back into the wall.

She had time for a single, muffled scream.

He went to serious work on her. She could feel the anger increasing in his iron hands and fingers.

And then the door was bursting open.

And two guards were grabbing him.

And tearing him away from her.

And one guard was bringing his wooden baton down hard across the back of Peter's skull.

And another guard was leading her, dazed and shocked and terrified, from the room to the assistant warden's office around the corner.

She didn't see Evelyn or Doris again that day.

After a long, rambling and apologetic speech from the assistant warden, she was taken out the back way, put into the rear of a panel truck so the press couldn't see her, and driven back to her motel.

There was a bar adjacent to the motel. Though she was not especially fond of alcohol, she had two very stiff drinks of whisky and then went back to her room, taking a turkey sandwich and a small bag of potato chips with her.

Without quite knowing why, she spent several minutes checking the locks on the doors and windows.

She had this image of Peter. She'd never known how much he hated her, how much he'd wanted to kill her.

But checking the locks . . .

Did she think he was going to somehow escape prison tonight and come kill her?

She took a long, hot, relaxing shower.

When she was toweled dry and ensconced in her favorite pink cotton pajamas – she had never forgotten her sweet mother's advice that dark-haired girls always looked good in pink – she slid between the covers, clicking on the TV remote as she did so.

She hoped there was some kind of mindless comedy on tonight. She needed that kind of escape.

She wished she'd never come up here now.

She wished she'd never seen Peter as she'd seen him just a few hours ago.

This was how she'd remember him. For ever.

The motel didn't have cable, just the three networks – which meant that she didn't have much choice as to programing.

She ate her sandwich and half the chips, and occupied herself with a rerun of a wooden romantic comedy.

But at least no women were being ripped apart in it.

At least no sociopath's face was filling the screen as he screamed the word 'bitch' over and over again.

She drifted in and out of sleep several times.

Thunder woke her.

Thunder had always scared her. As a child, she'd seen a Disney movie in which a little girl was lost in a vast and terrifying forest. Thunder and lightning had stalked the girl like the wrath of a dark and disapproving god.

A moment of disorientation: a motel room that still managed to look like 1958 right down to the pressed-wood blond furnishings.

Where was she?

Who was she?

Peter's face. Shrieking at her.

His hands. On her throat.

Guards racing in—

Homely, familiar images now: the potato-chip sack on the night-table next to her; her rain-speckled tan suede car coat hung to dry over the back of the desk chair; a bit of brown paper bag sticking up from the small waste-can to the left of the front door.

Her eyes moved to the dark TV. She needed some human contact, even if it was secondhand.

She found the remote and thumbed it to ON.

A newsman standing in front of the prison. Night. Rain. The reporter huddled beneath his umbrella, speaking into the microphone in his right hand. He wore a trench coat and looked suitably grim, especially under the stark TV lights.

'Unless there's a last-minute reprieve, Bev, the execution is scheduled to take place just about one hour from now. At midnight.'

An off-camera voice: 'Michael, why don't you tell our viewers how a prisoner is prepared for execution?'

The reporter nodded. 'Well, there really isn't anything remarkable about it, Bev. Most of the day, the prisoner spends with his loved ones. Then, after they're escorted out, the chaplain comes in and remains for some time with the prisoner. And then the prisoner is showered and shaved for the execution.'

'I'm not sure what "shaved" means in this context, Michael.'

'Well, execution by electrocution means that electricity is conveyed into the body at specific points. They shave an area on the prisoner's left knee, so the electrode will fit nice and tight, and then they shave a five-inch circle on the crown of his head so the metal cap will fit. By the way, he's given special trousers with the left seam cut from cuff to knee so they can place the electrode with no problem.'

'Then he's ready to be executed?'

'Just about. They take him to the execution chamber and sit him in the chair and get him ready and then the assistant warden comes in and reads the prisoner the death warrant. And then the assistant warden makes a final call to the Attorney General to see if there's been a last-minute reprieve of any kind. And if not . . . Well, if not, Bev, the prisoner receives approximately two thousand seven hundred volts AC and five amperes of electrical current – and he usually dies within a few minutes.'

'Usually but not always?'

'Well, there was a case last year in New York where the electrodes weren't fitted snugly and it took the prisoner more than twelve minutes to die – and he was crying out for help all the time. I'm told it was a pretty grisly—'

'Hold on, Michael. They're telling me something in my ear.'

The camera held on the trench-coated reporter. You could hear the protestors chanting off-camera.

Then: 'Michael, we've just been informed that the Governor's office – and this is official as of 11:07 p.m. – will not (repeat: *will not*) issue a stay of execution. So Peter Emerson Tappley will be put to death in the electric chair tonight in, according to the studio clock, just fifty-three minutes.'

Jill thumbed off the TV.

Sat there unmoving in her frivolous pink pajamas in this ancient, worn motel room that smelled of cigarette smoke and mildew, and whispered of loneliness and adultery.

Soon now, it would be over, the life of the man she'd once loved so much but hadn't really known at all.

Not a word of remorse for what he'd done: that's what bothered her most.

Not a single word of remorse.

She went to the bathroom.

When she came back, she found a *Honeymooners* rerun and made a singular effort not to look at her little portable alarm clock.

She didn't want to know.

She didn't want to mark his passing.

Ralph Kramden said, 'Honey, you're the greatest!' just as she heard somebody on the rainy drive outside let out a cowboy yelp. 'Yahoo! Fry, sucker, fry!' She hadn't wanted to stay in this rundown place but it was the only accommodation she could find. All the decent motels had been commandeered by the press.

'Yahoo!' somebody else shouted.

They were celebrating.

They sounded drunk, and absolutely delighted.

The Boogeyman was dead.

She did not sleep well, waking several times to the eerie shifting shadows, and the eerie shifting silence, of this battered old room.

She rose early, packed and checked out.

Just as she turned away from the registration desk, the desk clerk said, 'Oh, I forgot. Somebody dropped this off for you.'

A fancy buff-blue envelope. She recognized the author at once. Evelyn Tappley.

Jill didn't open the envelope until she was in her car.

There was a handwritten note in the middle of the elegant blue page:

I hope you're happy, you
bitch. You'll pay for what you
did to my son, I promise you.
Evelyn Daye Tappley.

Part One

Chapter One

21 October

His ass was tired. But then, when Rick Corday pulled a surveillance job, his ass was always tired. He lifted his right cheek now and scratched. It was numb. He'd been sitting too long.

He looked at the array of stuff he always took with him when he pulled surveillance. Wrigley's Spearmint gum. Life Savers peppermints. Johnson & Johnson Dental Floss. A penknife for cleaning his fingernails. A copy of the new *Guys! Guys! Guys!*.

His car phone rang. 'Uh-huh?' he said after picking it up.

'It's me. Adam.'

'She's still in there. Saw a couple of people carrying stuff in and out. She must have a session.'

'I have to go to New York.'

Corday didn't say anything.

'Are you still there?'

'What's this New York crap?'

'You seem to forget who I used to work for.'

'So that means New York?'

'I have to make a little correction on a job I did awhile back. Somebody else connected with the case.'

You might think, from some of the language, that Rick and Adam were cops. They weren't. Rick was a former employee of a large investigative agency here in Chicago, while Adam was a former Los Angeles police detective. One of the things they had in common was that they killed people. Sometimes for fun. Sometimes for profit. Rick always preferred the former.

'Nothing's going to happen.'

'Right.'

'I told you, Rick. I'm really trying to change.'

'So far I haven't noticed. I mean, you were pretty drunk when you got home the other night. And pretty late.'

'Perfectly innocent. Hit a few bars was all.'

'Right.'

'When we wrap this up – with Jill, I mean – how about we take a vacation?'

'Just you and me and one of your new friends, huh?'

'There's no sense talking to you when you're in this kind of mood.'

'This New York thing pisses me off.'

'I'll be back in a week. Just keep watching Jill. But don't do anything till I get back, all right?'

'Yessir, your highness.'

'You can really be hard to take sometimes, Rick, you know that?'

'And you can't?'

'I'll call you from New York.'

'Right,' Rick said. And broke the connection.

The sonofabitch, Rick thought. The unfaithful sonofabitch.

Chapter Two

24 October

He was there again on Tuesday, the man in the blue Volvo. As usual, he spent his time pretending to read a magazine. Every few minutes, however, he'd look across the street at the small two-story building that was both Jill's work studio and her apartment.

This was the fourth day in two weeks he'd been here, and this time Jill was ready for him.

Grabbing her 35mm Nikon with the telephoto lens, she snapped a couple of shots, then walked quickly to the back of the apartment and went down the stairs leading to the alley. She couldn't see his license plates from her window.

The smoky smell of October made her nostalgic for her girlhood. Hallowe'en pumpkins to carve. Costumes to try on – she'd always wanted to be Cinderella. And stories to whisper excitedly among the other kids about which neighbors were secretly monsters and had dungeons instead of basements – dungeons in which evil creatures of every kind imaginable lurked.

Now Jill was about to deal with a real monster.

The Lake View East area of Chicago was, as always,

getting a partial face-lift. Lake View dated back to the last century and today its homes and buildings replicated perfectly a charming and more leisurely era. The city planned to keep it that way, too. Today a crew was painting the benches in a small park area a merry green color.

At two in the afternoon, the street was crowded. A lot of artisans had moved in lately, combining living space with working space, so traffic was now more intense. Many of the small businesses used awnings as decoration and to lessen the hot Indian-summer sunlight. The street looked tidy and smart.

The blue Volvo was still there.

Jill walked half a block down the street away from the blue car then turned suddenly and started snapping pictures of it.

She took twenty shots in all, the long-distance lens allowing her to get several clear profiles of the man as he stared at her building, and even the trunk sticker that gave the name of the dealer who'd sold the man the car. She still couldn't get the license number because of the car parked behind it.

The air smelled of gasoline and cigarette smoke and heat. She sneezed. She had terrible allergies.

The man surprised her by suddenly starting his car and driving away.

She took a few more snaps of him as he drove off.

She worried that maybe he'd spotted her – but no, that was unlikely. From where he'd sat, seeing her emerge from the alley was virtually impossible. And her camera position had been completely out of his sight.

Satisfied that she'd gotten everything she'd needed – much more, in fact – she went back inside and got to work.

Jill had souped her first photographs while she'd been on

the staff of her high-school paper in Springfield. She had never gotten over the seeming magic of it all.

You had developing tank and printing frame and printing paper, you had printing trays and developer and stop bath and fixer, you had film clips and printing tongs and safelight – nothing remarkable about any of these elements when you looked at them individually. In fact, they were all disappointingly mundane.

But if you knew how to use them properly, if you became a skilled technician in the holy gloom of the darkroom, then you truly became a wizard because you could reproduce life as you saw it . . . and sometimes you could even enhance life and its dramatic effects, as she'd done from the first time she'd ever seen an Edward Steichen black and white photo. The great photographer had died in 1973, but his influence and style lived on in Jill and a thousand other Jills around the world.

She went right to work on the photos of the man and the blue Volvo. All the sights, smells and tiny noises of the developing process buoyed her.

She would find out who the man was and what he wanted, and then she would deal with him appropriately.

When everything was under way, and it was safe to make her call, she stepped outside the darkroom and lifted the receiver on the wall phone. The darkroom was in the rear of the first floor. At the front of the large ground floor was the studio itself. Lights, tripods, cables and props left over from yesterday's shoot littered the floor. She'd done stills for the Down's Syndrome Society, a freebie because she made a very good living and wanted to give something back. The lady from the Society had brought in six children suffering from the condition and each one of them had broken Jill's heart. She turned every photograph into a masterpiece of compassion. This was the kind of work she loved, but in order to do it – at least for now – she also had to shoot portraits of arrogant business leaders, pompous politicians and strutting jocks. Having an original Jill Coffey portrait of yourself was something devoutly to be desired in the Chicago area.

She thought of the old brick convent she wanted to shoot someday soon. It was kind of an old nuns' graveyard, all these ancient, wrinkled, honorable women pushed away even by their own church, and utterly forgotten. Jill wished to capture their sorrow and their isolation. She needed a three-day shoot to do it properly. She also needed a big-money project that would finance her three-day shoot.

'Kate?'

'Changed your mind about dinner tonight, eh? I knew you would.'

Jill hadn't had to identify herself. Best friends didn't need to trifle with such formalities.

'He was here again today,' Jill said.

'The guy in the blue Volvo?'

'Uh-huh.'

'Remember that football player I used to go out with?'

Jill laughed. 'The one who thought Burt Reynolds should try his hand at Shakespeare? What was that title you came up with? "Smokey and King Lear Go To London"?'

'Well, cultured he wasn't but what he was, was one mean psycho after he'd had a couple of drinks. Maybe I should call him up and have him give you a hand. Two drinks would be all it'd take.'

'He's probably a reporter.'

'Who – the creep in the blue Volvo?'

'Sure, from one of those TV tabloids. Remember three years ago?'

Kate might have forgotten already, but Jill certainly hadn't. One day as she'd been leaving an office building in the Loop, she'd noticed a short blond man with a slight limp. Then she started noticing him again and again over the next few days. Everywhere that Jill went, so went the short blond man with the slight limp.

Only after four days of this, and three useless calls to the police, was Jill able to find out who the man was and what he was all about.

She'd been in Neiman-Marcus and suddenly couldn't deal with him trailing her any longer.

Right there in the middle of the store, with ever so many disapproving matrons looking on, Jill had confronted the man and asked him exactly what the hell he thought he was doing.

A TV tabloid reporter. That was who he was. That was what he was doing.

His syndicated show was doing a piece on *My Husband the Serial Killer*, about three wives who'd been married to multiple murderers and how they'd coped with the aftermath of their husbands' trials, and their own public shame.

Jill had refused to cooperate, of course. But that had not mattered.

One sunny April morning, as she was sipping her first cup of coffee in her tiny breakfast nook and listening to all the spring-sweet birds, she saw her own image on the 11-inch black-and-white TV set she kept on the kitchen counter.

'Did you know that prominent Chicago photographer Jill Coffey was actually the wife of notorious serial killer Peter Tappley? How do wives of serial killers cope with their lives after their husbands have been put to death?' (Here Jill's photo was joined with the images of two other women.) 'Find out tonight when *Hard Facts* presents *My Husband the Serial Killer*.'

They hadn't needed her cooperation.

They'd just gone to a few old friends – and a few old enemies – and gotten most of what they needed.

And what they couldn't get from those sources, they'd simply made up.

The weeks following the *Hard Facts* story had been miserable for Jill. While many within the Chicago advertising community had known about her former marriage to Evelyn Tappley's son, it was rarely mentioned. Her talent and her general good nature had made her a lot of friends and nobody wanted to see her suffer for something over which she had had no control.

Peter had killed those women, not Jill.

But for the three months following the *Hard Facts* story, Jill had experienced her first taste of notoriety – and had hated it. The cynical and knowing gaze, the quick smirk, the whispers – she'd been treated to them all and had felt a curious shame, as if this was just the kind of treatment she deserved.

So this time she was going to stop it before it started.

This time she was going to find out which trashy TV show or newspaper the man in the blue Volvo worked for, and she was going to get an injunction.

Surely a judge would be sympathetic once she told him what had happened following the *Hard Facts* story.

Peter was now six years dead, and Jill wanted him to stay dead.

'You remember when you hired that private detective?' she said to Kate.

'Marcy?'

'That's right,' Jill said. 'Marcy. What's her last name?'

'Marcy Browne. With an "e" on the end. Why?'

'I'm going to have her check out this guy in the blue Volvo.'

'What about the police?'

'First of all, what am I going to tell them? That there's a man who sits in a blue Volvo on a very busy street and he irritates me? And second of all, I don't want anything official to happen. Official means the press will get involved because they'll hear about it somehow. I just want Marcy to find out who the guy works for and then I'll hire a lawyer and threaten some kind of legal action. If an injunction doesn't work, then I'll threaten a lawsuit. I don't want to go through it again, Kate. I really don't.'

'God, I don't blame you. I just hope Marcy can do something.'

'Well, she can find out who he is if nothing else.'

'You sure you don't want to have Chinese tonight?'

'Maybe tomorrow night. Anyway, what happened to The Hunk?'

Kate laughed. 'He's doing just fine, thank you.' Kate had been the most famous runway model to ever come from Chicago, glamorous, beautiful and a resolute heartbreaker. She changed men frequently.

Jill's phone signaled a call waiting. Convenient as it was, call waiting could also be a royal pain in the butt. Jill and Kate always joked that one day one of them would be shouting frantically, 'And the killer is—' But then call waiting would interrupt them and the identity of the killer would remain forever unknown.

'I'll be right back,' Jill promised, and she depressed the phone button.

A male voice said, 'Jill? It's me, Eric.'

'Hi.'

'You sound as enthused as always.'

'Eric, we just don't have anything to say to each other anymore. I wish you could try to understand that.'

She hated the whiny note in her voice but she was getting

exasperated with the man. When she'd come back to Chicago following the execution, she'd had little luck in establishing a freelance business. Eric Brooks had just left one of the big ad agencies to start his own, and he needed money. She gave him her modest inheritance and together they formed a partnership. Within a year, Brooks-Coffey was one of the hottest shops in the Midwest. Eric was creative, bold and relentless. He was also egocentric, dishonest and so driven to sexual conquest that Jill sometimes wondered if he weren't insecure about his masculinity. After three years, they'd parted company. She'd made enough money on the partnership to set up her own photography studio. But Eric still called every few months, always trying to sound as if they were old friends who just couldn't wait to be together again. That might be Eric's feeling on the matter but it certainly wasn't Jill's. He had never managed to sleep with her and so she became this overwhelming object of importance to him. Somehow, someday, he was going to slip her into his bed. He was obviously certain of that.

'I need you to come to my office.'

'For what?'

'Strictly business. We're doing a new corporate brochure about ourselves and it probably won't surprise you that I want to be the center of attention.'

As she listened to him, she played with a pair of long scissors with orange rubber-tipped handles. She couldn't remember buying these but maybe they were an old pair she'd forgotten about. Such were the mysterious ways of households.

'Eric, I'm on the other phone. Let me call you back.'

'Ten thousand dollars – that's the figure to keep in your head. Ten thousand, just for a few hours' work of shooting me in various setups at the office.'

The convent. The aged nuns. Of course! It was as if Eric had read her mind, the bastard.

She certainly couldn't just turn him down.

She'd at least have to think about it . . .

'How about my office in two hours?' Eric said.

She felt rushed, confused, resentful.

Damn call waiting, anyway.

Then she smiled at herself: that was certainly a mature response to her little dilemma. Blaming call waiting.

'I can't make it at five. Will you be there at seven?'

'Hey, babe, remember me? I'm the original workaholic. Of course I'll be here at seven.'

'All right, I'll see you then.'

She punched back to Kate. 'God, I'm sorry.'

'That's all right. I wanted to read that novel anyway. It was only six hundred pages and I had plenty of time while I was waiting for you.'

'Eric.'

'Eric Brooks?'

'One and the same.'

'That jerk. What'd he want?'

'Ostensibly he wants me to take his photo.'

'He's still trying to get you into bed, isn't he?'

'Maybe he's changed,' Jill said.

'Why can't guys like him be impotent?'

'But he's making it very difficult for me. He's offering me ten thousand dollars to shoot him for his corporate brochure.'

'I'd shoot him for a lot less than that.'

'You know that convent idea I told you about?'

'Uh-huh.'

'Well, for ten thousand dollars I could close the shop down an entire week and really do the convent photos right.'

'Then I guess it'd be worth it.'

'I mean, I've held him off for a long time now. I guess I could hold him off for a few more hours.'

'Just remember to wear that nuclear-powered chastity belt I got you for your last birthday.'

Jill smiled. 'God, Kate, thanks for being my friend. I'd go insane without you, I really would.'

'So you going to call Marcy?'

'Soon as we hang up.'

'That's Browne with an—'

'Browne with an "e".'

'Smart-ass.'

'I'd better get back to the darkroom.'

'Let me know how it goes with Marcy.'

'I will. I'll call you tonight.'

They hung up.

Jill went to the darkroom. She needed to do some printing and enlarging of the photos she wanted to show Marcy Browne.

Chapter Three

Rick Corday rented a small storage shed near the north side. The area had become so violent that he kept swearing to get a garage someplace else but as yet he hadn't gotten around to it.

Now, as he pulled up to his small shed, one of a hundred such sheds inside the cyclone fencing, he saw the two teenage boys he'd had some trouble with the last time.

One white, one black.

They'd called him a name he hadn't liked at all and he'd given them the finger.

As he'd pulled away, they'd thrown rocks at his car.

Now, getting out of the car, he observed them. They were a hundred yards away, near the entrance, watching him.

This wasn't a good time to harass him.

He was still very angry with Adam. Adam always played so many mind games. He knew Rick was a hypochondriac, for instance, so he was always telling Rick how pale and sick he looked. And when they watched TV talk shows, Adam always said, 'That sounds like you, Rick,' whenever somebody had some real head problems – like the guy that killed his mother and then skinned her and wore her around the house all day. And Rick, who was very insecure, always bought in. He was just too suggestible – believing virtually everything Adam told him.

Adam.

The bastard would never be faithful: never. Wouldn't even make the attempt.

Rick took his keys from his pocket, unlocked the shed, walked in and looked around. He heard the distant barking of angry dogs.

Rick was an orderly guy. Boxes were stacked neatly on either side of the small shed. He needed the one containing his winter boots and parka and windshield scraper – all the accoutrements to get through a Midwestern winter.

He took down the box. Hidden behind it was a small suitcase; a quarter of a million dollars was in it. He picked up the box. Then he went outside and locked the shed and turned around and looked at the two teenagers standing there.

One white, one black.

'You gave us the finger the other day,' the black one said.

'Oh, yeah?'

Rick just went on about his business, saying nothing more.

He opened the car door and slid the box in on the backseat.

And that's when the white one made his move.

Put his hand on Rick's shoulder. Tried to spin him around.

Rick brought his knee up and hit the boy square in the groin.

He pushed the boy over backwards.

All the kid could do was hold his crotch and roll around on the ground.

'Hey, man, you can't do that,' the black one protested.

Rick pushed his angry face up against the kid's face. 'Oh, yeah? Who's gonna stop me?'

The black kid kind of shrunk in on himself.

Rick got in the car and drove away.

The white one was still rolling around on the ground, clutching himself.

Chapter Four

Before the death of her first son, Evelyn Daye Tappley had generally been liked by her servants. She'd never been an especially warm woman but she was fair and tolerant, and always remembered birthdays and always tried to be accommodating when a maid or cook had family matters to attend to, and she was certainly liberal in the salaries she paid.

But this was many years ago, and in a mansion on the other side of Chicago.

Her husband Clark had died tragically in a car accident sixteen months following the death of young David. The police and family friends alike found the accident suspicious. Clark had been a virtual teetotaler, but on this night his alcohol content measured far in excess of the legal limit. 3He'd been alone, driving a familiar stretch of road, when his car left the highway and slammed into a tree at an approximate 75 mph. The coroner ruled the death accidental.

Three days after his death, in the Madison Street building from which he oversaw the family railroad dynasty (thank God his grandfather had decided to haul freight instead of humans), Evelyn found a letter in the middle drawer of the large oak desk she had given him the day he assumed the presidency of the corporation. Nothing in the note surprised her. In the past year, Clark had been subject to insomnia, depression, frequent impotence, frightening rages and curious lapses of memory. And crying jags. She had never seen a man cry so long or so hard. She comforted him when she could but he was beyond comfort. Their minister said it simply: 'He doesn't seem to be able to get over David's death.' And it was that simple. And that profound.

Margaret Connally was let go, of course. While Clark didn't blame her for David's death, he still couldn't bear to look at her because all he saw was David in his playpen and the timber rattler striking. The two other children had been Evelyn's idea. She was pregnant with Doris when Clark took his life. As for the note itself, it read:

Dear Evelyn,

I couldn't have asked for a dearer wife or better mother of my children. Please understand that I can no longer bear up under my pain.

I'm hoping that all those Sunday school stories of my youth are true, that I will soon be reunited with my little boy David once again. Please destroy this note and don't share its contents with anyone. I don't want the lives of Peter and our new baby ruined before they get started. With all my love, darling,

Clark

The mansion held too many memories for Evelyn and so, in the spring following Clark's death, she took her son and baby Doris to live on the former Piermont estate, a vast place of native stone situated high in the hills. As if nature with its rocky cliffs and impenetrable pines had not already made the place sufficiently inaccessible, Evelyn surrounded it with a high spiky wall and hired guards to patrol the perimeter twenty-four hours a day. Inside the mansion were all the latest electronic inventions to detect smoke and burglars. She owned one of the first security video camera set-ups in the world.

Evelyn became a recluse. No more Junior League, no more charity functions, no more trips abroad. She would always blame herself for what had happened to David. If she had devoted all her time to him, instead of trifling with things such as gardening, her son would still be alive today. As would her beloved Clark. To make up for her great sin – to wash, as it were, David's blood from her hands – she decided to devote every single waking moment to her children. They would never be out of her sight for more time than was absolutely necessary. They would never have secrets, for secrets meant that they could get into trouble without her knowing it, and they would live lives inextricably bound up with her own so that they could become a family such as the world had never seen before. Never again would she trouble herself with her own selfish pleasures. She would concentrate on her children completely.

And so she did.

And by the time Peter was four, the snickers and smirks and clucks of concern could be heard among those few friends who still had any contact with her at all.

She was too much of a good mother, Evelyn was. In wanting to protect her children – 'Now, you're sure you don't feel as if you're coming down with anything?' she'd sternly ask anyone who called to say they might drop by – she became their jailer. Peter was rarely allowed to play outdoors, and then only when he was accompanied by his mother. Doris fell from her bicycle when she was five years old and was not allowed to ride another one until she was twelve. Evelyn even controlled their pleasures. Peter, for instance, took painting lessons and piano lessons and dancing lessons – exactly what a refined and sophisticated mother would wish for her son, but not necessarily what a boy would pick if he had any choice in the matter. Doris was turned into a parody of old-fashioned 'female' virtue. She was taught to cook, sew, serve tea, sit quietly as Evelyn and Peter discussed things (Peter was David's surrogate, and as such he would always be more important than Doris), and to look pretty and proper even when she was running a fever or hacking her way through a terrible cough and cold.

And so they had their little world.

The children were taken to and from school in an imposing black limousine driven by a liveried driver who packed a snub-nosed .38 in a shoulder-holster. School friends visited only occasionally, and rarely did Evelyn approve of them. She encouraged her two children to be not merely brother and sister but best friends. Even when they were in high school, Peter and Doris hung out together. You saw them at the movie theater, the malls, the high-school games. There were a lot of jokes about them. They were both strikingly good-looking – indeed, they looked a great deal alike, with that kind of blue-eyed blondness that verges on the almost too-perfect – and they were quiet and insular to the point that many considered them arrogant.

When college came, Evelyn went through the charade of honoring Peter's wish to go to Harvard, but she had her doctor concoct an illness for her that would make Peter want to stay closer to home. He ended up going to Northwestern, as would Doris in a few years, and carried on living at home.

Three years after finishing college, Peter married Jill and his life was – at least as Evelyn saw it – forever ruined. Much against her will, Evelyn accepted Jill and invited her to become one of the family here on the estate. But Jill was coarse and of the world. After a year of this, she wanted to take up her old occupation of professional photography again. Work in the city. Oh, she'd come back home every night but invariably she'd bring with her the sins of the city – the violence, the disease, the vulgarity. The spirit of the mansion would be violated.

At this time, Peter began killing women. But Evelyn knew who was really to blame. Jill had betrayed Peter's faith. He'd always assumed that she would be happy living every day in the mansion, not needing to see others – especially not 'city' others – and when she betrayed him, Peter went insane and started stalking women . . .

At the same time that Rick Corday was going to check the contents of his shed, Evelyn Daye Tappley was just coming out of the front door of her mansion.

Her two servants, the pair who had been with Evelyn even while her husband had been alive, watched the small but robust woman go down the front steps and walk over to the shiny black 1951 Packard sedan that had belonged to Clark. His favorite car. And she kept it perfect.

She climbed in and started the engine. It ran flawlessly. She had it serviced every 1,000 miles.

The servants watched as she drove down to the gate where a gray-uniformed guard stepped forth. He gave her a little salute and then opened the gate.

Moments later, she was gone, headed west into the tall timber where the mausoleum lay, the mausoleum in which both Clark and David now rested, moved here when she came to this estate. Of course, now there was a third person interred there – Peter. Following his execution, she had brought the casket back here.

No matter what the weather, Evelyn drove into the timber once a day to pay her respects.

The servants looked at each other now and shook their heads. It was very sad, what Evelyn had done to her children in the name of protecting them.

Chapter Five

Shortly after leaving his shed on the north side, Rick Corday pulled his blue Volvo into the two-stall garage of a handsome suburban home with wood and stone accents, the closest neighbor being half a block away. In the windy night, the place was dark and just a bit ominous. But maybe that was because Rick lived here and knew about the basement . . . And what went on in the basement.

He went in through the kitchen door, glad to be home. He enjoyed this place, its sunken great room with fireplace and built-in bookcases and adjoining formal dining room with built-in china cabinets.

He went to the bathroom, relieved himself, washed up, and then took off his suit and did one hundred one-handed pushups. Then he changed arms and did one hundred more.

In his underwear, he sat on the edge of the double bed and dialed the phone, glancing at the brocaded gold wallpaper and Louis XIV furnishings that lent the room a formal if rather stiff elegance.

The air-conditioning made everything chilly. Too chilly, probably, for some people. But coldness had a productive effect on Corday and so he appreciated it.

On the night-stand between the beds, he saw the note,

the note that told him that his best friend, his good and true lover, had been cruising again.

He dialed a long-distance number.

'Hello,' said Adam Morrow.

'I'm ready to roll,' Corday said.

'Goddammit, Rick. I asked you to wait until I was there.'

'Everything's ready. We may not get this opportunity again.'

Adam decided to stay as cool as possible. 'So it's going well, then?'

'Professionally,' Corday replied, getting that hurt tone in his voice, 'everything is going fine.'

'What's that supposed to mean?'

'It means that the job is doing fine,' Corday said.

'The job is doing fine,' Adam echoed, 'but we aren't, is that it?'

Corday didn't want to say it, loathed his bitchy side, but couldn't stop himself. 'You know when you asked me to take some of your clothes to the cleaners? A note fell out of your pocket.'

Silence. Then, 'Are we reading each other's private mail now?'

'It's not private mail. It fell out of your pocket!'

'Same thing.'

'Seems you and some guy named Wyn became very good friends when you were in Miami a few weeks ago.'

Silence. 'I'm a lot better than I used to be.'

'True. Now you're only unfaithful every month. It used to be you were unfaithful every week.'

'You need to concentrate on the woman, Rick. Forget about us for the time being. We'll work it out.'

'Right,' Corday said. 'We'll work it out.' Then, 'You think you'll ever change?'

'I want to change. For your sake.'

'You should want to change for your own sake.'

Laugh. 'You've been watching Oprah again, haven't you?'

'I'm serious.'

'So am I, Rick. You listen to all that touchy-feely crap on TV and you think that's how everybody should be. A lot of very good relationships include one or both of the partners getting a little strange tail on the side. It doesn't mean that the relationship has to end.'

'So you're going to keep right on doing it?'

Sigh. 'I'm going to try not to, Rick. On that I give you my word. I'm going to try not to. That's the best I can tell you. That I'll try.'

Rick hated himself when he sulked. Professional, that's what he needed to be now. Professional. 'I'll see you in the morning then?'

'I'll be landing around ten o'clock.' Silence. 'Rick?'

'What?'

'I'm sorry you feel betrayed. It didn't mean anything to me. The guy's a dork.'

'Right.'

'He is. God, he peddles TV time. Some closet fairy who likes to strut around and tell you how he knows half the Miami Dolphins personally.'

'Do you want me to save the note?'

'Now what the hell do you think? I just told you what a dork he was, didn't I? Burn the goddammed thing.'

'With pleasure,' Corday said.

A few moments after hanging up, Corday had another one of his blackouts, a phenomenon that sometimes followed arguments with Adam.

He had to grab the back of a chair to steady himself. All was cold yet sweaty darkness as he clung to the chair to keep from falling over.

And from somewhere within himself came a voice crying out to him. He could not understand the words to this voice, but he knew that it was saying something vital and urgent.

After a time, Rick Corday went into the bathroom and threw up.

Chapter Six

The fading Hollywood star explained, in the course of the interview, that she had once been abducted by these strange-looking creatures that often landed in a spaceship in a nearby field, and that they had often given her enemas while she was aboard their ship. *The National Peeper* was the only thing Jill could find to read here at Marcy Browne's.

Then the office door burst open and in came one of the grungiest and most violent-looking women Jill had ever seen. She belonged on a direct-to-video poster for a B-movie called *Barbaria*.

The woman wore a sleeveless denim jacket, on the back of which was the insignia of what was presumably a motorcycle gang, The Marauders. On her right biceps, a tattoo repeated the insignia. Around each wrist was a miniature spiky dog collar that matched the much larger one around her neck. Her too-tight faded jeans were streaked and filthy. Her tight blonde curls resembled a hybrid of Shirley Temple and Madonna in one of the latter's many incarnations. She smacked gum with chilling ferocity. She came snarling and bow-legged into the outer office, fixed Jill with an icy blue gaze and said, 'Is that bitch in her office?'

Jill, abashed, couldn't find her voice. She stammered, cleared her throat and said, 'No, she isn't due back for a few minutes yet.'

'That slut. I never should've hired her to find out if my old man was porkin' Cindy. You know what that bitch did?'

'Cindy, you mean?' Jill enquired, feeling as if she were about eight years old and being intimidated by a giant straight out of the Brothers Grimm.

'Cindy? Hell, no, I mean Marcy Browne.'

'What did she do?'

'I think she was gettin' it on with my old man herself.'

'Oh, really?'

The woman glared around the neat but very, very tiny outer office – two battered secondhand filing cabinets, a desk that had one end propped up with books, and the most inexpensive black dial phone available these days – and she said, 'Hog Face fools a lotta chicks, you know.'

'Hog Face?'

'My old man.'

'Ah.'

Now they'd gone from the Brothers Grimm to *Alice in Wonderland*. The conversation was starting to get strange indeed. Jill squirmed, a nervous smile on her lips. She did not want to displease this woman in any way.

'I mean,' said the woman, 'you look at him and what do you see? He looks like three hundred and fifty pounds of blubber and he's got real bad teeth and when he's drunk, he kinda likes to beat up on chicks. I mean, he don't sound like the kinda guy most women'd be interested in at all, does he?'

This was like a trick question, Jill thought. She had to answer carefully, otherwise this Biker Mama might suddenly become even more psychotic than she was at the moment.

'Oh, I don't know,' she said. 'Some women have different tastes from others.'

The woman shook her head bitterly. 'Yeah, I wouldn't think that Hog Face'd get the chicks, either. But he does – and that's why I hired this little slut. To find out if he's been slippin' the salami to Cindy.'

For a long moment, the woman looked hurt and confused, then she lunged toward the cheap pressed-wood door which led to the inner office.

'I really don't think you should—' Jill started to say.

But the woman stormed into the inner office, shouting: 'You slut!' and hurled the door closed behind her.

No sound came from the inner office.

Jill sat perfectly still. She felt very self-conscious, as if the Biker Mama might be peering out of a hidden eye-hole, watching her.

Maybe she should try some other private investigator.

Maybe this Marcy Browne wasn't as competent as she'd seemed to Kate.

Jill stood up.

Sneak out of the office.

Sneak down the stairs.

Sneak away in her car.

Give Marcy Browne some kind of headache excuse if she called and asked why Jill hadn't waited.

That's what she'd do. Just sneak out right now – and hope she never saw the Biker Mama again, not even in her worst nightmares.

At that moment, the door to the inner office opened up. An attractive, honey-haired young woman in a white blouse, blue pointelle cardigan and fashionably long floral skirt stood in the door, smiling. 'You must be Jill.'

'Yes. Are you—?'

'How did I do?'

Back to *Alice in Wonderland* again.

Do? What was this young woman talking about?

'I'm afraid I—'

'The biker chick. Was I convincing?'

'You mean you were—'

Marcy Browne nodded and smiled. 'Last year at the National Private-Investigators' Convention in Las Vegas, one of the speakers suggested that we try taking acting lessons so that we could really go undercover when we needed to. So I've been going to this night-school acting workshop at Northwestern and trying out different parts.' The smile again, one of those quick and totally winning smiles. 'So how'd I do?'

'You did great.'

'I knew you'd be a tough audience and all. I remember Kate telling me that you directed a lot of TV commercials.'

'God, you really had me going. I thought she was the most disgusting woman I'd ever seen.'

'You like that "Hog Face" name I gave the guy?'

Jill laughed. 'Not to mention "slipping the salami". There's an elegant turn of phrase.'

'Well, now I can be confident that if I ever need to infiltrate a biker gang, I'm ready.' She effected the loud crude voice of Biker Mama. 'C'mon, Hog Face, slip me the salami real quick. I'm just a horny Mama tonight.'

'And they say romance is dead.'

'I've had a few dates who weren't all that far from being Hog Face,' Marcy said as she led them to the inner office.

'So've I, unfortunately.'

The inner office was much like the outer office except that two legs of this desk were held up by books, and the window was cracked and covered with masking tape along the fissure line.

Marcy said, 'This place is kind of a pit but it's all I can

afford right now.' When Jill didn't respond Marcy said, 'Now you're supposed to tell me that this place isn't so bad at all.'

'Oh. Right. This place isn't so bad at all.'

Marcy smiled her smile again. 'If we were in acting class, I'd give you a D for that last line. It wasn't convincing.'

Chapter Seven

Rick Corday did more than burn it.

After the note was charred black gossamer wings, he dumped them in the toilet and flushed them down.

Bastard. Unfaithful bastard.

He went back to the bed where he'd been propped up against the headboard reading the latest Tom Clancy novel. This time, instead of the novel, he picked up a manilla envelope from which he shook out two black-and-white photographs.

Everything about the man bespoke the kind of sleek ego that seemed endemic to the world of advertising. There was something silly and hollow and theatrical about these people – men and women alike – but they didn't seem to be aware of it.

This one, for instance.

Standing on the dock next to his yacht, wearing the whites and blue blazer of a man who had conquered several nations and would conquer several more before his time was finished on this world.

Eric Brooks.

Hardly to the manor born, despite an official bio that got more creative each year.

Father a worker at the Caterpillar heavy equipment

plant in Peoria. (Is this the same father you would later list as an astronomer, Mr Brooks?)

2.8 college average at the state university.

Three failed marriages, two paternity suits, and the loss of a major client because Brooks kept plugging the client's wife on the side.

Now sole owner of the only Chicago agency to ever win six Clios in one year.

Now sole owner of a Maserati, a Cessna that sat eight and a hunting cabin in Idaho that Ernest Hemingway had owned briefly back in the forties.

Corday looked at the second photo now.

Mr Brooks all gussied up in his handball T-shirt and his handball shorts and his handball scowl. Sweaty, gritty black-and-white, this photo, and how the macho Mr Brooks must love gazing upon it.

That's one tough hombre, that Mr Brooks.

Corday smiled.

He was going to ruin Mr Brooks' life and there wasn't a thing Mr Brooks could do about it.

Not a single solitary thing.

But first Rick had to stop by Jill Coffey's place . . .

Chapter Eight

'He wouldn't take a shower?'

'Not unless I refused to have sex with him.'

'You're kidding.'

'Uh-huh,' Jill said.

'Why wouldn't he take a shower?'

'He said taking a shower was just another example of how our totalitarian government had brainwashed us into being robots.'

'Wow.'

'So, anyway, that's how I met Peter. I just got so mad at Donald one night I couldn't take it anymore, and I put on my best dress and stockings and a garter belt, and I went out looking for a good time.'

So many years ago now, it seemed, Jill's college days.

She'd entered the state university just as the Flower Power movement was ending. Unfortunately, the boy she fell in love with, one Donald Franklin Spangler, had taken the considerable college fund his millionaire father had set aside for him, and recreated himself as a snarling student radical.

The first year wasn't so bad because Donald, for all his crazed rants against capitalism, was great in the hay and allowed himself to be dragged to various movies and rock concerts, even though he saw them as more evidence of how 'decadent' our system had become. Jill always wanted to point out the irony of a Marxist who drove around in a brand-new van his daddy had bought him and who owned many thousands of dollars' worth of stereo equipment, but why spoil his self-delusions? Hadn't Eugene O'Neill said that none of us could survive without them?

Her worst embarrassment that first year had been at an SDA rally in a small auditorium, where Donald had insisted on reading a poem to the assembly. He stood before them and said, 'The name of my poem is *Screw America*.' Jill started sinking down into her seat, hoping that nobody would notice her. This was going to be humiliating. Everybody would see Donald for the pretentious twit he sometimes was.

Screw America

Screw America, I say
Red White and Blue
Screw America, I say
Richard Nixon – screw you.

Screw America, I say
So loud and mean
Screw America, I say
Robbing our planet of everything that's green.

Screw America, I say
Killing the Red Man so proud and tall
Screw America, I say
I don't respect you at all.

At which point – God, she couldn't help it – Jill started

giggling. The poem was so sophomoric and Donald was such a melodramatic ass that Jill just assumed everybody else, even all these self-proclaimed Maoists, would find it equally funny. But then she started looking around. The poem wasn't over. In all, there must have been forty stanzas, each worse than the previous one. But everybody here seemed mesmerized. Absolutely downright mesmerized. Everybody in the little auditorium was on his feet except her. And they weren't giggling, they were crying – silver tears streaming down their cheeks as they repeated in a kind of Gregorian Chant, 'Screw America, I say!' every time Donald said it first. She had never forgotten that night, but she sure tried to.

There was even a second act to this farce. She stayed with him a second year. True, the rants were getting longer and crazier but she could abide it because he gave her plenty of time to study – he was always off somewhere marching in demonstrations – and because she didn't love him. He was an amusing companion and no more, perfect for somebody who didn't want any serious involvement – until he quit taking showers.

'So that night I went to this singles bar,' Jill went on, 'and there was this great-looking older guy there and this absolutely ridiculous thing happened to me.'

'What was that?'

'I fell in love with him.'

'God.'

'I couldn't believe it. He really was gorgeous.'

'That happened to me once, too. A gorgeous guy like that. God.'

Every few minutes, Jill would study Marcy. It was still difficult to believe that this slender, attractive young woman could possibly have been Biker Mama.

'So then what happened?' Marcy said.

'As soon as I got out of college that summer, he took me to the family manse where I met his mother and sister. The sister was great – or as great as she could be, anyway, in those circumstances – but the mother . . . Well, to be fair, she didn't like me any better than I liked her. She thought I was an evil woman, out to take all her little boy's money and pride.'

'But you got married, anyway?'

Jill nodded. 'Got married and was promptly locked behind bars for the rest of my life.'

'The family manse.'

'Mmm-hmm. Mother had come around to letting me be one of her honorary children. You know, stay behind the prison walls and do everything Mother told you to. But I couldn't do it. Not for any long stretch of time, anyway. I always had excuses to get out of there – my parents to visit, things like that. Then I sent in one of my photographs to the *Trib* photography contest and won first prize. People started offering me work and I took it. Over three years, I must have done a hundred assignments and really built a name for myself.'

'I'll bet Mother wasn't happy about that.'

'Mother,' Jill said, 'was furious.'

'How about Peter?'

'He was furious, too. He comes from a family where the women are blindly obedient. Whatever the husband says is the law. I told him we should move to Chicago and get our own place – his mother would send him on various business trips to make him feel that he actually had a career, but it was mostly makework things – and for a while there, I think he was actually considering it. But then the letters started coming.'

'Letters?'

'His mother paid somebody to write them and send them to me, I'm convinced of it.'

'What kind of letters were they?'

'Love letters – from this man who claimed to have slept with me several times while I was in Chicago working on photo shoots. Mother showed them to Peter, of course. Any idea he had of breaking away from her . . . Well, he wasn't going to move away with a woman who was a "harlot" as Mother liked to call "easy women." I think that's when he started killing those girls. He may very well have been using them as surrogates. He probably wanted to kill me.'

'Or Mother.'

Jill nodded. 'Or both of us. By that time in his life, he didn't like women very much.'

From there she detailed the sad years that followed soon after, Peter's arrest, the trial, the appeals, the execution. She finished by talking about the assault of *Hard Facts* on her privacy and life.

'God, that sounds terrible,' Marcy sympathized.

'That's why I want to find out who's been watching my place.'

'How'd you come to notice him?'

Jill shrugged. 'Ever since *Hard Facts* I look around at my surroundings: I try to notice everything. I started seeing this blue Volvo and got suspicious, so today I snuck down and took some photos of him.'

She handed Marcy an envelope and smiled. 'You won't find anything in there with great artistic merit.'

Marcy looked through the photos. 'No artistic merit, maybe, but these will be very helpful.'

'When I called you earlier, you said you hoped you could get to it right away.'

'Turns out I can. I have an industrial client who wanted

me to handle something for him but now he needs to put it on hold for a little while.'

'So you can start today?'

'Soon as you leave here, I'll call my old buddy in the Driver's License Bureau.'

'Great.' Jill stood up, remembering her appointment with Eric Brooks. 'I'd better get going.'

She put forth her hand. Marcy shook it.

'I sure hope that Biker Mama gets Hog Face back,' Jill smiled.

'Gee, I'm so pleased you liked what I did. A pro like you, I mean.'

'If your investigation business gets a little thin, there's always dinner theater.'

Marcy walked Jill to the door. 'You'll probably be hearing from me later tonight.'

Jill nodded and left.

Chapter Nine

Rick Corday had no problem getting into Jill Coffey's place. He owned a number of burglary tools.

Wearing a pair of latex gloves, he spent half an hour searching through her closets and drawers. He didn't need to do this but he enjoyed it. There was something sweetly pornographic about spying on somebody else's life.

A week ago, the range of his spying had increased when he'd let himself in here and installed a bug in her telephone, one he could pick up on an FM receiver from his motel room or, as earlier today, from his car. He'd heard her make her appointment with Eric Brooks.

A lot of dirty fun, spying on people.

The hell of it was, Jill Coffey seemed to be a pretty tame person. One time in New York, searching through the apartment of a highly-regarded female broadcasting executive, he'd come upon some of the most vicious S&M appliances his knowing and cynical eyes had ever seen. The belt with the tiny metal thorns had been the really impressive one. God, you could shred a guy's back with two lashes.

The bathroom offered even fewer revelations. Not a single vibrator in sight.

He went back into the bedroom to do what he'd come here for.

Find a skirt and blouse.

He selected a sandwash silk in electric blue for the blouse and a royal blue wraparound for the skirt.

Pantyhose – that would be a nice touch.

He searched through three drawers before he found a pair that had already been worn.

He wrapped these inside the skirt.

By this time, he had already made up his mind.

A better opportunity might never come.

It had to be tonight.

Before he left, he picked up the long scissors with the rubberized orange handles. He'd set them next to the phone the other day, knowing she'd be bound to pick them up. He dropped the scissors carefully inside a Ziploc bag.

Then he let himself out, reconstructing the security system that no doubt gave Jill Coffey such a great sense of well-being.

Chapter Ten

Church wasn't something Mitch Ayers had planned on. He wasn't the churchgoing type. From his Catholic boyhood he had a sentimental belief in a personal and caring God, but when he looked around at the predators he saw every day – Mitch being a homicide detective – he wasn't sure that Anybody was up there at all. At least, Nobody who cared much about all the sad, maimed, despairing creatures who crawled around in the mud below. But he needed a place to think and he'd been driving by and so, on impulse—

Took him three tries to remember the *Hail Mary* and he finally had to resort to a prayerbook to remember the second part that began, 'Holy Mary, Mother of God.' That part. The *Our Father* he had no trouble with at all, nor the *Glory Be*.

After he was finished praying, he sat back in the pew that was very near the front of the church. He liked the way the blue and red and green and yellow votive candles flickered in the dusky shadows. He liked the faint smell of incense on the quiet air. He liked the dignified beauty of the altar, sad Jesus on His cross looking out on His flock. He saw himself at three different times of his life in this very same church – as a twelve year old in white-and-black surplice and cassock serving High Mass with Monsignor O'Day, who always massacred the Latin language; as a twenty-four-year-old police rookie standing next to Sara Byrnes, the most beautiful girl in their graduating class at St Malachy's; and as a twenty-six-year-old father watching Monsignor O'Day sprinkle Holy Water on the forehead of tiny pink Frances, their first daughter. Following that there was the funeral of his father, and then the death of his beloved Aunt Lavina, and then the funeral of a one-time good friend and classmate Phil O'Herlihy, and—

And then Mitch and Sara Ayers moved away from the old neighborhood, out to a suburb where everything was sleek and sophisticated, and where over a period of a few years they seemed to change, somehow. At least Sara had. She took a job in administration at a hospital; she started flying to conferences and meetings all over the country, leaving the two girls more and more to Mitch; and three years ago, this same kind of lingering smoky autumn, she took a lover. He was a doctor and a handsome bastard and a rich bastard to boot and he seemed to represent something to Sara – some kind of approval that Mitch could never give her. To Sara, the doctor had been everything; to the doctor, Sara had been just one more affair. One night Jessica ran downstairs and told Mitch that Mommy was making funny noises up in her bedroom. Thank God for seven-year-old Jessica. Sara had intentionally overdosed on Xanax. Mitch called an ambulance. They got her to the hospital in time to pump her stomach. A week on the psych ward. A marriage counselor for them. Then a six-month trial separation. Sara's idea.

It had been during this time that Mitch met Jill Coffey. He'd liked her right away. There was a curious mixture of amusement and sorrow in those pretty dark eyes that fascinated him right away. And she was something of a smart-ass, so she made him laugh a lot of the time. He hadn't been honest with her. Told her that his impending divorce was a sure thing. Told her that he didn't much care about his wife anymore. They went out for several weeks and it was like being in high school again, the intensity of the romance and all the laughter. Jill surprised him one night by telling him that she was in love with him. And he'd been touched. For all her good looks and poise he saw that she was a very vulnerable person for whom loving and trusting someone was a very difficult prospect. But then Sara gradually decided that maybe it was time she gave her marriage another serious shot and if Mitch was willing . . .

Mitch never did get around to telling Jill that he loved her back.

What he did get around to telling her was that he thought maybe he should give it another try with Sara. He tried to make it sound noble. For the kids' sake, he said. '*You know – I've got to think of them first*.'

Noble.

Right.

So he moved back to suburbia and they did ten months together, ten fragile months, and then one night a month ago, Sara said, after the girls were in bed, 'I met somebody.'

'You what?' He could still hear the keening wounded sound in his voice, and was both embarrassed and ashamed.

'I met somebody. Not on purpose. I mean, I wasn't looking to. It just happened.'

And he did something he had rarely done.

He went down into the basement family room and closed the door and wept. Actually wept. So hard in fact that he thought he was going to throw up. And when he was finished, he lay back against the couch and looked at all the merry crayon drawings the girls had affixed to the wall with scotch tape, and then he started weeping again.

Round two.

At one point, Sara knocked gently on the door and said, 'Are you all right?'

'Yes,' was all he said. Quietly. No dramatics. '*Yes*.'

There was a round three. Around midnight. This one snuck up on him totally. He'd just gone upstairs and fixed himself a bologna and swiss sandwich and opened a can of Hamms and made himself comfortable on the family room couch for the second part of *Letterman* and then – bam!

And round three was worse than either of the other two because he was crying so hard he couldn't muster the strength or savvy to set down either his sandwich or beer. He held them all during this final attack of the weepies, literally crying in his beer.

Near dawn he went upstairs and got an hour and a half of turbulent sleep and when he woke up, he felt as if a dire fever had been broken. He looked over at the slender and very beautiful woman next to him and realized that just as she no longer loved him, he no longer loved her.

He was in love with that goddammed crazy photographer Coffey and she'd practically handed herself over to him and look at what he'd done to her.

He sat in the church of his boyhood, the church from which he took a sneaky agnostic comfort, and thought of Coffey, Jill Coffey. She really was sort of crazy in a lot of ways, and he realized that he could no longer put off what he'd been wanting to do ever since Sara had told him about her new Significant Other.

He was going to look up Jill Coffey and beg her to take him back.

Boy, was she going to be pissed when she saw him.

He apologized for using the word pissed and then got up and left the church.

Jill Coffey, here I come.

Ready or not.

Chapter Eleven

There was nothing like sex in the office.

Everybody on the other side of his door working their butts off, phones ringing, faxes humming, elevator doors opening and closing, conferences conferencing . . .

And where was the boss?

Well, the boss was in his big lavish CEO-type office, looking right out on the Chicago Cultural Center, getting a BJ.

Today her name was Cini. Not Cindy, which is what he'd thought she'd said last night when he'd taken her to the Brass Pump. Cini. C-I-N-I.

Three years in drama school, Mr Brooks. I know I can do it. I *know* I can.

They were never this bold till after he'd given them a few drinks. He always went to the casting sessions pretending that he was Very Concerned that they get the right actors and actresses for this Very Important Spot coming up, when what he really wanted was a new diversion. A new source for BJs.

So, pick one from rehearsals and kind of sidle her on over to the Brass Pump and if they *really* want to get that part . . .

Well, they can use their imaginations a little.

What do you think would please a handsome forty-two-year-old, very *virile* adman, anyway?

You want to know how virile he is, dig those framed photos of him on his African hunting trip when you're up in his office tomorrow. Sure, the colored boys did a little shooting of their own to back him up, but hey, he still brought the rhino down himself. God, he really digs that photo where he's standing with his right boot on the dead rhino's head. Is that virile or what? Who says admen aren't virile – some fag who works at the *NY Times*?

Last night, she'd had a little spunk in her, he had to give her that. He'd called the wife and told her he was working late (she didn't believe him, of course, but it was this little dance they did every night he was out prowling), and then he'd spent about an hour and a half trying to screw this little Drama Major Who Just Knew She Could Do The Part.

And got nowhere.

Felt her up a little, but hey, that was high school.

That was also as far as he got.

Till this afternoon when he called – she'd left her phone number – and invited her over.

'Did I get the part, Mr Brooks?'

'Hey, what happened to Eric?'

'Oh. Right. Eric. Did I get it?'

'I think so. I should know by the time you get here.'

'Is there somebody else?'

'Well, there's one other girl. She did a very good job with the lines.'

'Did you invite her up, too?'

'Yeah. But she'll be here before you. You'll be here last. That's always best.'

'It is?'

'Sure. The last person is always freshest in your mind.'

'Yeah, I guess that's right. Well, see you around five.'

Told his secretary that he was expecting a young lady just at closing, and the secretary all tee-hee intercommed another secretary and said, 'Guess who's going to be having a little sex in his office tonight?' and that secretary called another secretary, who called another secretary, who called . . .

He knew all about it, how word got around, and he loved it, positively loved it because it was all part of the image.

Biggest new advertising tycoon in Chicago in twenty years. Pilot. Hunter. Ranch owner. Crony of NFL quarterbacks, senators, movie stars.

And one killer ass-bandit.

Everybody pretended they hated ass-bandits but they secretly admired them because secretly that's what they wanted to be. Even chicks wanted to be ass-bandits when you came right down to it.

And so the girl – Cini – had come up here tonight and she'd done just what he'd wanted her to do (he felt so powerful, a chick doing him that way) and now she was finished and fixing herself up.

He stood at the window and looked out at the gathering autumn dusk, the shadows falling between skyscrapers, the first faint evening stars.

She said, 'So do I get the part?'

He smiled. 'You bet.'

'Oh God, wait till I call my mom!'

He slid an arm around her. 'You going to be around your apartment tomorrow night?'

'Sorry. Got a date.' She walked back to the door and picked up her blazer. She had wonderful breasts displayed in that sheer blouse of hers. She picked up her coat.

'Anything serious, your date?' He realized that he sounded – preposterously – hurt. No business of his how she spent her nights. But still, he felt spurned. Lonely, even.

She smiled. 'I have a boyfriend, Mr Brooks.'

'God, are we back to Mr Brooks?' He was irritated. 'And this boyfriend of yours, what would he do if he knew—'

A sad smile. 'He knows you have to do certain things you might not really want to do, in order to get a certain part.'

She went to the door, put a slender hand to the knob. Last night she'd looked a little sluttish to him, but today there was a kind of dignity to her. He hated women with dignity. You couldn't push them around without a great deal of effort.

'So you didn't really want to do it?'

She looked at him. 'What's the difference, Mr Brooks? I did it, didn't I?' The gaze narrowed. 'You're not going to take the part back from me, are you? I mean, I fulfilled my part of the bargain.'

Hurt. Pain. Great crashing waves of self-doubt. Didn't this girl know who he *was*? Didn't she know about his powerful *friends*?

'Jesus, I can't believe this.'

'I really should be going, Mr Brooks.'

'You just came in here and very cynically had sex with me and— You probably don't even like me much, do you?'

'I'm late, Mr Brooks. Sorry.' She opened the door.

'You know, that's just what you deserve. You know that, don't you? I mean, the way you're talking to me now, I should take that part right back from you, this minute, and there isn't a goddammed thing you could do about it.'

This time, the look was a glare. 'I did what you wanted me to, Mr Brooks. Now do I still have the part or not?'

'Bitch,' he muttered to himself.

'I'll call the casting director, then, and tell him that you decided to go with me.'

She started through the doorway, paused, and then said, 'I wasn't trying to hurt your feelings, Mr Brooks.' The quick sad smile again. 'I really wasn't.'

Chapter Twelve

'Tappley residence.'

'Mrs Tappley, please,' said Rick Corday.

'May I say who's calling?'

'Mr Runyon.' That was the code name she knew him by.

'One moment, please.'

She came on at once. 'Good evening, Mr Runyon.'

'You asked us to keep you informed.'

'Yes.'

'We're just about to get the project underway.'

'I see. I hadn't heard from you or your partner for some time. I was getting concerned.'

'Everything is fine.'

'So it will be – soon?'

'Very soon, Mrs Tappley. Very soon.'

'And you'll keep me informed?'

'Oh, you'll know about it, Mrs Tappley. I promise you that.'

'You're certain you've thought it through?' This was more like the Mrs Tappley Rick Corday had talked to before. He knew her attorney, Arthur K. Halliwell, who had set all this up. Rick had never met Mrs Tappley, but she was certainly formidable over the phone.

'We've thought it through carefully,' he told her now. 'We couldn't have asked for a better set-up.'

'I've waited a long time for this.'

'I know you have, Mrs Tappley.'

'I just want everything to go right.'

'It'll go fine, Mrs Tappley. I promise.'

This was one of the few times he'd heard both age and grief in her voice. Her son had been executed. She'd never recovered. All she had, as the lawyer had said, was her anger and her desire for vengeance. And those things could sap you of all reason and all strength.

'Good luck, then.'

'Thank you, Mrs Tappley. Talk to you soon.'

Chapter Thirteen

She went to Fat Camp six years in a row, Cini did, and each summer lost somewhere between fifteen and thirty pounds. Over the first two months of school, she put those pounds right back on. Between her junior and senior years in high school, her last year at Fat Camp, she actually gained twelve pounds over the course of the summer. She was five feet six and weighed nearly two hundred pounds. Whenever Cini was depressed about her weight, her mother always said the same thing: 'But you have such a pretty face, dear.' The frustrating thing in all this was that Cini's father was a heart specialist, a man who could tell you all about what excess weight could do to your health. His warnings, which her mother usually softened by sneaking in with a powdered donut or a Snickers when Dr Powell had gone, did not seem to have an undue effect on Cini. At school, there was kind of a Fat Girls group. It cut across all lines of race, socio-economic status and intelligence. The girls had three things in common. They were fat; they did not want to be fat; boys made fun of them. Some boys even referred to them collectively as 'The Whales,' thus disputing the myth that most boys start to grow up a little as they near graduation. Even in this group, Cini was an outsider. She felt that the others were brighter and cleverer than she was, and so she tended to be quiet whenever anything important was discussed, like what time to meet at the mall or who could get the van tonight or which night they were going to the grand opening of the Ample Lady, which was where girls of their size shopped.

The year she turned nineteen, Cini was hit by a car. She was crossing a street over near Northwestern, not really watching where she was going, just hurrying to get out of the chill March rain, and here this car suddenly appeared. Cini was too big to move with any skill. The car, a new Chevrolet, slammed into her and knocked her down. She was unconscious by the time her head collided with the wet pavement, and she would remain unconscious for more than three months. Later on, her parents told her about all the extraordinary steps they had taken to save her life, including Daddy's old friend Dr Weintraub flying up from Dallas and virtually babysitting Cini during the most critical two weeks of the entire process.

Cini woke up on a sunny May day and looked out the window. She was not sure who she was, where she was, or what had happened. Then she looked down at her body and realized she was dreaming. She weighed scarcely half of the real Cini. No more than 100 pounds. She screamed. This dream was too weird, too real. Nurses came running, shoes squeaking, diving for her bed to see what had gone wrong.

'Help me wake up, please. I'm scared,' Cini said to the first nurse who took her hand.

'You *are* awake, Cini. You've been unconscious for almost three months but now you're finally awake.'

'But my body – My weight—'

The nurse smiled. 'I'll have the doctor come in. I'll also call your parents and have them come over right away.'

It was simple enough, explained the doctor who came in.

They'd decided to help rid her of her excess weight as they also slowly tried to woo her out of her coma. He told her about all the fractures she'd sustained, then about all the damage her cranium had suffered. She was lucky to be alive, he said.

On 3 August of that year, the first time Cini was permitted to leave the house by herself, she put on a blouse and a pair of jeans and looked at herself in the mirror and grinned her ass off. Her very shapely ass. She was not just a pretty face these days. She was a pretty body, too.

She spent three afternoons in a row at the mall. God, she loved it. All those young guys looking her over. Smiling. Nudging each other. Even whistling a few times. It was still like a dream. A few times she thought about calling some of her old friends but she was afraid they'd take one look at her and hate her. You know, as if she'd betrayed them in some way.

She enrolled in Northwestern. Her freshman year, four different boys asked her to the homecoming dance. Good-looking boys. Prominent boys. One of them was even a senior. She felt like an imposter, one of those aliens in sci-fi movies who can disguise themselves to look appealing to earthly eyes. Didn't they know that deep down inside she would always be a charter member of The Whales?

The phone calls, the party invitations, the movie dates never stopped. God, it was wonderful. So wonderful. Then she had to go and spoil it all by meeting Michael Laine, a guy who had so many good-looking girls that she was just one more . . .

And when he dumped her, she got this notion about making him jealous by getting herself cast in a TV commercial. Becoming a star . . . So she signed up with a talent agency and started going to castings. It was incredible. She must have gone to forty auditions over a month and a half and got not a single call back to read or test for the part.

Her old depression returned. She started eating excessively again. She became frantic about getting a part in a commercial. Getting a part would prove something to her. Prove that she really wasn't deep down still a Whale. That she was just as desirable as she had been feeling there for awhile. She had to get a part. *She'd do anything to get a part . . .*

Chapter Fourteen

Jill was able to rush from the reception area before the young woman came out of Eric's office. With the door partly opened, Jill had been able to hear the last minute of their conversation. She didn't want to embarrass the girl by being in the reception area.

Having once been half-owner of this agency, Jill knew exactly where to go. There was a nook that the art department used as a coffee hutch near the back of this floor. Jill went there and poured herself some coffee.

Her impulse was to leave. It had been a mistake coming here, of ever thinking she could work with Eric even if it was for the sake of the convent.

Eric hadn't changed at all.

For many years, she'd tried to rationalize his behavior. Men were under such pressure to be macho and studly. She'd told herself that Eric was simply a victim of these cultural forces, that within himself there was goodness and kindness and tolerance.

But the way he'd just spoken to the girl told Jill that nothing had changed at all. Nothing.

As she walked toward the front of the office, carrying her cup of coffee, she flashed on her old days in advertising. She'd never been suited to it. The number of awards ad people gave themselves was enormous – and told you how important they deemed their work to be. The new generation of ad people, far from being apologetic for pushing products that were either useless or downright destructive, celebrated themselves as artistes. The ad magazines were filled with chest-thumping editorials about advertising being today's most important art form. It was a laughable premise, but ad people and clients alike had a vested interest in deluding themselves that they and their work mattered in the scheme of things.

She was glad to be gone.

No more laughing at lame commercials; no more dull meetings about cost-per-thousand and focus group research and test market results; no more enduring lightly-veiled propositions from clients, and palace intrigues led by young turks as full of themselves as ballerinas.

It was over; she had been released early for good behavior.

For all that, she had to admit that the offices were beautiful. Eric had leased an additional floor and it was gorgeous. There was custom woodwork throughout, with full-height solid wood doors, gray fabric-covered walls, and patterned and bordered carpeting. In the reception area, fluorescent downlights lightly tinted the plum-stained mahogany. The blue-green and plum and gray furnishings lent a final touch of elegance.

Eric sat on the edge of the reception desk. When he saw her, he cocked his head in the boyish way he knew that some women liked and said, 'You're still the sexiest woman I've ever known.'

'Oh God, Eric,' Jill said, 'knock it off, will you? I'm here on business, remember?'

He was crushed. He spent half his life being crushed. For all that he liked to pose with one foot on a dead rhino, he had a frightfully fragile ego. He looked at her now as if she'd slapped him.

'Eric, I came here because you said you wanted me to take some photographs. Let's just stick to the subject and everything will be fine.'

And she couldn't help herself. She smiled. Eric was a raving jerk but there was a teeny-tiny part of her that felt protective of him. He thought he was a killer but he was just a Chicago kid who'd gotten very very lucky. She knew a few real killers. Eric wasn't even close.

She put her hand out. 'Let's try and get along, all right?'

He laughed. 'Same old Jill. One tough cookie.'

She waved an arm around. 'I can see why you want to be photographed in here. It's beautiful.'

'You should see the bills from the decorator.'

'*Mr Blandings Builds His Dream House*.'

'What?'

'An old Cary Grant-Myrna Loy movie,' Jill said. 'About a couple who build their dream house and go broke in the process.'

'Why don't I give you a tour?'

'Great. I'd like that.'

As they started walking, he said, 'What was the name of that movie again?'

'*Mr Blandings Builds His Dream House*.'

'With Cary Grant?'

'Right.'

'I always heard he was gay.'

She laughed. No, Eric hadn't changed a bit. Try and talk about a movie you liked and he ended up reducing the subject to farfetched gossip.

It was like the time she'd told him that Mike Royko had written an especially good column in the *Trib* about babies being born drug addicts.

'Yeah,' Eric had said, not caring at all about the matter of drug-addicted babies, 'but I bet Royko doesn't make half as much a year as I do.'

After she left Eric Brooks' office, Cini Powell found a restroom on the same floor and went in and brushed her teeth. She wished she could throw up.

She'd actually gone through with it.

Actually gone to that creep's office and let him—

As she stood there with rabies foam from the toothpaste covering her mouth, her blue eyes filled with tears and a lone silver drop traced down her perfectly shaped cheek.

Tonight she'd lost her virginity. Well, technically speaking, she'd actually lost her virginity two years ago, when she was twenty, in a beach house on a Wisconsin Lake, to a twenty-one-year-old named Chuck who kept saying, 'God, were you really a virgin till tonight?' Obviously ole Chuck was pleased with himself. Bagging a virgin these days was no easy task, not unless you made a habit of dating twelve year olds.

That was losing her physical virginity.

Losing her spiritual virginity, which is what she'd done tonight, was a far more serious matter.

All so she could get a part as a talking mannequin in a commercial for a trendy local department store.

All so she could make Michael Kenneth Laine, law student, basketball star and relentless woman-chaser, sorry that he'd ever dumped her.

At least, that had been her plan . . .

But now, for the first time since she'd seen the casting notice in the *Tribune* want ads, she realized that not since she'd walked in on Michael making love to that girl in his apartment had she been quite sane. Had she been quite herself – her *real* self.

Until now. Until she'd looked into the mirror and realized the enormity of what she'd done on the top floor of this building. Just twenty minutes ago.

She brushed her teeth some more.

She wanted to rinse out her mouth with alcohol.

She wanted to go to Confession, something she hadn't done since moving out of her good upper middle-class Catholic home four years ago. She wanted to find a closet somewhere and hide in there and never come out.

God, how could she have done that? Not even Michael was worth debasing herself for this way. All for what? So he might catch a little glimpse of her in a sexy body stocking on TV, pretending to be a talkative mannequin?

What could she possibly have been thinking?

She walked over to the third stall along, opened the door, sat down on the closed lid, and proceeded to sob.

The tour took fifteen minutes.

He told her the price of everything. Parquet flooring was this much. Track lighting that much. Custom-fabricated niches this much . . . And so on.

Good old Eric.

When they were back in his office, he said, 'So what I want are some really sexy shots of me in various departments. You know, looking cool as usual.'

'Cool. Got it.'

'But businesslike.'

'Cool but businesslike. Check, boss.'

He glanced at her. 'You know what?'

'Here it comes.'

'Can you take a nice boy-girl compliment?'

She sighed. 'What particular compliment did you have in mind?'

'That you look sexy as hell in that aqua blouse.'

'All right. Compliment accepted. Now let's get back to work.'

The hurt look again but this time Jill felt no pity for him. He was letting his lust run way ahead of his reason. She sensed he was about to put the serious moves on her again, and hoped she was wrong. Because if he did try anything, she was likely to get very angry.

'Why don't you go over and stand by that window?' she suggested quickly. 'That'd make a nice shot, with all those buildings in the background.'

He went over and stood, the Chicago skyline spearing into the dusk sky behind him. This was Jill's favorite time, twilight – magical, when all of night's promise lay ahead.

'How's this?'

'Great,' she said. 'Now try the other window.'

He took several steps across to the west window. 'Whatever happened to that cop you were seeing?'

Mention of Mitch Ayers caused Jill to shut down completely for a moment, as it usually did. She froze. Then, 'It didn't work out.'

'I heard you were really in love.'

'Turn to your right.'

'Don't want to talk about it, huh?'

'Now turn to your left.'

'He dump you or what?'

'Now walk out on the balcony and jump.'

He laughed. 'Guy must've really gotten to you, the way you're acting.'

She walked over. He had to be angled just right for a shot like this to work. She liked to walk through her shots, rehearse them, so that the actual shoot went faster.

She touched Eric's elbow and turned him toward her and that's when he grabbed her and pulled her to him. Before she could gather herself to protest, his mouth found hers and she felt his hot tongue passing between her lips.

She pulled back and slapped him with a ferocity that startled even her.

'You bitch! What the hell do you think you're doing?'

After a long moment, Jill walked to the door and said, 'I guess I don't need to tell you that I won't be doing that shoot of yours.'

'God, Jill, I'm sorry. I really am.'

'No, you're not, Eric. You're not sorry at all.'

A genuine sorrow filled her. Sometimes people baffled her completely. Eric would always remain unfathomable to her. All the high-school macho games he played. Becoming a real adult seemed to hold no appeal to him whatsoever. He would always be one of those aging boy-men you saw so often in sports and politics – and advertising.

'Jill.'

But she didn't stop.

Walked out through the reception area.

Found the hall and walked to the elevator.

A young woman emerged from the restroom at the far end of the hall. She looked upset, and Jill could tell she had been crying.

Eric came up. He looked miserable, but she felt no sympathy for him at all. 'Jill, please, you have to believe me. I really am sorry. Really I am.'

She turned to him. 'Don't make this worse than it has to be, Eric. Go back to your office and let me wait here alone.'

He started to argue but saw that it was no use.

He shook his head, ran a hand through his hair, and then walked sullenly back to his office. He obviously hadn't noticed the young woman standing by the restroom at the opposite end of the hall. She was watching both Jill and Eric.

Jill and the woman looked at each other down the long corridor. Then the woman opened a door marked STAIRS and disappeared.

A few minutes later, Jill's elevator car came. She boarded it and was gone.

Chapter Fifteen

Corday knew he should have been concentrating on the job ahead but he couldn't. He kept thinking of how Adam had been unfaithful. Again. After all those promises.

Then he saw Jill.

Time for work.

Couldn't afford to worry about Adam anymore. Or the jerk Adam had spent time with in Miami.

He waited until Jill had disappeared beyond the door leading to the ramp, and then he moved.

Across the lobby.

To the elevator.

Up to pay a visit to Mr Brooks.

Cini had just reached the lobby – hurrying because the deep shadow and the hollow echoing sound of her footsteps unnerved her – when she went to reach in her purse for a Kleenex . . . and realized that she didn't have her purse with her. She always carried her toothbrush in her coat pocket so she hadn't missed her purse. But now—

Her purse.

Upstairs.

Eric's office.

Of course.

Dammit, anyway.

She turned, saying a dirty word she'd been trying to break herself of, and walked back up the stairs.

Chapter Sixteen

'You seem a little preoccupied.'

'I guess I am.'

'Want to talk about it?'

'No big deal, I suppose. Just having a few problems with my business partner.'

'Business partners can be a real pain.'

'Maybe I'll have another drink,' Adam Morrow said. 'I mean, if you don't mind.'

He'd met his new friend just an hour ago in a Village bar. Now he was having drinks in his new friend's apartment. His friend kept casting an anxious eye to the darkened bedroom beyond, but Adam was too worried right now to think about sex.

He just had this awful feeling that finding the note had undone Rick, and that Rick might do something stupid.

Something that could end their perfect record.

'Why don't you let me freshen that up for you?' Adam's new friend said, taking the glass from his hand.

Adam scarcely noticed.

If only he hadn't had to fly to New York at the last minute to take care of a loose end on the last job.

Rick, for all his skills, got so emotional at times that he didn't think clearly.

Early tomorrow Adam would be on a plane headed to Chicago. Just so long as Rick didn't do anything crazy tonight . . .

'Here,' said Adam's new friend. 'Maybe this'll mellow you out a little.' He smiled. A very white smile. An actor's smile. 'Then maybe we can get to know each other a little better.'

Chapter Seventeen

'Will there be anything else, ma'am?'

'Not for right now, Emma. Not for right now.'

Emma thought how you didn't often hear Mrs Tappley's voice this soft and sentimental.

But tonight she sat in the darkened den watching all the old films of her son Peter when he was growing up.

How she loved those old films, Emma thought.

Some nights Mrs Tappley would stay in the den until midnight, and sob with such great pain and loss that Emma herself would begin to cry.

Losing a son that way, in the electric chair.

No wonder the woman watched the old films so often, and cried so hard.

Chapter Eighteen

There was always risk, and Corday loved it.

In Los Angeles, he had once been trapped in the hold of a ship with two drug dealers he'd been hired to kill. They each had automatic weapons: Corday had only a knife. They had some fun with him, chasing him across the hold, laughing when he tripped and fell – but they had not counted on his intelligence. When he fell, he pretended to bang his head, and become unconscious.

At first the dealers accused him of faking. '*Hey, man, get up, we ain't gonna fall for that old trick*.' But after a few minutes, the mood in the hold suddenly turning tense, one of the dealers walked over to the fallen man and leaned down to see if he could hear breathing. Corday put the knife deep into the dealer's right eye, then pulled the dealer down on top of him, snatching the man's weapon. Even before the other dealer could figure out how to fire without hitting his buddy, Corday had killed them both, firing until the automatic pistol was empty and the hold an echo chamber of fired rounds.

There was risk tonight, and Corday loved it.

He rode up to the floor where Eric Brooks had his office and stepped off the elevator.

Plum and gray walls; plush plum carpeting. Nice. Not so

nice was the lavish painting of Eric Brooks that made him resemble Clint Eastwood. That kind of bone-clean manliness. You'd think a guy would be embarrassed to parade his fantasies publicly like this. '*Hey, outside I'm this kind of nerdy jerk – but inside, I'm Clint Eastwood.*'

Corday looked around.

Nobody in the hall.

Listened for cleaning people. Vacuum or toilets flushing as they were being cleaned. Heard nothing.

Tugged on his latex gloves.

Walked up to the massive wooden door with the name ERIC BROOKS engraved in it. Another touch of humility.

The gray and plum motif continued inside. Corday didn't know anything about interior decorating, but these sure were fancy digs. Eric Brooks might be a weenie but he was a successful weenie. Had to give him that.

Corday went deeper inside to where a group of furnishings were arranged in the center of a vast open area. The general reception was regaled with even more evidence of Eric Brooks' ego. Here were framed hunting photos of him. Corday smiled. God, the guy really *was* a weenie. Great white hunter. God.

From the reception area, Corday turned right, taking a hallway down several yards then turning left. Here was the reception area and inner sanctum of the King himself.

Corday stood still, listening again.

A voice. Inside Eric's office.

Corday moved swiftly, silently to the partially opened door.

Eric. Laughing. 'You treat ole Eric right, he'll treat you right.' Beat. 'Remember that afternoon I gave you a grand just to go blow on clothes? Well, that could happen again some time. I mean, if you're nice to old Eric.' Beat. 'Babe, I know you're trying to give your marriage a serious shot but just a quick lunch tomorrow is all I'm asking. You know, in my office.' Half beat. 'Right. Like the old days.' Half beat. Giggle. 'I'll introduce you to Mr Bill again. You can give him a nice big kiss. You remember Mr Bill, don't you?' Half beat. 'Good, because he sure remembers you.'

Eric made it so easy.

He was so caught up in laying out his plans for lunch tomorrow that he didn't hear Corday come up behind him.

Eric: 'Anything special you want for lunch? Besides Mr Bill, I mean?' Giggle. 'You want me to tell you what I want for lunch?' Giggle. 'He's pulling into the driveway? You better go, babe.' Beat. 'Around noon would be great. Bye, babe.'

Eric hung up without turning around.

Then he got up from his desk and walked to his window and looked out over the Chicago skyline.

Still unaware of Corday behind him.

Corday smiled.

Great white hunter.

Guy is standing just a few feet behind him with a deadly weapon and the sonofabitch doesn't even hear him.

Corday walked around the desk and perched himself on the edge of it. 'Evening, Eric,' he said.

Brooks turned, startled, stunned. 'Who the hell are you?'

'Death,' Corday said. 'At least for you, I am.'

'Is that supposed to be funny?'

'No. It's supposed to be the truth.'

'How the hell did you get in here?'

'You think I could get me one of those photos of you in your great white hunter outfit – for my own personal collection, I mean?' Corday smiled. He had a wondrously icy smile and knew it. 'How many native boys did it take to bring down that rhino?'

Eric hesitated a moment, looking left, looking right, then plunging for the phone.

Corday clamped an iron hand on Eric's wrist.

Eric glared at him a moment then lifted his hand from the receiver. When Corday let go, Eric started rubbing his wrist. Corday was one strong guy.

'Fifty bucks says your sphincter goes.'

'What the hell are you talking about?' Eric said. But he knew what Corday was talking about. Knew damned well.

'The medical examiner always told me that when the sphincter goes, it's just an autonomic response. Doesn't mean you're a coward or anything. Just as many brave guys have their sphincters go as cowardly guys. At least, that's what the medical guys tell me. But you know what? I don't believe them. I think a really brave guy could control it. Even when he's in so much pain he can't even feel anything anymore.' Corday paused. 'Fifty bucks says your sphincter goes.'

Eric's right hand had started to twitch. 'There isn't a lot of cash up here. I could maybe scrape up five, six hundred or so.'

'Didn't come for cash, Eric.'

He screamed then, a high piercing animal scream, a recognition of the final darkness closing in. 'Then what the hell are you doing here?'

Corday took the scissors from his pocket. 'I already told you that, Eric.'

Eric started running his hands through his thinning hair, pacing off little six-steps-and-back tattoos on the sweetly carpeted floor. He paused and said, 'This is my wife, right? Hiring some hit guy to take care of me? Right? Am I right?'

'Eric, a great white hunter like you should know that a "hit guy" like me could never tell who hired him. Us "hit guys" just don't do things like that, Eric. Sorry.'

Now both of Eric's hands were twitching. His eyes were filling with tears.

'I don't want to die. Please. I know you think I don't have any guts, but – but I don't want to die. I'll do anything you want me to. I promise.' Beat. 'I have kids. And a wife. Think of what it'd do to them if I died.'

'You see them a lot, do you, Eric? Your wife and kids, I mean.'

'Every chance I get.'

'Sort of like *Ozzie and Harriet*, I'll bet.'

'What?'

'You know, good faithful wife, good faithful husband.'

'Oh. Right. Absolutely.'

He didn't even stand up, he was close enough sitting on the edge of the desk to stab the scissors deep into Eric's chest.

Eric didn't even come up with a very good scream.

He seemed so shocked he couldn't really do anything but stand there and cover the hole in his chest as blood began to spurt and spray through his fingers.

Corday angled away, so he wouldn't be sprayed.

'Please,' Eric muttered, 'please.'

Corday wasn't sure what Eric was 'pleasing' him about but at this point he didn't much care.

The kill was at hand.

The only thing Corday liked more than the risk was the kill itself.

Indeed indeed.

He eased himself from the edge of the desk and took two steps over to Eric so that he could put the scissors in at an angle this time. Right at the base of the skull.

This time Eric's scream was a little better but it was short-lived because paralysis was setting in. Corday knew the exact spot to effect that. And that's just where the scissors had gone.

By now, there were small puddles and pools of blood on the floor, and the fabric walls were getting blotchy from the spurting geyser escaping from between Eric's fingers.

'You ever kill a puma, Eric? I hear they're really tough. Some hunters tell me they're the toughest of all.'

This time he stabbed him in the stomach.

Had to look like a frenzy kill.

Lots and lots of wounds.

Hatred accumulated over a long period of time suddenly bursting forth.

Eric put up bloody hands so Corday could not cut him but by now Eric was too weak to do much of anything.

He slumped back against the wall.

'Eric, you'd make this a lot easier for both of us if you'd just stand still. You really would, babe.' Corday smiled. 'I heard you calling that woman on the phone "babe." You like being called "babe?" Huh? You like it, Eric?'

This was a good one.

Right in the old larynx.

For a milli-second, Eric looked like that famous painting *The Scream*; his eyes bulging in horror, his mouth open wide – but no sound coming out.

Hard to make a sound when some nasty man has just plunged a pair of scissors deep into your throat.

Poor baby.

Eric slid to the floor.

He was dead by the time his haunches settled into the deep carpeting.

All was silence.

Corday knew better than to stay around.

He worked quickly.

From his pocket he took the Ziploc bag with the pair of scissors identical to the ones he'd used on Eric.

He held the new scissors between thumb and forefinger and carried them delicately to Eric.

He dipped the scissors in blood, then inserted the tips of the scissors into various wounds, collecting not only blood but cotton from the shirt and skin from the stomach, both things the medical examiner would expect to find on the murder weapon. He inserted the scissors into all the major wounds.

Then he placed the bloody scissors several feet from Eric.

This section of the office was a mess by now, especially the wall, blotched blood looking like Rorschach tests in some places.

Then it was time to go.

And go quickly.

Part Two

Chapter Nineteen

Cini had never much liked elevators. As a little girl she'd heard a news story about a Loop elevator car falling twenty-six floors. A woman visiting from Iowa had died from injuries two hours later. The newsman, trying to reassure everybody, talked about how uncommon this was – less common than being struck by lightning was the example he used – but Cini could never ride an elevator car now without a few moments of anxiety bordering on hyperventilation.

But not now. She was concentrating so hard on her game plan – retrieving her purse and getting out of the office without letting Eric Brooks lay a finger on her – that she paid no attention to the faint whining sounds of the powerful elevator system, nor to the way the car shimmied every half-floor or so, nor to the way the doors didn't part for long, long moments after the car had reached the top floor.

Ordinarily, she would have wanted to scream for help and start pounding on the door.

But now . . .

Now Cini got off the car and stood in the eerie silence of a Loop office building after closing hours. The corridor leading to the Brooks Agency's door was long and empty, and the wall-sconce indirect lighting, bouncing off the grid and tile system of the ceiling, produced a curiously alien brilliance.

She started down the corridor.

She was halfway there when the elevator doors rumbled shut behind her. She turned, startled, just as the two doors came together.

Just had to get this over with . . .

Just had to get out of here . . .

She no longer cared about the TV commercial – or even Michael – anymore. She'd been so foolish . . .

As she started to open the door, she thought she heard a noise. A muffled shout, perhaps. Or scream.

She listened, hearing only the faint buzz overhead of the electrical system.

She went inside. The main reception area looked neat and empty, the massive front desk situated in front of a row of Clio awards the agency had won. The awards were kept in a glass case that was lit from inside and gave everything a theatrical-accent light.

The corridor leading right was the one she wanted. At the far end of that she would find Eric Brooks' own smaller reception area, and his impressive digs.

She had taken eight steps when she heard the scream and recognized it immediately as belonging to Eric Brooks.

Without wanting to at all, she edged closer to his office and there, framed in the doorway, were two men. One was Eric Brooks. His face, chest, hands were covered with blood and he was cowering backward over his desk, holding his hands up to stop the bloody scissors from stabbing him again and again. The man with the scissors was tall and angular and handsome in a hard way. All she could think of was the actor James Coburn.

Eric saw her but the killer didn't.

Eric tried to call out her name, wave an entreating arm in her direction.

But the killer was so intent on killing that Eric didn't have a chance, particularly after the man plunged the scissors deep into the area just below Eric's Adam's apple.

This was very different from the kind of violence you saw on TV programs. For one thing, both men were kind of clumsy. The killer stumbled a couple of times in his frenzy, and Eric, for his part, kept making a kind of wheezing *braying* noise, like one of the dusty old donkeys she used to ride at the Illinois State Fair. The killer made sounds, too. And that's what they were – *sounds* – not fine fancy words put in his mouth by some screenwriter. He grunted, he groaned, he yelped, he yipped – and when his blade struck home, he made curiously ecstatic sounds . . . 'orgasmic' would not be too strong a word. His cry was pure pleasure as the scissors went in and out, in and out—

Eric's head flopped backwards, soon followed by his entire body, his arms waving for balance as he fell across his desk, the killer staying right with him, ripping the scissors from the trachea area and plunging them once again into Eric's chest.

She was afraid she'd scream.

She was afraid he'd see her.

She ran.

She ran back down the narrow corridor to the main reception area then across the lobby to the front door.

She ran to the elevator and pushed the button ten, twenty, thirty times. But the elevator doors did not part. She kept glancing back over her shoulder, to see if the front door opened. To see if the man with the bloody scissors was coming for her—

She pressed the elevator button ten, twenty more times. Then, more in frustration than anything else, she started banging her fists on the elevator doors until she realized how crazy she was being. He'd hear her for sure.

She ran to the neat red overhead sign that read: FIRE. Flung back the door. Started down the stairs two at a time. Stumbled once, slamming her knee painfully against the edge of a concrete step. Swore. Started to cry. Swore at *herself* this time for being such a sissy. No time to cry. Only time to run.

Run.

She ran.

Chapter Twenty

He stood across the street from Jill's apartment, staring up at the only lighted window. She passed by it occasionally, her slender body provocative in silhouette. Probably wearing her Danskins.

Eric Brooks was less than an hour dead.

Full night now. Traffic a steady flow of lights and the smells of gasoline and rubber. The occasional booming, blaring radio.

The sidewalks were full, too. Lovers. He'd had a lover once. Been faithful, too. At least for a time. But then—

He watched the window.

He was going up there soon.

Very soon.

Chapter Twenty-One

Jill looked longingly at the fireplace. With autumn setting in, it was nearly time for a fire. But she hadn't bought any logs yet, nor cleaned out the grates.

Tomorrow, she thought. Tomorrow.

Her argument with Eric finally starting to fade – it took her a long time to calm down once she'd been angered – she went into the kitchen for a glass of Chablis.

She'd spent a good share of last year's photography profits having custom-cabinets installed. At that time, she'd still had dreams of marrying Mitch Ayers. Following the divorce, Mitch would be poor. This would be a perfect place for them to start a marriage.

Or so she'd thought.

Now, reaching into the open refrigerator for the bottle of wine, she forcefully willed Mitch from her mind.

She wasn't dishonest with herself: she knew she wasn't over him completely yet. But one day she would be and when she was – well, maybe she'd meet somebody even nicer who wanted to move in here.

Somebody who actually *would* move in.

Not run back to his wife.

She carried the wine goblet into the living room. She enjoyed the eclectic nature of the furnishings in there – the antique fireplace mantel contrasting with the shining hardwood floors and off-white sofa.

She put on a Kenny G CD and strolled over to the window for her peek out at the street below. She'd always liked the excitement of this particular thoroughfare: it reminded her of her high-school days. She'd done a lot of cruising up and down streets in the company of boys determined to despoil her. But—

She smiled. In college, it got even crazier, though it was still kind of funny. All that spluttering of Donald's. All his protesting. All his *bring-down-the-Government* talk. And all the while living on a big fat inheritance.

Then she saw him.

Across the street.

Looking up here.

She didn't have a detailed look at him but she was sure he was the man in the blue Volvo.

She wished she'd heard from Marcy Browne, the private investigator. Wished she knew who this man was for sure. And what he wanted.

What if he wasn't a TV tabloid reporter?

What if he were something far more ominous?

She let the drape fall and walked back to the fireplace mantel. Now that he knew she was aware of him, maybe he'd leave. Maybe he'd get scared that she'd call the police.

She sipped her Chablis. Her heart was pounding and she resented being upset again. Eric was enough for one day. She didn't need this, too.

She charged across the room to the window, swept back the drape and glared out into the night.

Gone.

He was gone.

She let the drape fall again and walked across to the hutch where the phone rested.

She consulted the number she'd written on her phone pad this afternoon.

'Marcy?'

'Uh-huh?'

'This is Jill Coffey.'

'Oh, hi. Excuse all the pig noises. I just ran over to McDonald's and bought myself a little dinner.'

'That's fine – go right on eating. I just wondered if you'd gotten any information yet on the Volvo.'

'Not so far. I'm waiting for Nate to call me back.'

'Nate?'

'Yeah. Cop friend I have. He's going to run the number for me.'

'Oh.'

'But he got stuck doing something else for his boss first. He says he'll run it soon as he can. You sound kind of nervous.'

'I am. He was across the street just a few minutes ago.'

'Guy in the Volvo?'

'Uh-huh. Except this time I didn't see the Volvo. This time he seemed to be on foot.'

'Maybe you should call the cops.'

'Not yet. I'm going to give it a little more time.'

'I'll get back to you as soon as I can. Damn.'

'What's wrong?'

'I just knocked over my malt. Spilled it all over the desk.'

'I'm sorry.'

That was when the bell at the bottom of the stairs rang, the stairs that led to her apartment.

'You hear that?'

'Your doorbell?' Marcy Browne said.

'Yes.'

'You have any way of knowing who it is?'

'Not till I get down to the door and look through the eyehole.'

'Maybe you better call the police.'

'I can do better than that.'

'How?'

'I've got a .38. I'm going to get it and go downstairs.'

'You want to leave the phone off the hook so I can hear what happens?'

'That's a good idea. I'll be back soon.'

She rushed into the bedroom, searched in the second drawer of her night-stand, and found the .38.

She went to the front door, opened it and went down the stairs. In the dark.

Now her heart was really hammering.

She kept flashing on the man in the Volvo.

Maybe he had a gun, too. Maybe he'd shoot her right through the door.

The hall was narrow and dusty. She sneezed. Great. Fine time to sneeze. You're supposed to feel independent and strong with the cold gray metal of a gun in your hand and then you go screw it up by sneezing.

She reached the small vestibule.

Walked to the door.

Peered out the safety eye.

It took a moment for her eye to adjust in the darkness, then she made a small gasping sound.

It was a man she'd seen across the street just a few minutes ago, but it wasn't the man in the Volvo.

It was Mitch Ayers.

Chapter Twenty-Two

Cini hid on the sixth floor.

She snuck in from the back stairs and found a darkened corner at the far end of the sixth-floor hall where she could huddle in the shadows and hope that the cleaning crew didn't spot her.

Had to think things through.

Carefully. Sanely. So much at stake now.

Even in panic, she realized that she couldn't just leave her purse up in Eric's office. Eventually, the police would get there and find it. And then she would be dragged into the case.

God, she could just imagine the interrogation . . .

And after the bar, you went back with Eric to his office?

Yes, sir.

Why?

(Obviously lying) *He, he wanted to show me some commercials he'd done.*

I see. He couldn't have shown you the commercials during regular business hours?

I guess I never thought of that.

Were you aware of Eric Brooks' reputation?

Reputation?

He was quite the ladies' man.

I see.

In fact, he was notorious for making love to women right in his office.

Oh.

Did you make love to him in his office, Ms Powell?

(Pause) *No.*

You hesitated.

I wouldn't call it making love.

What would you call it, then?

Please, do I have to tell you what happened?

This is a murder investigation. Of course you have to tell us what happened.

Well, he, I— I mean—

Ms Powell?

(Silence)

Cini?

(Silence)

You have to tell us the truth. Maybe not right now, Cini. But eventually.

And she would have to tell the truth. About what she'd done, there in his office. Just so she could get a part in a commercial. Just so she could make Michael jealous. It would be in all the newspapers, and on all the TV stations – and all the radio stations. She could hear the disc jockeys laughing about it now. This was the sort of thing they loved. She would be a laughing stock to all of Chicago. Or maybe even worse . . . Maybe David Letterman or Jay Leno would start making jokes about her—

She had to go up and get her purse.

Nobody must ever know what she'd done in Eric's office tonight. Nobody. Ever.

She'd take the stairs again. Walk very quietly. And when she got to the top, she'd listen very hard. The killer was probably gone by now. They didn't usually hang around. Not on television, anyway.

She moved away from the shadows of the corner.

Walked toward the FIRE sign at the far end of the hall. She'd have to go back up there and get her purse. Go back up there and try very hard not to look at Eric. He had been so bloody the last time she'd seen him.

She reached the door. Eased it open. Started climbing.

She just hoped that the killer watched enough TV to know he shouldn't be hanging around up there.

Chapter Twenty-Three

'I don't suppose it matters that I'm sorry.'

'Not anymore it doesn't, Mitch.'

'You wouldn't take any of my calls.'

'There wasn't anything to say. You were a married man, and I don't go out with married men.'

'I made a mistake.'

'Yes, I think you did.'

'And it's too late to do anything about it?'

'God, Mitch, what did you expect I'd do when you came over here tonight? Welcome you with open arms? Ask you to move in? Call up all my friends and tell them I'm having a party for the man I love?'

'I really do love you, Jill.'

'I thought that before. And then you went right back to your wife.'

'It didn't work out.'

'She found somebody else again, didn't she?'

'Well . . .'

'Oh great, Mitch. You're on the rebound a second time?'

'Not on the rebound. It's done, it really is. I don't love her: I love you.'

'I need some more wine.'

'So do I.'

'This really makes me mad, Mitch, you coming up here this way. "Good old Jill. She'll be there."'

'It isn't like that at all.'

'Oh no? Then why didn't you call before you came? I'll tell you why. Because I wouldn't have let you in, that's why. Right?'

'Well . . .'

'*Right?*'

'I suppose.'

'It just really makes me mad.'

'You said that.'

'Yeah, well, I'll probably say it a few more times before I kick you out.'

'I wish you'd calm down.'

'You do, huh?'

'Yeah, I do.'

'Well, I'm not going to calm down.'

'Oh, no?'

And that was when he took her in his arms.

And that was when he kissed her.

And that was when she felt all sorts of things she'd hoped she'd never feel again. At least, not with Mitch Ayers.

'You did a nice job.'

'Thanks.'

'It's really attractive up here. Looks like you've changed everything.'

'Just about.'

This was half an hour after their first kiss and twenty minutes after their second kiss and ten minutes after their third kiss.

She'd be all right for a little while, thinking how good it felt to be in his arms again and to kiss him, and then she'd erupt once more, think of how he'd dumped her, and then she'd go across the room and sit in the big armchair alone, which was where she was now. Mitch was across the room on the couch.

'So where's your wife now?'

'Ex-wife.'

'You're divorced?'

'We will be.'

'Just like last time.'

'You're not very good with sarcasm, Jill. A little heavy-handed.'

'You're not very good at keeping your promises. Maybe that makes us even.' She shook her head. 'God, I hate it when I sound like this. The Victim. I'm not a victim.'

'I know you're not.'

'I'm an intelligent woman perfectly capable of running her own life.'

'I love you, Jill.'

'The next time you say that, I'm going to get some kitchen matches and set your tie on fire.'

He laughed. 'Still crazy, I see.'

'Look who's talking!'

'I'm really nervous. Are you really nervous?'

'I'm beyond really nervous. I need a couple boxes of Prozac.'

'Even if you won't ever see me again, I'm glad I came over.'

'Well, I'm not going to tell you that *I'm* glad you came over.'

'You sure?'

'Positive.'

He smiled again. 'You're beautiful.'

'No, I'm not.'

'Well, you're very pretty then.'

'Pretty I'll accept. Beautiful, no way.'

'I prefer pretty.'

'This isn't working.'

'What isn't working?'

'You know, what you're trying to do to me.' She really did feel wretched. She wanted to throw him down the stairs – and at the same time she wanted to cling to him, too.

'What am I trying to do to you?'

'Make me like you.'

'You don't like me?'

'Not anymore.'

'I'm really not trying to make you like me.'

'Then how come you keep looking so damned cute?' This time it was Jill who smiled. 'I hate you, Ayers. Do you understand that?'

'Then how come you're smiling?'

'Because I'm glad to see you, but that doesn't mean that I don't hate you.'

He looked down at his big hands. 'I need to ask you something.'

'Ask me what?'

He looked up at her. 'To forgive me.'

The playfulness was over. For both of them.

'I don't know if I can, Mitch.'

'Would you be willing to try?'

'I'd have to think about it. And I'm not just being difficult. I don't know if I could ever trust you again. You've been honest with me, so I'll be honest with you. I love you more than I've ever loved anybody, Mitch, but I don't know if I'll ever feel comfortable with you again. I'll always be waiting for you to go back to your wife someday.'

'That's not going to happen.'

'Then maybe it'll be somebody else you'll leave me for.'

'Every relationship has risks, Jill. You know that.'

'I'd need some time to think. And maybe I won't want to go back, Mitch. Maybe I won't be able to go back.'

'I know, Jill. All I'm asking you is to think about it for a while.'

He stood up.

She felt both relief and panic.

This apartment was going to be awfully empty without him.

The way it had been awfully empty the first time he'd walked out on her.

She went to him and took him to her, hugging him rather than kissing him. She didn't want passion, she wanted tenderness.

And he seemed to understand that.

He didn't try to kiss her. He simply held her.

'Is it all right to tell you I love you?'

'It's all right if you want me to set your tie on fire.'

He eased away from her. 'I guess I'll just have to take that chance.' He leaned forward and kissed her softly on the forehead. 'I love you, Jill.'

And then he was nothing more than retreating footsteps down the dark stairs, and out into the noisy night.

Chapter Twenty-Four

Cini put her fingers on the fine curved metal handle of the fire door. All she had to do was pull it open, step out into the corridor, walk down to the Eric Brooks agency, go inside and get her purse.

What could be simpler?

The killer was still here. She just knew it. Could *feel* it.

This was what half her mind told her. The scaredy-cat half. The half that had always gotten her laughed at by more adventurous girls. This was the Cini who was afraid of swimming, flying, fast bicycle-riding, thunderstorms and dogs any bigger than a small poodle. And these were only a few of the things she was afraid of.

Then there was the other half of her mind or, more precisely, personality. This half told her she was being silly. No competent killer would hang around after murdering somebody. And from her look at him – she would not forget his face even if she lived to be 108 and was brain dead – he certainly appeared competent. *Slash slash slash*. He had used those scissors with terrifying virtuosity.

All she had to do was
take hold of the handle
and

open the door

and

A noise. An echo.

Her first impression was that it was on this same floor, but when she heard the voices distinctly, followed by the roar of the industrial-size carpet cleaner, she realized that the noise was coming from the floor directly below.

An office building like this one would have several cleaning crews working simultaneously. This crew probably worked the top three or four floors, which meant they'd be up here not too long from now.

She had to hurry.

Get into Eric's office, get out.

Before the cleaning crew saw her.

Cini took a deep breath. She told herself she was being perfectly silly about the killer. Her fingers formed a claw on the curved handle of the door. She opened it and stepped out into the corridor.

Empty.

Never before had emptiness struck her as such a beautiful and glorious sight.

No scouter-ahead for the cleaning crew.

No killer coming at her with bloody scissors.

She turned right, straight down the hall. Walking fast.

She opened the front door to the advertising agency and went inside.

This time the silence, the emptiness came at her in a rush. Thrum of electricity. Rapping of skittering October wind on windows. Rumbling thunder, faint down the dark sky.

Past the reception desk, she went. Down the proper corridor to the proper office. Pausing now at the small reception area in front of Eric's office.

He was going to be in there, Eric was. All bloody. All dead.

She needed to tap into the strong, confident part of herself. The part that had only emerged when she lost all that weight following her accident.

A deep breath. Tightening her hands into fists.

Dead. She was strong enough to deal with dead. Even stabbed-dead. Even bloody-dead.

She marched promptly into Eric Brooks' office, saw him lying on the floor and then clamped a hand hard over her mouth so she wouldn't scream.

Oh my God.

He lay sprawled face up, a dozen or more slashes and cuts on his face and hands alone. In the torso, he must have been stabbed maybe two dozen times. His clothes were soaked with blood, dark and gooey in some places, shiny and almost pink in places where the bleeding was more superficial. The killer had even slashed Eric's cheeks, defacing him. The odors were awful. She remembered reading an Ed McBain novel about how murder victims frequently emptied themselves in the course of their violent death.

She made a Sign of the Cross.

She hadn't liked him – and liked herself in relation to him even less – but she knew he had a family and so it was really for them that she was crossing herself.

And then she had a terrible thought: What if he wasn't actually dead? What if he had survived all the wounds and still enjoyed faint life?

She didn't want to touch him in any way, that was for sure.

She didn't even want to place the 911 call in case it would somehow be traced back to her.

But she didn't want to leave here without at least having tried to determine if he was truly dead.

She did the only thing she could think of.

She sort of tiptoed over to him and said, in a voice little more than a whisper, 'Eric, are you dead?'

Nothing.

She leaned down. 'Eric, are you dead?'

Nothing.

She listened for any faint exhalation.

Nothing.

She watched his eyelids for a full minute.

Not a flutter.

She watched the bloodiest part of his entire torso, his belly.

It did not move.

'Eric, are you sure you're dead?'

Nothing nothing nothing.

'God, Eric, are you absolutely sure?'

The stench was really starting to sicken her.

She took one last look at him, decided that he was really truly absolutely dead, and then started searching around for her purse.

She found it on the far side of the couch. She remembered she had put it on the arm: it must have fallen off.

She walked quickly out of the office, angling her head so that she did not have to see Eric.

She wanted to forget this night completely. And forever.

Chapter Twenty-Five

Doris always felt the need to apologize for the mansion.

While she didn't have a job, she did go to the city frequently for her charity work, where she was inevitably asked to dinner by handsome bachelors intrigued by the lovely, somewhat frail, dark-haired woman who would someday come into the entire Tappley fortune.

Occasionally, though she knew her mother would disapprove, she accepted their invitations, allowing herself to try out the restaurant of the moment.

Inevitably, the subject of the manor house came up, the manor house that had fascinated Chicago for nearly four decades.

She pulled up to the looming iron gates now, the house hidden behind shag pine and oak and birch, and thumbed the opener for passage.

She swept up the half-mile curving drive and there, sprawling on forty-seven acres of starry prairie night, was the spectacular Georgian brick home of gracious living room, formal dining room, state-of-the-art kitchen, paneled library and family room with fireplace and French doors to the terrace and pool. In all, the house had a dozen bathrooms, eight fireplaces, a sauna, and servants' quarters that were very nearly as well-appointed as the manor house itself.

She took her parking place in the garage and then stood for a moment staring out at the night. Every few weeks she vowed to start hiking again. For her, hiking was peace. No one to feel beholden to, not even Mother.

She immediately felt guilty.

This was not a time when her mother needed bad thoughts circulating in the air.

Tomorrow was 14 October, the night her brother Peter had been put to death in the electric chair. Six years ago tomorrow night.

Whenever the date approached, her mother became almost frenzied with her grief and melancholy, shutting herself off in the den where she watched old family films of Peter. A bitterness came up in her mother that almost made her a stranger. She went from a sleek older woman gracious and tutored in the best of society to a haggard and angry crone.

Doris might have been more understanding if only her mother could have accepted a simple fact – that Peter was guilty. Doris had fought this truth, too, for nearly two years. But during the trial it became apparent that Peter had indeed murdered those girls. She did not want to see him die – she knew by now that he was insane and could not hold out against his compulsions – but nor did she want him set free, as her mother so devoutly wished. Not that Evelyn Tappley didn't have suspicions; sometimes she bitterly blamed Jill Coffey for what Peter had done, inherently admitting at these moments that Peter *had* killed those girls. She went back and forth in a kind of delirium about the subject. All that mattered to her was that, guilty or not, her son, her beloved son, had been stolen from her. And Jill Coffey was somehow responsible.

Doris looked up at the wheeling stars, and inhaled the last of dying summer on this autumn night, and listened to the horses down by the barn neigh as night rolled on. Life had become so strange over the past six years. Her two-year marriage had faded now and she was so accustomed to being defensive about her occasional date – 'Maybe somebody actually likes me for myself, Mother, instead of my money: have you ever considered that possibility?' – that she'd given up even those. Now it was just her charities and her three horses and the house and the two annual three-week vacations she took with her mother to Europe. By now, Doris had made her peace with loneliness. The morning mirror, the light that never lied, told her she was becoming gray of hair and fat-cheeked and lined. Her beauty, which had been considerable, was sliding into a mere memory of beauty, a kind of matronly hint of better days. There were times when she wanted to complain to someone about her life, but who could listen without laughing? No matter what she said, they would remind her of the manor house, of the servants and gardeners, of the family empire that grew ever more vast, and of the fact that she would someday own it all.

There was an owl on the night suddenly, and it sounded just as isolated as she felt. She listened to it for a long moment, one lonely being recognizing another, and then she went inside.

'How long has she been in there?'

'A little over two hours.'

'Did she have any dinner?'

The maid shook her head. 'I tried.'

'I'm sure you did, Martha.'

'Those films, you know. The old ones.' Martha was sixty, stout, gray-haired, gray-uniformed. She was always touching the small silver cross at her neck. Perhaps there were vampires in this house that needed warding off.

'You want me to try her again with some dinner, miss?'

'No thanks, Martha. I'll try her myself.'

'Yes, miss. Good luck.'

This was a house of high ceilings, two sweeping staircases, spectacular decorative moldings, carved mantels and arched windows. It was also a house of vast and intricate echoes; as Martha walked away in her sensible brown oxfords, the high hollow echoes of her passage filled the air.

Doris knocked on the double mahogany doors leading to the den. From inside, she could hear her mother crying softly as the videotape unspooled.

Doris went inside, stood in silhouette in the doorway.

'Hello, Mother.'

Evelyn looked up, daubing tears with a lace handkerchief. 'Remember this?'

Peter was not quite ten when this footage was taken of them in the family swimming pool on a hot July day. The remembered smell of chlorine filled Doris' nostrils. And then the smell of scorching sunlight.

On screen were Doris and Peter, both skinny, somewhat gangly, both grinning into the camera. There was a fairytale aura about this – a better time in a far land where fathers lived for ever and sweet little boys did not grow up to become killers.

For a moment, Doris felt the same kind of suffocating melancholy her mother must experience whenever she watched these old films. But instead of letting it smother her, Doris escaped from it, came back to the present.

'Martha told me you didn't eat any supper.'

'I'm not hungry, dear. It's nothing to worry about.'

'Well, you're wrong, Mother. It *is* something to worry about. You didn't eat lunch, either, as I recall.'

On screen now, Peter was riding his bike down the sweeping driveway, sunlight dappling through the summer trees.

'He was so handsome.'

'Yes, he was, Mother.'

'This is all her fault. I know you don't like me to say that, but it's true. If he'd never met her, Peter would be living in this house with you and me today.'

Doris didn't want to argue. All she said was, 'I'm going to have Martha make you a turkey sandwich and a salad.'

But Evelyn was off in one of her reveries. Staring at the screen – the image was now that of Peter playing basketball on the outdoor court his mother had had built for his twelfth birthday – she said, 'But she's finally going to get her come-uppance. Don't think she isn't.'

'And how is that going to happen, Mother?'

Evelyn looked up at her. The crone look was on her again. Beady, shining, crazed eyes. Thin, bitter mouth. 'I've arranged for her to be dealt with in a very fitting way. And that's all I'm going to say about it.'

Doris felt her stomach knot. Her mother was telling the truth, not merely bluffing. Evelyn Daye Tappley never bluffed. Powerful people like her didn't have to.

Doris stared at her mother for a long moment, not knowing what to say, and then finally: 'I'll have Martha get your sandwich.'

But her mother was already watching the screen again, lost in the perfect memories of her perfect little boy.

Chapter Twenty-Six

After leaving the Loop via the Dan Ryan Expressway, Cini took an exit different from her own and pulled up to a 7-Eleven store whose lights she had seen from a distance.

She knew there was only one way she could cope with what she'd seen just a while ago in Eric Brooks' office. Some people would have picked up a glass of whisky; others would have engaged in sex. For Cini there was only one salvation. Junk food.

She surprised the Pakistani clerk by picking up one of the red plastic hand carriers. Virtually nobody ever used the hand carriers in here.

She wanted something from every basic food group – pastry, candy, potato chips, ice cream.

She didn't even try to stop herself, didn't even try to say, You're going on a binge again, Cini, and you're going to destroy that beautiful thin body of yours.

God, Cini, stop before it's too late.

But she was in the throes of a desire that she could no longer control. Did not *want* to control.

She started at the pastry section, picking up a box of Hostess powder donuts then a box of Little Debbie filled oatmeal cookies then grabbing a half dozen Colonial bear claws in cellophane wrappers that were gorgeously sticky inside from all the gooey sugar frosting.

The candy section came next. Cini specialized in chocolate. She selected a quarter pound Hershey bar with almonds, a King Size Baby Ruth, a bag of mini-Mounds, a bag of mini-Almond Joys, a Milky-Way King Size, two boxes of Boston baked beans, three boxes of Good n' Plentys and two long dealies of Switzer's red licorice.

At the ice-cream counter, she filled up her entire red plastic hand carrier with six quarts of Haagen Dazs of different flavors and then a vast box of Drumsticks. She really liked the nuts they sprinkled on the top.

There was a black customer at the counter when Cini got up there. She was nervous; she couldn't help it. Black people who weren't dressed in suits and ties (male) or nice dresses (female) scared her. She'd seen a black hatemonger on TV a year ago and he'd convinced her that in every black heart was a yearning to kill white people. Cini knew that this wasn't true, that most black people were decent citizens and not really all that much different from herself, but the trouble was, how did you tell the occasional hater from your good ordinary person? They didn't wear little tags that said HATER. Only too late did you find that they had guns or knives and were in the process of killing anything that moved and was white. You saw it on TV all the time.

The black customer, who was probably fifty, shook his head when he took his lottery ticket from the Pakistani clerk and checked the number. He smiled at Cini. He had a great smile – wry, intelligent and friendly. 'And here I was gettin' ready to retire, too,' he said, nodded goodnight to Cini and the clerk and left.

Cini put the hand carrier on the counter.

The Pakistani laughed. 'Such a slim girl. Such a big appetite.'

'I'm having a little party tonight,' she lied. 'Some friends are coming over.'

Yeah, she thought. They don't like beer or bourbon or marijuana. They're Switzer's licorice junkies. Life in the fast lane.

She was already back to her Whale days. Always lying to clerks about why she was buying so much junk food. Ashamed of herself but unable to stop.

The clerk started ringing everything up.

He needed one of the big bags to get everything in.

The total came to $44.39.

My God!

That was another thing about being a Whale. You were always broke from buying junk food. No joke. Linda, another one of the Whales, once spent more than $200 in a single weekend on pastries alone. She estimated she had consumed more than 50,000 calories that weekend. She forced herself to vomit, as usual, but she began vomiting so violently that she actually puked up blood. She called Cini in absolute terror. Cini met her at the Emergency Room. She had done no permanent damage but the young female intern did convince Linda to try the Eating Disorder Clinic. Linda lasted seven weeks there and then started bingeing again. Last time Cini saw her, Linda weighed more than 220 pounds and was doping herself up constantly on tranquilizers. Being obese was a great big joke to people who didn't suffer from it. But for those who did . . .

Cini wrote out her check and handed it over. The clerk rubber-stamped the back of it and then began filling in the information he took from Cini's driver's license.

Cini hefted her bags and started out to the car.

Behind her, the clerk said, 'You be careful with all that junk food, missy. Don't want to ruin that figure of yours.'

Cini smiled and walked out the door. The night smelled of cigarette smoke and gasoline. She set the bags on the passenger seat and then walked around and got behind the wheel.

The tears came instantly – hard, hot, harsh tears that made her grab the steering wheel with such force that it bowed beneath the sudden pressure.

She was going to do it again.

Start the eating again.

The gorging that would take her back to obesity.

For the first time since the urge had seized her, she thought: *I don't want to do this. I really don't.*

But then she started the car and backed out of the 7-Eleven and headed in the direction of her apartment.

Before she had gone three blocks, she had ripped open the King Size Baby Ruth bar and was cramming it into her mouth.

Chapter Twenty-Seven

The scalpel is made of stainless steel and feels cold as death to the naked hand.

The same can be said of the other instrument the surgeon chooses on this overcast morning in Berlin, a knife of ten inches in length and two ounces in weight.

The surgeon likes the heft of the knife in his hand. Not many mortals are allowed to cut up a human being in this fashion and get paid for it. And paid so well.

He begins.

Chapter Twenty-Eight

I cut her up real good and the bathtub runs maybe an inch-and-a-half deep with her blood and that's when I get the idea of taking her out and then just sitting in there.

So I take her out and set up her bled body on the closed toilet, like maybe she's having a tinkle or something, and then I get in the tub and sit in her blood and light myself a Pall Mall and stare out the window at the dusk.

The dusk always makes me melancholy as hell but it's a dangerous melancholy, one I've never been able to explain to anybody. Things are just so fucking sad and nobody seems to understand that.

And I'm drunk, which doesn't help.

Drunk and sitting in an inch-and-a-half of some woman's blood and there's a sad spring night breeze coming in through the window and some goddammed sad black rhythm and blues song on the radio and then I start talking to her.

Asking her about herself.

I've never really found out anything about any of my victims.

She sits there, kind of propped up, all blue of skin and

deeply bloody of wound, and she just stares straight ahead in her stunned, dead way.

And I'm talking to her because I'm so drunk and because the melancholy is on me and when it's on me I just want to be held and held tight and then suddenly I'm jumping out of the tub and I grab her and break her arms until they fit around me and then I start dancing with her, the way I used to slow-dance back in high school, with a big embarrassing erection that brushes against the girl every few seconds or so. I'm dancing with this dead woman in my bathroom and the worst thing is that it makes me feel better.

Not so lonely.

At least for a time.

The night breeze feels good.

And I don't feel so scared now.

I just dance and dance and dance.

Chapter Twenty-Nine

Sister Mary Margaret decided to stop at the corner news stand and get herself a magazine.

Black and white habit flowing in the October night, she approached the small kiosk where the dumpy man in the ratty cardigan sweater and the big cigar butt stood talking to another male customer about – what else – the Bears.

The night smelled chill; in the autumn scents were traces of winter.

Sister Mary Margaret listened and shivered as the two men made dire predictions about how the season would turn out.

Traffic raced by. The night was alive with an energy that was both exciting and terrifying.

She scanned the magazines. So many promises they made. How to lose weight. Get a man. Find God. Make your erection last longer. Double the profits on your investments. Make your children like you. It was all sort of sad and desperate, the splashy magazines and their even splashier pledges.

Sister Mary Margaret cleared her throat.

Stan, the guy who ran this magazine stand, glanced over at her and said, 'Hey, Sister, sorry. I didn't see you standin' there.'

The good Sister, who was a very shy lady indeed, kept her face tilted down, ostensibly so she could scan all the newspapers Stan had laid out across the front of his counter. 'That's all right. You've got so many interesting things to look at.'

'So what can I get for you, Sister?'

'I wondered if you had a copy of *Hustler*.'

Stan glanced at his football pal. Both men looked shocked.

'I don't think I heard you right, Sister.'

'I thought she said *Hustler*,' said the football pal.

'Yeah, so did I.'

'I did,' said the nun.

'*Hustler*?' Stan repeated. 'With the broads and everything?'

'Yes,' Sister Mary Margaret said, 'with the broads and everything.'

And it was then that she reached up and looked Stan right in the face and said, 'Boy, did I have you going.'

'God, Ralph – look, it's Marcy!'

'Marcy Browne!' his football pal said. 'The chick private eye.'

'I'll be damned,' Stan said.

'I'm sure you will be,' Marcy said.

'What's with the nun stuff? You undercover?'

'Something like that.' The grin again. 'Plus I just wanted to see what you'd do if some nun came up and ordered a copy of *Hustler*.'

'You sure had me goin',' Stan said admiringly. Then, 'So you really want a copy?'

'Are you kidding? That sleazy rag?' And Sister Mary Margaret walked huffily away.

Marcy really dug this acting stuff. It was fun.

* * *

Once she was back in her office and dressed in her own clothes again, Marcy heated up some soup in a pan on her hotplate and then sat with her feet up on the desk, sipping Campbell's tomato soup from a Spiderman mug and reading a copy of *American Ballerina*.

Only her mother knew that Marcy had always wanted to be a ballerina. She'd seen *The Turning Point* with Shirley MacLaine when she was twelve years old and ever since . . . But, her Dad being a steelworker and all, Marcy didn't come from the proper social background anyway. After being told by his wife that Marcy needed ballet shoes, Ken Browne had said, 'What the hell'm I supposed to do about it, Candy? Go out to Sears and charge her a pair.' Right, Dad. Ballet slippers at Sears.

But that hadn't been the only thing to hold her back. Even worse than having a dad who thought that Sears sold ballet slippers was being a girl who had absolutely no dancing talent whatsoever. Sweet little face. Sweet little body. But no talent at all.

She slogged through three years of training until one day Nick, the dance instructor, finished his session with Marcy and asked if he could see her mother alone. Mrs Browne came over and Nick looked right at her and burst into tears. 'I can't do it anymore, Mrs Browne. She's driving me crazy. She's a great kid, your Marcy, but she moves like a moose.' At which point he put his head on Mrs Browne's shoulder and proceeded to weep.

The subject of dance was never again mentioned in the Browne household. The ballet slippers were given away; the costumes were packed in a trunk. And Dad was relieved that they didn't have to watch any more PBS dance shows where guys walked around in very tight pants and big cast-iron nut-cups. Those guys made him extremely uncomfortable.

So all that was left of that era for Marcy was her fondness for *American Ballerina* magazine.

She loved it. Pored over every single page, fantasizing that she was every one of those agile, fragile princesses up on their toes and breaking all those artistic hearts.

Not for Marcy Browne Paris or Vienna or Rome, or any other noted dance city of the world. No, for Marcy Browne it had been Hilton Community College and Criminology 101, Crim 102, Crim 103 and Crim 104, putting in her first years as a security guard (minimum wage and no health insurance) at Montgomery Wards (or 'Monkey Wards' as Dad always called it) and then three years with the Night Shift Detective Agency, where she'd mostly followed around unfaithful spouses, and then that teeny tiny inheritance from Aunt Paula – just enough to start her own teeny tiny agency . . .

Now, she hoisted her Spiderman cup, finished off the tomato soup and then glanced at the dusty wall clock directly across the office.

It was time to check out Jill's place again. Marcy hadn't promised – and couldn't deliver – twenty-four-hour surveillance, but since she was wide awake she might as well run by Jill's apartment, just on the off chance that the blue Volvo had put in another appearance . . .

She went to her closet, chose an outfit, dressed and then walked outside to her car.

She just hoped her Dad never saw her in this get-up. The tight black micro-skirt was slit right up to her hipbone, and the white peasant blouse was cut so low her breasts practically stood up and waved at people.

Dad, being Dad, would probably try to have her arrested. 'Teach her a lesson,' as he would put it.

Marcy got in her car and drove to Jill's. On the way over, four different guys tried to pick her up at stoplights.

Chapter Thirty

The house felt emptier than usual.

After leaving Eric Brooks' office, Rick Corday stopped in for a drink at a neighborhood bar, then went to the supermarket and bought several bottles of Evian water and ten very lean slices of beef together with a loaf of dark rye bread.

Now he stood just inside his front door and wished that Adam were here. Loneliness came easily, too easily, to Corday; sometimes he felt completely isolated, as if he were an alien spy left on a planet of suspicious strangers.

He clipped on the light and came inside. Not even the manly grace of the leather furnishings and the Remington prints helped much this evening. Their home seemed as cold and barren as a motel room.

He put the groceries away and then went into the bathroom and stripped down to his underwear. He wrapped everything he'd worn to Brooks' office into a bundle and then tied it with string. There was an incinerator at the dump he used sometimes. He'd go there in the next day or so and destroy all these things.

He put on a blue button-down shirt, jeans and cordovan penny-loafers and started down the hall to the living room.

But halfway there, he paused, and looked with nostalgia and anxiety into the darkness of Adam's bedroom. They each had their own rooms. Adam's was verboten. Even the cleaning lady had been instructed not to go in there. One day, Adam had caught Rick looking for a shirt to borrow and he'd become so enraged that Rick thought he might have gone temporarily insane. '*I never want you in here again. Never!*' he'd screamed.

But Adam was out of town.

And Adam had cheated on him again.

And Rick felt like a little excitement tonight.

Adam was a very mysterious person. Rarely did he talk about his background, for example, except to say that he'd grown up in the Midwest. For all that they were partners, Rick always sensed that there were many vital things he didn't know about Adam: things which Adam would never tell him.

He took a deep breath.

This was like disobeying your parents, doing the one thing that was going to really infuriate them.

Another deep breath.

He started into Adam's bedroom.

Found the overhead light switch and turned it on.

Adam was as untidy as a little boy. Piles of dirty clothes everywhere; an uneven stack of paperbacks on the night-stand; a half-finished wine cooler next to the bed; the bed itself unmade.

Rick had to smile.

An untidy little boy, that was Adam. Or at least, a part of him, anyway. Rick didn't like to think about the other parts. The secretive part. The cold part. The cruel part. Especially the cruel part. Adam had a tongue like a meat cleaver and wasn't slow to use it when you had displeased him.

Now Rick was going to learn more about Adam.

He went in and walked around, taking in the air. This was very special air: Adam's own private air.

No framed photographs to divulge the past. No college yearbooks to rummage through, and get sentimental over. No dusty military uniforms to hint at where you'd served.

Impersonal. Very much like Adam himself.

Soon enough, Rick got tired of walking around. He had the itch to get his detective work underway.

Here I come, Adam, ready or not.

The chest of drawers – that promised to be a mountain of information. People put all kinds of things in their chest of drawers.

Another deep breath.

Exciting. Scary.

Fingers on the ornate knobs of the chest's first drawer. Slide the first drawer open. Peek inside . . .

Socks. Black socks, blue socks, argyle socks. Maybe two dozen pairs of socks.

But was something more interesting hidden beneath them? Rick reached inside – the drawer smelling of sawn pine and coarse to the touch from being unfinished – and started to push his hands all the way down to the bottom of the drawer. He found –

Socks.

Damn.

Just like Adam to build up your hopes and then disappoint you with socks.

Maybe drawer number two . . .

Drawer number two was underwear.

Plain white jockey shorts, buff-blue boxer shorts, even a pair of red bikini underwear, though Adam hated all things effeminate and fussy.

Maybe beneath this tumble of underwear was hidden –

Nothing.

Nothing at all.

More sweet aroma of sawn pine. More feel of rough, unfinished wood. But – nothing inside.

Two more drawers to go.

This was like a treasure hunt. Or a game show.

Two more to go!

And that was when the phone rang. Rick jumped in terror and panic, as if his mother had caught him doing something extremely unpleasant and unwholesome. He fled the bedroom, clipping out the light and trotting down the hall to the living room to pick up the phone there.

'Mr Runyon, please.'

He said, and quite angrily, 'How did you get my number, Mrs Tappley?'

'My attorney, of course.'

'He promised that he wouldn't tell anyone how to reach me.'

'I pay my attorney a great deal of money, Mr Runyon. He can't afford to keep secrets from me.'

He said, 'Is somebody else on this line, Mrs Tappley?'

'What?'

'This connection sounds funny.'

'You must be a very paranoid man, Mr Runyon.'

'I want to hang up now, Mrs Tappley.'

'And I want to know how things went – you know, tonight.'

'Watch the news later on.'

'I really resent your attitude, Mr Runyon.'

'I don't give a damn what you resent, Mrs Tappley.'

And with that, Rick Corday became the only person in Chicago history to ever hang up on Mrs Evelyn Daye Tappley.

* * *

A half hour later, still angry that Mrs Tappley had his number, still certain that Adam had gone to New York simply to cheat on him, Rick Corday got in his car and decided to drive past Jill Coffey's place.

He wanted to make sure she was home.

So the police wouldn't have any trouble finding her.

This was such a tidy little job. It did a heart good to know that it was, at least upon occasion, capable of genius.

Chapter Thirty-One

Doris did not hang up until both her mother and Mr Runyon had done so. Then she gently cradled the phone and left the den. She'd heard her mother, in her private office, call somebody. Doris had then immediately ducked into the library and lifted the receiver.

'*Watch the news later tonight,*' the man named Runyon had said. What had he meant by that? What had her mother hired him to do?

Earlier tonight, her mother had said that Jill Coffey was 'finally going to get her come-uppance' and the words had frightened Doris.

Her mother was old and bitter and had the resources to destroy virtually anybody.

Had she finally gotten around to destroying Jill Coffey?

No use asking her mother directly. The woman would never tell her. But Doris had to find out somehow. Jill Coffey didn't deserve her mother's wrath. Her only crime had been that she hadn't fitted into the Tappley household, where Evelyn Tappley was the absolute lord and master.

Nobody deserved to be destroyed for that.

Nervously, Doris went downstairs to the den. She needed one of her rare drinks of alcohol. Perhaps, in fact, she needed two.

Chapter Thirty-Two

Andre Sovic always knew that someday he was going to be important. When he was in grade school, he figured he was going to be important in high school, and when he was in high school, he figured he was going to be important in college. But he wasn't important in college, either, because this really aggravating little war called Vietnam got in the way. As the son of poor Polish immigrants, Sovic had nobody to take his part when his summons came from the draft board, so off he went to war. It was a fine and noble calling, a war, and as much as the mother and sister were heartbroken, as much as the old man was secretly afraid, off Andre went. He didn't become important in the war. He sat on his butt in a supply depot in Saigon and typed up requisitions. Back home, there were no parades, no newspaper interviews, not even any big family gathering. But why should there be? As yet, Andre Sovic had not proved himself to be important. He went to work at the GM plant, got married to a Polish girl with a set of charlies that were truly eye-popping, and then spent the next sixteen years (they now had four kids) in happy oblivion. Then he got laid off permanently (why couldn't they just say 'fired' and have done with it) from GM and spent just over a year collecting unemployment checks and getting sick of the soap operas his wife watched all day. Andre Sovic was still not an important man.

He was thinking of all this as he got off the elevator tonight. Maybe he was wrong. Maybe he'd never be important. Maybe this was simply the fanciful notion of some dumb polack kid from Chicago wearing his khaki uniform with the little Ajax Janitorial insignia above his lapel, jaunty dark brown Ajax Janitorial cap on his head, and Ajax Janitorial vacuum cleaner in his right hand.

He went up to the wooden door marked ERIC BROOKS, was surprised to find it unlocked, and peeked inside.

'Hello?' His voice sounded kind of eerie in the stillness.

He wondered why the door was unlocked. Brooks was usually the last one out of here (a lot of times he had babes with him, *beautiful* babes) and he always locked up.

No answer.

He went inside.

He was scared. He didn't know why.

Odd, too. All these months going up and down inside dark skyscrapers and he hadn't once got scared.

But tonight, now—

'Hello?'

What was he scared of? Guy goes off and forgets to lock the door. Big deal. Probably had some babe on his arm who made him forget everything else.

He went into the plum-colored reception area. Paused. Heard nothing. Decided to take a right and go down the short hall leading to Brooks' own office.

'Hello!'

Didn't want to find Brooks bopping somebody on his desk or something. Didn't want to get fired.

By now he was right up to Eric Brooks' office. The door was open.

He peeked in.

The first thing he saw was the blood sprayed and splashed all over the gray fabric wall.

The second thing he saw was Eric Brooks' head sticking out from behind the desk. On the floor. At a very odd and painful-looking angle.

The third thing he saw were the bloody orange-handled scissors several feet from Eric Brooks' head.

'Oh God,' said the formerly unimportant Andre Sovic. 'Oh God oh God oh God.'

Took him three minutes to gather himself sufficiently to lift his communicator from his belt and talk to his black bastard of a boss.

'You botherin' me again, Sovic.'

'You gotta get up here.'

'You got some chicks up there, all right. Otherwise forget it.' Then he seemed to sense Sovic's mood. He dropped his street-jive accent and said in a perfectly normal middle-class voice, 'What's wrong, Sovic?'

'Just get up here. Please – get up here real fast.'

Andre Sovic had become important at last. To the police, who would question him. To the press, who would quote him endlessly. To his family, who would forever more tell stories about the night Dad found that rich guy all cut up in his office.

But as Andre Sovic looked at the bloody body, he wondered if he really liked being important after all.

Not even in Vietnam had he seen corpses this savagely cut up.

Chapter Thirty-Three

Marcy Browne had been sitting there in her cute little hooker costume for maybe thirty, thirty-five minutes when the blue Volvo showed up.

She had been listening to a country and western station – the title of the last song being 'I Cheated With My Body But Not My Soul' – because she planned on taking up line dancing very soon. Line dancing was becoming very big in the United States among people who fancied themselves real cowboys and cowgirls, though it was highly unlikely that a real cowboy would ever have done a dance called the Tush Push.

She was thinking about Tush Pushes, her mind drifting the way it always did when she pulled surveillance, when the blue Volvo eased past her on the opposite side of the street.

She spotted the guy driving immediately.

Same white-haired James Coburn kind of guy as in the photo Jill had given her. Same deep blue Volvo Jill had described.

She sat up good and straight, still feeling a little self-conscious in her hooker get-up, turned on the lights and prepared to make a U-turn.

The blue Volvo wasn't stopping at Jill's but it was slowing

so the guy could look at the second floor and see that Jill was home.

She started into her U-turn.

This was great.

Real excitement.

The kind of thing that happened to TV private eyes all the time but that almost never happened to them in real life.

An honest-to-goodness tail job!

She was going to get his license number and then she was going to follow him and then—

And then, because she'd been so excited she hadn't seen it coming, the gray Plymouth drove straight into her. Marcy had been halfway through her U-turn and—

There was a great and calamitous ripping and rending of metal, a loud and ugly shattering of glass, and an angry blast of horn that could probably be heard half a mile away.

Only now did Marcy realize what had happened. She'd swerved out into the traffic lane without seeing him coming.

He was big, truck-driver big, and mean, thug-mean, and he fairly tore off his door getting out of the car. He stalked up to her with ape-drooping arms and said, 'You little bitch, I should slap the shit out of you.'

It was enough to make her want to go back to community college and find herself a new line of work.

Chapter Thirty-Four

After Mitch had left, Jill went downstairs to the darkroom and developed some film from an agency shoot she'd done a few days earlier.

As she worked, clipping the film up to dry, she tried very hard not to think about Mitch Ayers. Or how, despite all her words to the contrary, she'd been happy to see him tonight. Even worse, she sensed that he just might be telling the truth – that his long and difficult and failed marriage might finally be over at last.

No. Don't get sucked back in.

This was how it went for an hour, yin and yang, to and fro, back and forth. She wanted to see more of Mitch; she dreaded seeing more of Mitch. Mitch was honest and trustworthy; Mitch was selfish and deceitful.

This was one of those times when she wished she'd had more experience with men. In all, she'd slept with five men in her life, one of them (she smiled wryly) who wouldn't take a shower unless she threatened to cut him off from sex. She didn't really have enough experience to know if Mitch's behavior was typical of a man in the middle of a divorce, or whether Mitch was just cynically using her.

She concentrated on work, developing six contact

sheets. She had to get back to the client in the next few days. Like most ad men, he believed in starting projects only a few hours before they were due.

She was just choosing shots, marking off the preferred ones on the contact sheets with a grease pencil, when she heard a loud pounding on her apartment door.

She thought of two people: Mitch or the man in the blue Volvo.

This time she didn't have her gun.

She had to go up the stairs to her apartment then back down a different set of stairs to the ground-floor door.

She peered out through the eyehole.

Kate stood there, shivering in the chill wind.

Jill took off all three locks and opened the door.

Slender, regal Kate, who might have been a taller version of Audrey Hepburn if only she weren't such a rubber-faced wise-ass, looked suspiciously subdued. Despite her years as a highly paid runway model, Kate usually opened with a dirty joke or two. But tonight there were no smiles, no joke.

'Have you been listening to the news?'

'No,' Jill said. 'Why?'

'Eric Brooks was murdered tonight.'

'*What?*'

Kate nodded somberly, drawing herself deep into her cape-like black coat.

'Let's go upstairs. Get WGN on. Their news starts in a few minutes.'

'Prominent Chicago advertising executive Eric Brooks was found murdered in his office in downtown Chicago tonight. Police aren't saying how he was killed or if they have any suspects. Witnesses at the scene at Brooks' office say there was a great deal of blood on the floor and carpet, indicating an act of extreme violence. We'll bring you a live update later in this newscast.'

Jill thumbed OFF on the remote.

The two women sat in silence, sipping at the dregs of Mr Coffee Jill had poured them.

'You saw him tonight, right?'

'Right,' Jill echoed. She felt dazed, unreal. For all that the crime rate was going up in Chicago, she had remained untouched by it. A friend of hers had once been robbed in a parking ramp, while another friend had found evidence that somebody had tried to jimmy open her back window, but the worst of it – the muggings, the stabbings, the shootings – had not touched her.

And now this.

She wanted to feel bad for Eric: that was what she was really struggling with. She wanted her dislike of him to subside so she could feel an appropriate sense of loss, but all she could summon now was rage at violence of this sort, and real sympathy for Eric's wife and children. This was the kind of event that would mark the girls for years, if not for life.

And finally she even felt sympathy for Eric. He had been an insecure and manipulative man but despite that there had been some genuine good times, and because of Eric she'd been able to go on her own as a photographer. His business acumen had given her the money she'd needed.

'What time did you leave?'

Jill didn't realize, until Kate's question had floated unanswered for a few seconds, that her friend had even spoken.

'I'm sorry. What was that?'

'What time did you leave Eric's office?' Even in a simple white button-down blouse and designer jeans, her shining dark hair touching her shoulders, doe-eyed Kate looked gorgeous.

'About seven-thirty, I guess.'

'Maybe you should call the police.'

'Yes, I guess I should.' She shook her head. 'God, I just can't believe it.'

'I had a friend in college, her brother was murdered like this. She said that even years later, she couldn't believe that somebody had killed him. She kept waiting for him to show up on her doorstep one day.'

'His poor wife and kids.'

'And poor Eric. I got the impression from the TV story that they must really have done a job on him.'

'You want more coffee?'

'If you wouldn't mind. I'd just gone out to get something to eat when I heard about Eric on the car radio, so I drove right over here.' She patted her stomach. 'It keeps growling.'

'I've got a stale donut in the cupboard if you're interested. Or a fresh apple.'

Kate grinned. 'Now knowing me, Ms Nutrition, which do you think I'd like? Fresh apple or stale donut?'

'Stale donut.'

Kate clapped her hands together like an exuberant child. 'Correct. Very good guess.'

As Jill prepared another pot of coffee, and set Kate's donut on a saucer, she thought again of Eric's widow and his children. Especially his children.

She said a silent prayer for them.

Chapter Thirty-Five

Mitch Ayers wanted to live in a kinder, gentler era and his choice in rental videos reflected this fact.

After leaving Jill's place, he declined the pleasure of meeting some cop buddies in a bar and instead went to Video Crazy where he rented comedy tapes with W. C. Fields and Laurel and Hardy, and a Warner Brothers one which included two Daffy Ducks, two Elmer Fudds and three Bugs Bunnys.

Mitch was from the last generation that went every week to Saturday afternoon matinées. This was in the mid-fifties when big shiny cars disgorged howling mobs of suburban kids in front of downtown theaters. He'd always been especially keen on comedy, Jerry Lewis, Francis The Talking Mule and Ma and Pa Kettle being among his favorites.

For nostalgia's sake, he'd even rented a Ma and Pa Kettle tonight.

He lay on the couch in a jogging suit, a can of Schlitz on the pressed-wood coffee table, trying hard to lose himself in Fields' *The Bank Dick*. Usually, Mitch had no trouble being transported back to the early part of the century when men were still gentlemen and women were still ladies.

But every thirty seconds or so he'd find his mind drifting back to Jill and what had happened at her place tonight. Much as he wanted to tell himself that it had gone well, that she hadn't kicked him out anyway, he'd seen how much he'd hurt her. He remembered disappointing his youngest daughter once by forgetting her birthday. He would always remember her face that day – just as he would always remember Jill's face tonight.

He loved her: he was more sure of that than ever. The question was, even though he knew she loved him, would she take him back? Would she give them another chance?

The phone rang.

He felt a ridiculous surge of hope. Maybe it was Jill, inviting him back over tonight. *All is forgiven*.

Ridiculous was the operative word. Unless she had recently soaked her vocal chords in two packs of Winstons and a pint of Old Grandad a day, this was not Jill.

'I thought you were goin' out with some of the boys tonight?' Lieutenant Sievers drawled.

'Decided to turn in early. What can I do for you, Lieutenant?'

'You know a lady named Jill Coffey, right?'

'Right. Went out with her for several months.'

'Tell me about her.'

'No, you tell me about her.' He felt anxious suddenly, and angry that his boss hadn't explained why he'd called. 'Why are you asking about her?'

'Her former business partner was killed tonight and I understand she was up in his office around the time it happened. Her name was in his appointment book.'

'Are you talking about Eric Brooks?'

'One and the same.'

'Killed?'

'Stabbed to death. Stabbed several times, in fact. I'm told the crime scene is a real mess.'

'You're not telling me you think Jill had something to do with this, are you?'

'All I know, Mitch, is one of the homicide boys said that he thought you'd known her at one time and would I call you and get your general impressions.'

'My general impressions are all favorable. She's a very nice, kind, appealing woman.'

'Sounds like you might be sorry you're not still seeing her.'

'I am, as a matter of fact.'

'Well, we'll have to ask her some questions.'

'I'm sure she'll be happy to cooperate.'

'She got a temper?'

'Not a very bad one.'

'She really hated this guy, huh?'

'Hated is a little strong. She didn't admire him much.'

'Then why'd she go see him tonight?'

'As you said, you'll have to ask her some questions.'

'I'd invite you along but I don't think that'd be a good idea. Professionally speaking, I mean.'

'Neither do I.'

The Lieutenant paused. 'Now don't go gettin' all bent out of shape about this next question, all right?'

'I'm ahead of you. As far as I know, they were never lovers.'

'You pretty sure of that?'

'Pretty sure, yes. I mean, I think he hit on her a lot but it didn't do any good.'

'When he hit on her, would that get her pretty stirred up, you think?'

'If you mean angry, yes, I suppose it did. But not angry enough to stab him.'

'Are you sure about that?'

'I told you, Lieutenant, she's not the type.'

'I appreciate the information, Mitch.'

'She's a very nice woman. Tell homicide to take it easy with her.'

'Like I said earlier, I guess it's a good thing you're not going along.'

'Yeah,' Mitch said. 'I guess it is.'

After hanging up, he put in a different tape and lay back down again. But not even Daffy Duck's famous lisp could amuse him now.

More than he wanted to admit, he was concerned about Jill Coffey.

Chapter Thirty-Six

Cini was just opening her second box of Good n' Plentys when the phone rang in her apartment.

'Hi, honey. We were just wondering how you were doing.'

Oh great, just what she needed. Mom and Dad. Much as she loved them, she hated the way they constantly called to see what she was up to. She'd once overheard them refer to her to a next door neighbor as their 'problem child.' And she'd resented them ever since.

'I'm doing fine.'

'You sound funny.'

'I do?'

'Like you're eating something.'

'Oh. Right. Yes, I've got something in my mouth.'

'Your mouth?'

'A Good n' Plenty.'

'A Good n' *Plenty*? I didn't think you ate things like that anymore. You remember what Dr Steiner said.'

'"Well-balanced food cuts down on the craving for junk food, Cini." And Dr Steiner didn't say it, you did.'

'I really don't appreciate that tone of voice, Cini. I am, after all, your mother. And the man standing next to me is, after all, your father.'

'Yes, and I am, after all, your daughter.'

'I don't appreciate being mocked, either. I'm going to put your father on the line.'

Ultimate threat. At least, when Cini was growing up: *I'm going to put your father on the line.*

Her father came on the line.

'Is everything all right, honey?'

Oh yes, Daddy, everything's just fine. I had oral sex with a man just so I could get into a commercial, and now I'm starting to pig out again. Everything's just fine. Oh, and I almost forgot: I saw that same man get murdered tonight.

'Everything's fine.'

'I really don't appreciate it when you upset your mother.'

Cini sighed. 'I'm having a hard time right now, Daddy, that's all.'

'Then for God's sake, Cini, when you're having a hard time, why don't you call us and tell us about it?' Pause. 'What're you eating?'

'A Good n' Plenty.'

He inflected it just as her mother had done. 'A Good n' *Plenty*?'

'A pink one.'

'Honey, Good n' Plentys aren't exactly what Dr Steiner had in mind when he put you on that maintenance diet after your accident.'

'I'm only eating one.'

'Scout's Honor?' God, that was so Daddy, asking Scout's Honor, the way he used to when she was eight.

'Two, then.'

'Two?'

'I've had three, Daddy. But I'm crumpling up the box and throwing the rest away. Can you hear me crumpling the box?' She put the Good n' Plenty box next to the receiver and started twisting and mashing it. 'Can you hear that?'

'I just don't want to see you start overeating again. You were so happy there for such a long time. And you looked so good.'

'I won't start again,' Cini said, feeling sorry for him. That was the weird thing, no matter how hard she tried she couldn't feel sorry for her mother. But Daddy she could feel sorry for all the time. 'I really won't, Daddy.'

'I'm taking you at your word, honey.'

'You should.'

'I want to put your mother on now and I want you to apologize to her.'

'I didn't do anything to apologize *for*, Daddy.'

But she could picture him. He'd be looking furtively at his wife and smiling, pretending that everything was just fine on the phone, pretending that Cini just couldn't wait to apologize and be all smiles again.

Cini smiled at this sad but endearing image of her father. 'All right, Dad. Put her on.'

She could hear her mother whispering – protesting – in the background. She didn't want to talk to Cini anymore than Cini wanted to talk to her. Finally, she took the phone. 'You know how it upsets your father when we argue.'

This was about as close as her mother would ever come to apologizing.

'I'm sorry, Mom. I'm just feeling down, I guess.'

'Any reason in particular? Is it Michael?'

'I think Michael and I are all through.'

'He didn't look like a very serious young man to me, Cini.'

'I know, Mom. You told me that many times.'

'And whatever's making you depressed, Good n' Plentys aren't going to help.'

'I know that, Mom.' She decided to tell a whopping big

lie, one that would make them all feel better and get her mother off the phone very quickly. 'This talk has helped a lot.'

'It has?'

'Uh-huh.'

'So you're really going to throw those Good n' Plentys away?'

'Uh-huh.'

'And get back on that diet Dr Steiner put you on?'

'Uh-huh.'

'That makes me feel much better, Cini.'

'Me, too, Mom.'

'Your father and I love you very much.'

'I know you do.'

'Now you sleep tight.'

'And don't let the bedbugs bite. That's what you always used to say.'

'G'night, Cini.'

'G'night, Mom.'

Soon as she'd hung up the phone, Cini tore into the Good n' Plentys. Then she started on a pint of the Haagen Daz strawberry ice cream. She had a long way to go before she finished eating everything she'd bought earlier tonight.

Chapter Thirty-Seven

The drill is the most frightening of all his surgical instruments in appearance. Difficult to imagine how the human body, so delicate and vulnerable, could possibly withstand an assault with a 3/8″ Skil model running 110 volts with a bit that looks capable of ripping through steel.

The surgeon wraps his hand around the drill handle.

The drill is his favorite of all instruments.

And so he begins.

Chapter Thirty-Eight

Adam's new friend had gone to sleep in the bedroom. Adam came walking out, buttoning his shirt, ready to leave.

He looked out the window to the phone booth on the street below. He'd call Rick Corday from there. Rick had been pretty upset about finding that note from Adam's one-night stand in Miami. Rick was such a child. He could never seem to grasp that loving somebody was very different from merely sleeping with someone.

As he found his trench coat and let himself out the door, Adam also started wondering how things had gone tonight with Eric Brooks. Not exactly a good time for Rick to be upset, his mind wandering, or his need for violence to surge again.

Much as Adam felt superior to Rick – smarter, better organized, far more focused, certainly more mature and, let's face it, *much* better-looking – his mate had one area of clear superiority: he loved violence far more than Adam ever would.

Adam and Rick had met in a gay bar in Chicago and then started hanging out. This was four years ago. One night several weeks into their relationship, Rick saw a young woman walking alone on a dark street and he said, 'You ever thought of killing anybody?'

'Sure. Who hasn't?'

'What if I told you that I've already killed somebody. In fact, several somebodies.'

Adam, who was driving, smiled. 'What if I told you that I'd killed a few people, too?'

'Really?'

'Really.'

'God, that's fantastic.'

Adam, ever the cynic, said, 'What if one of us is lying?'

'Huh?'

'What if I'm telling you the truth but you're lying?'

'That I didn't really kill people before?'

'Right. Then I'd be confessing to murder – and you'd just be lying.'

'Sort of like *Strangers on a Train*.' Rick smiled. 'But I really have killed somebody.'

'So have I,' Adam said. 'But how're we going to prove it?'

'Two blocks back.'

'What?'

'That chick. Two blocks back. That's how we're going to prove it.'

'What about her?'

'Let's go back and get her.'

'You're serious?' Adam said.

'Very serious.'

'Then what?'

'Take her out to the country and kill her.'

'Just like that?'

'Just like that. We're supposed to be killers, remember?'

A few minutes later they came around the corner of the block where the woman was walking.

'Go past her,' Rick instructed. 'Drive down to the next block. There's an alley there.'

'Good idea.'

Adam drove down to the alley, turned in and then parked the car in deep shadow. He killed the lights but left the motor running.

They got out of the car. It was misting. The alley smelled sweet-and-sour of garbage. A tomcat came down it carrying a mouse in his mouth.

They walked up to the edge of the alley. Pressed themselves flat against the wall. Listened hard for footsteps.

Nothing – nothing – then –

Footsteps.

High heels.

Coming fast.

Coming right toward them.

Adam thought how crazy it was. He was really going to kill somebody again. The ultimate risk . . .

'Let her get past us a couple of feet,' Rick hissed.

Adam nodded, his heart slamming against his chest. God, if something went wrong—

But it went just fine.

When she got three feet past them, Rick virtually leapt on her, clamping his hand over her mouth and dragging her back into the alley.

As soon as they were in shadow, Adam grabbed the woman's feet. They carried her quickly to the car.

Adam set her feet down and popped open the trunk.

Rick picked up a loose brick from the alley and smashed it against the side of the woman's head. She went limp.

They got her in the trunk and drove away.

Rick gave directions. They drove for nearly an hour,

finally coming to a stop at a deserted stone mansion. Rick explained that it had once been an artists' colony but had burned down. A huge red barn, sagging westward now with age, sat adjacent to the charred and empty mansion.

Adam drove into the barn.

He climbed out into darkness. The barn smelled of wet hay and animal feces.

They got the woman out of the trunk and took her into one of the stalls where horses once slept.

She was still breathing, but not with any great energy or regularity.

Rick found a rusted lantern and got it going, hanging it on a peg above the woman.

Adam watched as Rick ripped all the woman's clothes off and then proceeded to rape her. All the time he was having her he was also hitting her, again and again and again in the face until nothing recognizable was left of her looks. Adam wanted to say something but was, frankly, a little afraid of Rick at the moment.

When Rick was done, he stood up and nodded for Adam to take his turn. Adam's first impulse was to decline but then he felt that icy ripple of fear down his back.

This was one intense guy, this Rick.

Adam took his turn.

But he didn't hit her and he finished as quickly as he could.

When he was done, he stood up. Rick was gone.

The woman moaned.

From out of the darkness, Rick said, 'You want to finish her or shall I?'

'Be my guest.'

'Afraid, huh?'

'No, I'm not afraid.'

'You really kill somebody before?'

'Yes.'

'Then kill her.'

'Maybe you're the one who's afraid.'

Rick laughed. 'Hey, pal, we're talking about you here, not me. Finish her.'

'How?'

'However you want to.'

The others, he'd cut their throats. 'I don't have a knife with me.'

'Kick her.'

'Where?'

'Where the hell do you think kick her? In the head. Right about the temple.'

'In the head?'

'Sure. Just pretend you're punting a football.'

'You've done that before?'

'Two or three times.'

'What's it like?'

'You know, when your foot makes contact with the skull – it's a real satisfying feeling.'

'Wow.'

'Do it.'

Adam nodded. Maybe it would be fun, after all.

He stepped up to the naked woman sprawled on the hay beneath him. Her face really was gone now, just blood and broken bones. Her moaning got fainter and fainter.

Rain pattered the leaky barn roof; a lonely dog barked somewhere nearby; the engine of a plane could be heard faintly, faintly.

'Go ahead.'

He was hesitant at first, self-conscious with Rick watching, but then he did it, one quick short violent kick, and he had to admit, it really was satisfying.

'Wow,' he said. 'You were right – about how your toe feels when it connects with the skull.'

'Kick her again.'

'Really?'

'Sure. Probably take a couple times to do it right.'

He kicked her again.

This time her head canted a little, as if it wanted to roll away.

'You think she's dead?'

'Why don't you make sure?'

'You mean another one?'

Rick laughed. 'They don't cost you anything, do they?'

He kicked her again, just above the temple.

The tip of his toe felt her skull start to go this time.

'She's dead.'

'I'll make sure for you.'

'You want to kick her?'

'Sure,' Rick said.

He kicked very hard.

Blood started pouring from her nose.

'Man,' Adam said, 'you really gave it to her.'

Coming down the stairs now, six blocks from a fashionable area of restaurants, Adam thought back to that night two years ago and shook his head. He enjoyed taking risks, but within reason.

But Rick, when he got down or depressed, or angry with something that Adam had done—

Adam stood for a moment on the corner taking in the fresh night air. Well, as fresh as you were going to get in New York City, anyway.

The lighted phone booth reminded him of a million *films noirs* he'd seen over the years. How he loved them. Bogart. Robert Ryan. Lawrence Tierney (who maybe had the greatest *noir* face of all) . . .

Hearing his footsteps echo in the night, turning up the collar of his trench coat, tilting his head against the bitter wind . . . he felt like a character in a *film noir* himself.

When he got to the phone booth, Adam took out his wallet and his Ma Bell credit card and went to work.

Four minutes later their phone was ringing back in Chicago.

Ringing and ringing and—

Adam got a bad feeling.

He could see Rick being so upset about the latest of Adam's dalliances (well, the latest till he'd arrived here in New York) that his mate went out tonight and did something stupid.

Rick was always a wild card.

Always.

Adam replaced the receiver.

Then he was out of the booth and walking again, a character in a black-and-white film circa 1948, one with a lot of blue and lonely sax music . . .

Chapter Thirty-Nine

'Excuse me.'

Jill had been in the middle of buttering a piece of wheatbread she'd bought fresh from the bakery earlier that day, and exchanging some choice gossip with Kate, when her phone rang.

She picked it up. 'Hello?'

'Hi. It's me, Mitch.'

She glanced at Kate, feeling guilty, the way she had when her older brother always smirked about her boyfriends calling the house.

Kate seemed to know immediately who it was.

'I'm sort of busy right now, Mitch. Kate's here.'

'This is business, Jill.'

'Business?'

'Yes. You heard about Eric Brooks?'

'Yes.'

'Well, my boss is going to question you, probably later tonight.'

'Isn't that normal? I mean, I was up there, seeing Eric.'

'Anything noteworthy take place?'

'Not really. Excuse me a second.' She covered the yellow receiver, the yellow matching the walls of the kitchen, and said to Kate, 'The police are going to question me.'

Kate frowned. 'Boy, that's all you need. Publicity again.'

To Mitch, Jill said, 'This is all routine, right?'

'I hope so.'

'You don't sound sure.'

'My Lieutenant is – well, I don't know if you remember me talking about him, but Lieutenant Sievers isn't exactly a criminology genius. He's very old-school. And he tends to pursue the first person who looks like a good suspect.'

She thought of tabloid journalists hiding in wait wherever she went. Could it all happen again?

'Eric was alive and well when I left there.'

'I'm sure he was.'

'Do you have any advice?'

'Don't let him rile you. The Lieutenant, I mean. He's very good at making people feel guilty, even when they're not.'

'God, I'm not looking forward to this.'

'Maybe . . .' He paused. 'Maybe I could come over and give you a little moral support.'

She glanced at Kate, still feeling embarrassed about talking to Mitch in front of her, probably because she knew that Kate still disliked Mitch for what he'd done to Jill.

She did not want to say what she said next. But somehow the words came, symbols of all the loneliness and tenderness and emptiness she'd known since Mitch had so abruptly left her life. 'I'd like that.'

'I'll be there in twenty minutes.'

She hung up and said to Kate, 'I guess I'm going to have company a little later.'

Kate looked at her levelly. 'You sure you want him coming around again, Jill?'

Jill smiled sardonically. 'That's the funny thing. I *do* want him coming around again.'

Chapter Forty

Doris spent an hour on the phone talking to a college classmate who'd called a few weeks earlier. Doris hadn't gotten a chance to return the call till now, which gave her the perfect opportunity to be in the second den, the smaller one, that her mother used as an office.

As Doris and her friend Amy went through the latest on divorces, births, re-marriages and promotions, Doris carefully examined everything on the green felt desk pad, and then began working her way through the desk drawers.

She wanted to find something with the man's name on it. *Runyon*.

'And did you hear about Sally Wasserman?'

'No,' Doris said, trying to stay alert as she talked and searched. 'But she's such a decent person, I hope it's good news.'

'New breasts.'

'Sally Wasserman? That must be just a rumor.'

'No rumor. I've seen them with my own eyes.'

'Maybe she's just wearing padded bras.'

Amy chuckled. 'No bra's this padded, believe me. Plus, they sit straight out.'

'Maybe I should look into it myself.'

'You? You've got great charlies, Doris.'

'"Charlies?"' Doris laughed. 'God, where did you hear that?'

'That's what my ten-year-old calls them when he thinks I'm not listening to him talk to his totally sexist little friends. I think we're raising a generation of male chauvinist pigs.'

'Well, is there anybody we haven't worked over?' Much as Doris had always liked Amy, she always felt slightly degraded after talking to the woman. They had a tendency to make uncharitable remarks about other people and that wasn't exactly the image Doris wanted of herself. Living at home with a dominating mother didn't exactly make her an ideal person herself, so she shouldn't criticize others for the way they chose to live their lives.

Amy said, 'And how about Robert Fitz—'

But before Amy could launch into a job on hapless fat Robert Fitzgerald, Doris said, 'Did you hear about Helen?'

'McGiver?'

'Uh-huh.'

'No, what? Her husband dump her?'

'No. She got promoted to chief of staff at her hospital in Florida.'

'And that's it?'

Doris laughed. 'Oh, right, I guess I forgot to add that she's figured out a way to have sex while she's operating on a patient. She's sleeping with all these sexy young interns and—'

Runyon!

Name, address, telephone number neatly typed on a sheet of letterhead.

But that wasn't the most surprising thing.

It was who the letterhead belonged to that shocked Doris.

Third desk drawer, left side.

'You all right?'

'Fine.'

'You sure, Doris?'

Doris tried to recover. 'I just looked up at the clock.'

'You have to go?'

'I'm afraid so. I just remembered that I promised my mother I'd help her with something.'

Pause. 'How is your mother?' Amy's voice always got very tight whenever she mentioned Mrs Tappley.

Doris knew that whenever Amy discussed her, she clucked about Evelyn. Old shrew. Keeping her daughter a prisoner like that. So selfish. That was the funny thing. Doris knew that Amy really liked her. They'd always been something like best friends, and yet Amy completely disapproved of how Doris let Evelyn control her life.

'Oh, she's fine. Getting older. You know.'

But for once Amy didn't deliver a cryptic speech about how much a prisoner Doris was in her own house.

'It's sad, isn't it?' Amy said. 'Seeing your folks get old. I looked at my mother the other day, and I suddenly realized she's becoming this little old lady. It really scared me, how vulnerable she looked. I wanted to hide her somewhere, so Death couldn't find her. You know?'

'I know exactly.'

'Oh hon, I'm sorry I run people down all the time. I know how much of a gossip I am, and I know how much that bothers you.'

'I don't hang up, do I?' Doris said. 'And I gossip just as much as you do.'

'Thanks for saying that, hon, even though you know it's not true.'

'This time, I owe you the call.'

'Take care of yourself.'

'You, too, Amy.'

Doris sat back and stared at the letterhead. Two other names were typed on it, further down the page:

ADAM MORROW

RICK CORDAY

The names were followed by the same Chicago address and phone number.

But it was the name on the letterhead that held Doris's attention.

Arthur K. Halliwell
Attorney At Law

Arthur Halliwell was one of the most successful attorneys in Chicago, and had been the family's personal lawyer since the days that Doris' father had selected him to guard and administer the Tappley fortune.

Arthur Halliwell was one of the most respected men in the state. And the wisest. And the most conservative.

Doris couldn't imagine him ever helping her mother do something as illegal as get Jill Coffey into some sort of trouble . . .

'She'll get her comeuppance,' her mother had said earlier.

Still so bitter. Still so angry.

Doris could easily picture her mother contriving some kind of plan to ensnare Jill – but Arthur Halliwell helping her . . . ?

Doris slid the letterhead back into the drawer and closed it quietly.

She wanted to see her mother pass on with as much grace as possible. She did not want Evelyn to waste her remaining years pursuing some insane dream of vengeance.

Of his own free will, her brother Peter had crossed the state line into Indiana where, on three different occasions – and perhaps more that nobody knew about – he'd murdered and eviscerated three young women. And the state of Indiana had put him to death.

Jill Coffey had had nothing to do with any of it.

It was time Evelyn was made to understand that.

And understand it once and for all.

She left the den, climbing the grand staircase to the second floor and her mother's room.

Chapter Forty-One

Rick Corday watched the man knock on Jill's ground-floor door. He wondered who he was. This was his second visit tonight.

He waited until Jill appeared silhouetted in the yellow light of the doorframe and invited the man inside.

Rick then got out of his car and crossed the street. He had parked almost a block away from Jill's.

He walked up to the man's car and shone his light inside. All the forms, the nightstick and portable siren told him immediately what the man was. A police detective.

He walked back to his car. He wanted to eat something. A hamburger with lots of onions would be good. And he wanted to think about what this meant, that Jill Coffey had a friend who was a police detective.

Chapter Forty-Two

The call came just a few minutes after Mitch got to Jill's apartment. The kettle had just started to whistle. Jill poured water into her cup then made the long stretch to grab the phone.

Just before she heard a voice coming from the other end of the phone, Jill remembered something that Mitch had told her a long time ago – that Lieutenant Sievers did his best interrogation work on the phone. Sievers felt that a phone was much more relaxing for most people, and that they therefore tended to tell you more than they might have in person. Lieutenant Sievers, Mitch said, had received more than half a dozen murder confessions over the phone during his twenty-some years on the force.

'This is Lieutenant Wayne Sievers.'

'Good evening, Lieutenant.'

A pause. When he spoke, he sounded irritated. 'Our mutual friend Mitch Ayers told you I'd be calling, I assume.'

'Yes. Yes, he did.' She put her hand out and Mitch took it.

'You know about Eric Brooks?'

'Yes, I do. I'm still having a hard time making myself believe it.'

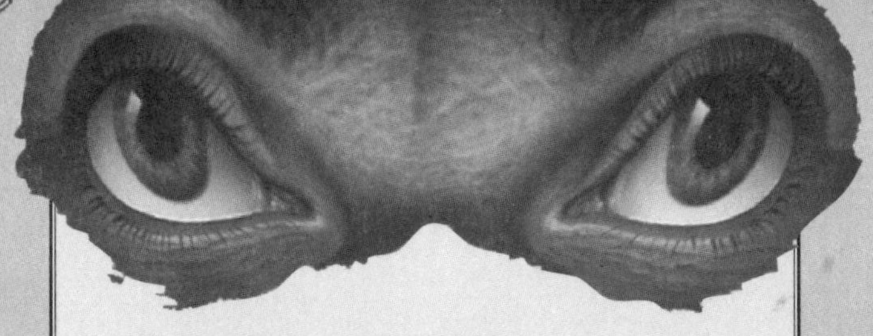

'Why's that?'

'I saw him just a few hours ago and he was alive. I still can't believe—'

'Were you two alone?'

'Yes.'

'What was his mood?'

'Oh, he was – Eric. You know.'

'No, I guess I don't know, Miss Coffey.'

'There was always something Eric wanted, and he always seemed agitated when he couldn't have it.'

'Was there anything in particular he wanted this evening, Miss Coffey?'

'Not that I know of.'

'Did he want you, Miss Coffey?'

She looked at Mitch. He made a big Happy Face, indicating she should do the same.

'I've already talked to some of his co-workers, Miss Coffey. They told me that he had always been interested in you romantically.'

'I wouldn't say "romantically."'

'Oh, then what would you say?'

'Sexually. But I didn't take that as any kind of compliment.'

'Why not?'

'Because Eric was fascinated with any woman who wouldn't sleep with him. I suppose he just couldn't imagine how we could say no to all his charms.'

'Was he charming, Miss Coffey?'

'He could be. But he could also be very manipulative and cynical.'

'Why did you two split up as partners?'

'There's no easy answer to that.'

'Then give me a complicated one.'

'Well, there was the sexual problem.'

'That being what exactly?'

'That he kept trying to get me into bed.' She looked at Mitch and shrugged. She felt as if she were saying the wrong thing.

'I see.'

'And we had argued a lot about the types of work I was doing. I'm a photographer and that's what I love doing and that's what I wanted to do, but Eric was trying to turn me into some kind of executive. I didn't want that.'

'I'm told you had very stormy arguments.'

'I can't deny that.'

'Did you have an argument tonight?'

She hesitated. 'I wouldn't characterize it as an argument.'

For the first time, a frown wrinkled Mitch's forehead.

'Then how would you characterize it?'

'Eric wanted to seduce me.'

'And you didn't want him to?'

'No, I didn't.'

'What happened?'

'Nothing, really. Before I went up there tonight, I'd had some hope that maybe Eric had changed. You know, grown up a little.'

'But he hadn't?'

'No. He was – Eric.'

It was all clear, of course, how Eric had forced a kiss on her and how she'd slapped him. She wanted to tell Lieutenant Sievers about this but every time her lips began to form the words—

Her slapping him.

And storming out.

And shortly thereafter, Eric murdered . . .

Jill remembered what Mitch had said about Lieutenant Sievers – how he was one of those cops who pursued the first serious suspect he came upon. She'd heard about cops like that. They spent all their efforts making a case against one person while not considering any other suspects.

So she didn't tell him about Eric's kiss, or her slapping him afterward.

'So you weren't intimate tonight?'

'Not just tonight, Lieutenant. We were never intimate.'

'How long were you there?'

'Fifteen minutes, something like that.'

'Did you see anybody else in the offices?'

'No.'

'Did you see anybody in the lobby or on the elevator?'

'No.'

'Did Eric receive a call when you were there?'

'No. But—'

'But what, Miss Coffey?'

'When I first arrived—'

'Yes?'

'There was a young woman just leaving Eric's office.'

'Could you describe her, Miss Coffey?'

Jill described her.

'Did she see you, Miss Coffey?'

'No, I don't think so.'

'Then she left?'

'Yes.'

'Did everything seem all right between them?'

'When I first got there, I waited outside Eric's door. I just heard the tail end of their conversation.' She told the Lieutenant everything she'd overheard.

'So Eric seemed angry?' the Lieutenant asked.

'No, that's too strong. Combative is more like it.'

'That's a strange word to describe a social relationship.'

'Not where Eric was concerned. He made a lot of sexual demands on you – a lot of innuendo, a lot of what he considered to be sly hints – and you had to fight back. Combative isn't too strong a word for how it felt.'

'So you saw this young woman there and then not again?'

'Once more.'

'When?'

'As I was leaving his office. I walked to the elevator, and she was standing there waiting for one to arrive.'

'You're sure the outer office was empty?'

'As far as I could see.'

'The elevators there have very distinctive bell tones. Did you hear the elevator bell?'

'No.'

'You're positive?'

'Positive.'

'And on the way down?'

'I saw nobody.'

'And you never actually saw this woman get on the elevator? You just saw the door close?'

'That's right.'

'So when you left, Eric Brooks was alive.'

'Very much so.'

'And you went where, then, Miss Coffey?'

'Straight home.'

'And you've been there ever since?'

'Yessir.'

'I appreciate all this, Miss Coffey.'

'We're done?'

'For tonight, anyway. I'm sure I'll have follow-up questions.'

'Lieutenant Sievers?'

'Yes.'

'I didn't kill him.'

'I'm glad you didn't, Miss Coffey.'

'I want you to believe me.'

'You seem like a very nice person, Miss Coffey.'

'One more time so there can be no misunderstanding: I did not kill Eric Brooks.'

'I'm writing that down in my notebook. "Miss Coffey says she did not kill Mr Brooks." There, duly noted, Miss Coffey. I hope you get a good night's sleep.'

Then he was gone.

And Jill sat in the echoes of their conversation feeling very much the way Lieutenant Sievers wanted her to – like a murderer.

'Ceremonial cocoa,' he said, 'sort of like a Japanese ritual.'

She smiled wearily.

As a little girl, whenever Jill had been feeling depressed or anxious, her mother had made her cocoa, usually pouring it into her very special Lone Ranger mug, that Jill had inherited from her older brother Jason, who was then a military adviser in a faraway land called Vietnam.

'Still got that old mug of yours, I see,' Mitch said.

'Always with me in my darkest hour,' she said. Then, 'I wish Jason were.' Her brother had been killed in Vietnam in 1964, just as the war had become a political issue domestically.

They sat on the couch, in front of a TV screen filled with David Letterman. Neither of them paid much attention to it.

Twenty minutes ago, Jill had finished her conversation with the police but even now her stomach was in knots and she felt her hands spasm every few minutes. It was starting all over again, she thought. Even though she was innocent of murdering Eric, the press would love this story: the wife of a serial killer now suspected of being a killer herself.

'I appreciate you making me the cocoa,' Mitch said gently. 'It tastes great.'

She looked at him. 'Like the old days?'

'Just like the old days.'

'They were good days, that's for sure.' Her right hand rested on the knee of his dark corduroy jeans.

'Best days of my life, Jill. They really were.'

She started to move her hand but he gripped it. 'This is kind of like high school. I want to make a pass but I'm afraid to.'

She smiled. 'I guess I'm feeling the same way. I want you to make a pass – but then again, I don't want you to make a pass.'

'We don't need to make love. I'm not asking for that.'

'I know you're not, Mitch. It's just I'm – afraid. We get close again and you'll leave.'

'I want to marry you, Jill.'

She laid her head against the back of the couch, stretched her long legs out on the coffee table and said, 'Could we just sit here and hold hands for awhile?'

'Sure.'

'And just listen to Letterman?'

'Sure.'

She laughed. 'You're awfully agreeable for a cop.'

'They're making us take all these public relations courses. Whole new approach. We kill people with kindness instead of bullets.'

'Does it work?'

'Not so far. The public I'm trying to kill won't even let me kiss her.'

'Maybe she will in the next fifteen minutes or so.'

'You want to synchronize watches?'

She laughed again. 'God, that feels great.'

'Laughing?'

'Uh-huh.'

'Well, maybe I should stop by more often. It'll give you a lot more to laugh at.'

'How about one kiss?'

'My pleasure.'

'But not open-mouthed.'

'What kind of guy do you take me for anyway? I've got more self-respect than that.'

They kissed.

No open mouths.

It made her dizzy.

She pulled away. 'Maybe we shouldn't have done that.'

'Yeah, maybe we should have waited for the full fifteen minutes. I think we still had fourteen to go.'

'I want to hate you.'

'Well now, that's a nice neighborly thing to say.'

'You really hurt me.'

He didn't say anything for a long time, just stared at the TV screen without seeing anything and finally said, 'I'm sorry, Jill.'

'That's the terrible thing.'

'What is?'

'I believe you. That you're sorry. And I don't want to believe you.'

He turned on the couch and took her slowly in his arms. 'You should believe me, Jill. You really should.'

After they had finished making love, they snuggled beneath the covers and listened to the wet chill wind slap against the windows.

She couldn't get enough of his touch, or the familiar way he felt pressed against her, the smell of his hair, the gruff feel of his chin. He was one of those men who needed to shave twice a day. At this moment, he was lover, friend, brother and confidant and she loved all of them equally.

They were going to get married and love each other forever more. There might be children, and there would certainly be a rambling rustic house as idyllic as those she always saw in the romantic movies of the thirties and forties – a true retreat from the wickedness and pain of the world, a place where sunsets were unspeakably beautiful, and lasted for days at a time, a kingdom where the crystal blue lakes remained untouched by industrial pollution. She closed her eyes and imagined such a realm, with herself as the princess and Mitch, of course, as her prince. The only trouble was, reality always intruded. Here was this handsome fairytale prince – who was always in need of a shave.

'I don't think he believed me,' she said.

'Who?'

'Lieutenant Sievers.'

'About what?'

'The girl who came into Eric's office. I think he thinks I made her up.'

'This is all a formality, honest.'

'He didn't sound like it was a formality.'

'He's just trying to scare you. That's second nature to cops.'

'Remind me not to buy any tickets to the policemen's ball next year.'

'You won't have to.'

'Why not?'

'Because by then you'll be married to a policeman. And you'll get your tickets free.'

'I'm getting scared again.'

'Of Sievers?'

'Ummm. Of Sievers. And you. And us.'

'It's going to work this time, Jill. Honest.'

'Will you come visit me in prison?'

'Don't talk like that. That isn't funny.' Pause. 'In fact, don't talk at all.'

Before they made love a second time, he simply held her there in the darkness. And eventually she started feeling better, not scared, and safe. Definitely safe.

Holding Mitch was even better than holding her Lone Ranger mug.

Chapter Forty-Three

At home, Rick went to the dry bar, had two quick drinks of JB Scotch, and then decided to go back to Adam's room and look through the drawers. This time, he wouldn't let anything interrupt him.

But as he reached the hallway, he wondered if he should do it. No matter how hard he tried to leave things just as they were, he knew how angry Adam would be if he found out.

But no, dammit. He knew very little about Adam and now the man's background had begun to interest him a great deal. Who was Adam Morrow, anyway?

He walked to the bedroom door.

Clicked on the light.

Adam really was such a slob.

Rick went in.

Straight to the bureau.

But he couldn't help it. He felt guilty. A naughty little boy, that's what he felt like.

He bent down to the third drawer. That's where he'd left off, right? The third drawer.

He opened it and saw handkerchiefs and cufflinks and tie bars and mementos of weddings and mementos of birthday parties and mementos of New Year's Eves and so on. A junk drawer, that's what the third drawer was.

He sifted through everything but, as he'd suspected, the contents were of no interest, except for what they revealed about Adam. A pack rat, that was Adam. Not major league but minor league at least.

There was one more drawer.

He wasn't expecting much.

All these months, he'd thought of how neat it would be to sneak into Adam's room and go through his drawers and find—

Engraved swizzle sticks? Paper accordion-fold party hats? Gag napkins with dirty jokes on them?

God, he hoped there was something worth looking at in the fourth drawer.

He opened it and pulled it right out. Except for one small white envelope tucked in the far corner, the drawer was empty. Wow. All this room and just this one teeny-tiny envelope.

Wonder what's in it?

Either it's so important that it deserves its own drawer – or it's so unimportant that Adam just tossed the envelope in here and forgot about it.

He lifted the envelope up.

Surprisingly heavy.

Rubber band around it.

Took off the rubber band.

Looked inside.

And found – photographs.

All the photographs showed the same boy at various ages.

A handsome boy. Bright-looking.

Many of the pictures showed the boy playing in the grounds of a fantastic mansion.

Rick realized how little he knew of Adam's background.

He turned some of the photos over, to see if there was any kind of identification on them.

Peter Tappley.

This was written on six or seven of the photos.

A few of them were also dated.

And then, darkness – a cold sweat breaking out across his face and under his arms. Blackout . . .

He groped frantically for the bureau. Supported himself while the darkness moved through him like a terrible disease.

Then, slowly, he was able to stand erect. Able to see clearly again. Able to stop shaking.

Slowly, he went back to examining the pictures. He went through each and every one of the photographs, occasionally checking for names and dates on the back.

Following the very last photo, he found a newspaper clipping.

He unfolded it.

HEIR TO TAPPLEY
FORTUNE DIES IN
ELECTRIC CHAIR

Peter Tappley, one of two heirs to one of America's greatest fortunes, was put to death in the electric chair last night, after both the Supreme Court and the Governor refused to grant any more stays of execution. Witnesses say that the execution went off without any problems. Coroner J. K. Whitsone pronounced Tappley dead at 12:14 a.m., CST.

There was more but Rick didn't read it.

He put the pictures back in the envelope and the

envelope back in the drawer. The newspaper clipping he slipped into his pocket.

He left the room, turning off the light.

Rick took great pride in the way he had soundproofed the basement. He had brought his CD player down here and turned on a Sousa march until the speakers began to wobble from the fury of the music. Then he'd gone outside to see if he could hear it and – nothing. Perfect.

The utility room he walked through was big and cold and pretty much empty; some appliances, the furnace, and a stack of cardboard boxes were its only furnishings. At the far end was a door leading to a storage room.

He looked at the door, then walked down to it.

He opened the door, groped around and found the light switch, and flipped it on.

Hard as he'd tried, he hadn't been able to clean all the blood from the concrete floor and walls. Lots of faint red splashes remained.

Fortunately, he had spent a lot of time fixing up the drainage system, altering the soil stack that emptied into the main drain beneath the house. In three years, he'd killed seven women in this basement room. While he'd carted most of the body parts away, pieces of meat and organs were inevitably carried down the drain to the main drainage system. He'd had some problems at first, but once the soil stack had been rigged differently, they were solved.

The axe stood in the corner. It was a thing of beauty, at least to Rick – the equivalent of Excalibur. Dried blood lovingly streaked the 36-inch-long handle as well as the 5-inch cutting face. At night, watching TV, he often filed the head of the axe then used a whetstone on it. It was always sharp, always ready for use.

He went over and picked it up, stroked the long silken handle with obscene pleasure. He had a pretty good idea of who he'd be using this on, and soon.

He angled the inside of his thumb against the edge of the blade, his own blood mixing now with the blood of his victims. That's what we all came down to in the end, anyway. Blood and bone and meat and shit and come, all sinking into the oblivion of the ground.

He was aroused, then, and unexpectedly, the way he used to get as a teenager.

His need overwhelmed him and he hurried upstairs.

He kept the small black box of videotape velcro'd to the bottom of his mattress. It would take somebody a long time to find it. A long, long time.

He went swiftly to the living room, put the tape into the VCR, switched on the TV and then turned off all the other lights.

He knelt in front of the TV, as the images and then the screams struggled to grainy life on the home video.

He'd done this many times before.

He filled his hand with his sex and began pleasing himself.

The video had been taken in the basement with this skinny red-haired waitress he'd dragged all the way back from Wisconsin in the trunk of his car. He'd sedated her for the trip.

But he revived her when they got back here because he wanted to get it all on video. And her fear was a big part of the pleasure.

He'd mounted the camera on the tripod and then set to work.

She lay in the middle of the floor, right by the drain, naked and all trussed up. She had spunk, he had to give her that, the way she rolled left then right and then tried to kick her feet out. She had to know she didn't have a chance.

The camera got some good sexy angles of her as she rolled around naked like that. They were so good he always thought he was going to faint from pure pleasure when he saw them. She had a great little rump.

Then this guy came in. All in black. Right down to a black executioner's mask. Very dramatic. Freaky.

But what you really noticed about the guy was not his clothes but the axe.

Long, curved handle; blood-splashed head.

Rick and his axe.

She screamed so much the video microphone started woofing: it couldn't handle all that shrillness. She knew just what was about to happen . . .

He knelt in front of his TV now, pleasing himself more and more, faster and faster, as the axe descended and took her head off.

He watched it roll down the slanting floor toward the drain . . .

And then the man in the black executioner's mask – that's how he thought of it, like the guy in black wasn't really him but an actor, like, say, Warren Beatty or somebody – went to work on the rest of her . . .

And now, as the late-October wind tore at trees and shrieked into attic windows . . . now Rick knelt before his TV, his breath coming in gasps, as he watched the executioner finish the job.

The darkened living room was filled with shifting beams of light as the screen bloomed with various colors . . . and as Rick Corday cried out in ecstasy.

Chapter Forty-Four

Adam Morrow lay awake in his hotel room listening to the muffled sounds of the Manhattan midnight thirty stories below him.

He was being silly, paranoid.

Everything would be fine.

He had had several stern talks with his friend Rick Corday about taking crazy risks.

The worst Rick would do was go get drunk somewhere and come on to some guy. And most likely the guy would say no, for there was something disturbing about Rick; something that had initially excited Adam but that now gave him pause, greater and greater pause, actually – and then Rick would insult him and storm out.

Then he'd go home and get even drunker by himself.

Good old Rick.

Getting time to dump him, actually.

Sleep came to Adam, then, as he assured himself for a final time that he had cured Rick of his impulsive and insane risk-taking . . .

Sleep . . .

Chapter Forty-Five

Following the death of her husband, Evelyn Daye Tappley had erected in her room a canopied bed of such proportion and craft that even a queen in a medieval kingdom would have been envious. In the manner of the ancient Egyptians, Evelyn had had her bedposts carved with intricate figures of myth such as unicorns and satyrs, and the bed itself hung with velvet and silk from the Orient.

It was here, when she did not wish to address mere mortals, including her daughter, that Evelyn Daye Tappley spent long hours in pajamas of the finest silk, sipping wine imported from French vineyards so celebrated that even international movie stars had a difficult time getting on the preferred customer list, and looking at photo album after photo album of her beloved second son Peter.

She was here how.

Doris knocked.

'I'll speak to you in the morning,' Evelyn said from the other side of the door.

'We need to talk now, Mother.'

'I'm in bed. Don't you have any respect for that?'

'I'm coming in, Mother.'

'Damn you, you have no right to treat me this way!'

But Doris waited no longer. *Could* wait no longer. If her

suspicions were correct, her mother had done something that was both vile and exceedingly stupid.

The only light in the large shadowy room came from within the interior of the canopy itself, a light appended to the headboard of the vast bed.

Doris walked over and said, 'I want you to tell me about this Mr Runyon.'

Evelyn's dark eyes blazed. 'So you were listening on the extension.'

'Mr Runyon, Mother. I want you to tell me about him. And I want you to tell me what Arthur Halliwell has to do with all of this.'

Even this late in her life, Evelyn Daye Tappley had a firm and shapely body. In the dainty silk pajamas, the body looked thirty years younger than its owner.

On Evelyn's lap was a photo album – all color photos, of course – of Peter's ninth and tenth summers. Evelyn had been an inveterate documenter of her children's young years.

'He was a handsome boy, wasn't he?' she said dreamily.

'Yes, he was. Now tell me about Runyon.'

'You know, his birthday is coming up. Peter's, I mean.'

'I know.'

'I assume you'll go to the mausoleum with me.'

'Perhaps, Mother. But first—'

Her mother glared up at Doris. 'You know what? The older I get, the more I wonder if you weren't jealous of Peter. I wonder if you weren't jealous all these years and I didn't understand it until recently.'

'You're changing the subject, Mother.'

'If you weren't jealous, you'd go to the mausoleum with me.'

'There's paying respect – and then there's morbidity.'

'And I'm morbid?'

'You're there every day, aren't you?'

'And that's morbid?'

'Of course it is.'

Doris did not realize until it was too late what her mother had just done. There was a button on the side of the bed for summoning a servant. She had just pressed it. Martha would be here soon. Evelyn would have Martha stay with her so Doris couldn't ask any questions.

'You're very clever, Mother.'

Evelyn smiled. 'I like to think so, anyway, dear.'

'We're going to talk about Runyon.'

'Are we?'

'Jill doesn't deserve this.'

'You know what I just said about you being jealous of your brother?'

'Don't be ridiculous.'

'If you weren't jealous then you'd agree with me that that little bitch should be punished.'

'She's a decent woman. She did everything she could to save her marriage.'

Evelyn smirked. 'Oh yes, Jill Coffey – a veritable saint, isn't she?' But she was angry now and could no longer control it. Her eyes grew wild again. 'Don't ask me about Runyon. Runyon is entirely my business, not yours. And I don't want you snooping around in my desk anymore, either.'

'I just can't believe that Mr Halliwell would have anything to do with this.'

'You're naïve about people, Doris, and you always have been.'

A soft knock. Martha came in.

Evelyn said, 'Why don't you fluff my pillows and straighten the blankets and help me get ready for bed?'

'Yes, ma'am.'

Evelyn smiled at Doris. 'I'm sorry, dear, but with Martha here, I'm afraid we can't talk.'

Doris and Martha glanced at each other. Martha was wise in the ways of Evelyn Daye Tappley.

'I'll talk to you in the morning, then, Mother,' Doris said, and turned away from the bed.

As Doris left the room, Martha gave her a weary little smile.

Chapter Forty-Six

Jill heard the noise about 2 a.m. She eased herself out of bed so as not to wake Mitch, and went to the window. In the alley that ran along the side of her house, she saw the darkened shape of a police cruiser. No headlights. Two uniformed officers with long flashlights. Walking to the dumpster. Opening the lid. Aiming the beams inside. One of the officers pulling on a latex glove. Reaching down into the dumpster. Feeling around like a kid searching a treasure box at a grade-school ice-cream social – feeling around blind for the best prize.

While the one officer, a woman, held the beam, the other, a man spent the next few minutes rummaging through the dumpster. Not a job Jill would want. The officers made faces at each other sometimes, indicating that the dumpster did not exactly smell of Chanel No. 5.

She knew they were looking for something to tie her to the murder. Mitch had once told her that the police frequently spent a lot of time going through garbage cans and dumpsters during the course of murder investigations. Something reliable often turned up.

The male officer found something.

His partner brought the light in closer.

He dug deeper.

Then he lifted something up for inspection.

Even from here, she recognized it. Her electric-blue, sandwashed blouse. But now there were dark stains all over it.

The officer folded it and put it in a large clear evidence bag.

Then he went back to the dumpster.

Behind her, Jill heard, 'What's going on?'

'Police,' she said softly.

Then Mitch stood next to her, smelling of sleep, his big hands on her thin shoulders. He felt warm and safe.

The female officer went back to shining her beam straight down inside the dumpster.

This took a few minutes longer than the blouse had, but eventually the male officer fished out another piece of her clothing – her blue wraparound skirt. From this distance, Jill was unable to tell if the same dark splotches stained the skirt.

The officer placed the blouse carefully inside another evidence bag.

'Is that yours?' Mitch asked.

'Yes,' Jill said.

At this point, the female officer returned to the patrol car and made a call on the two-way. Her colleague came over and listened to her talk. When she'd finished, obviously having received instructions of some kind, the two officers started walking up and down the ancient brick alley, deep in shadow and lined with dumpsters and stoops, shining their lights along the ground. They might have been astronauts on the moon on some arcane mission that civilians couldn't comprehend.

But Jill comprehended all right: they'd found her electric-blue blouse and her royal-blue skirt, and now they were looking for more evidence.

'He's already decided that I killed Eric. Sievers, I mean.'

'I didn't say he made his mind up that fast, Jill. He's a very competent cop.'

'They found my blouse and skirt in the dumpster.'

'I know, but—'

'I think there was blood all over the blouse. There may have been some on the skirt, too. This is crazy, Mitch. I didn't wear either that blouse or skirt tonight. Somebody's trying to make it look as if I killed Eric.'

'What did you wear?'

She told him.

'Did anybody see you in that outfit?'

'I wore a long coat. They couldn't see what I had on.'

'Not even the skirt?'

'The coat's a lot longer than the skirt.'

'Let's just go back to sleep. I'll talk to Sievers in the morning.'

'Should I get a lawyer?'

'It probably wouldn't hurt.' He sighed. 'That isn't exactly what you wanted to hear, was it?'

'No.'

She looked out. They were working the far end of the alley now, their beams faint as lightning bugs in the gloom.

'Still there.'

'He'll probably put some more people on it tomorrow. I want to work on it all I can but I'm on the Allbright case full-time – you know, the socialite murder. Sievers is getting a lot of heat about it.'

'I don't understand why they're doing this.'

He frowned. 'A suspect's residence or place of employment is important to check out.'

'"Suspect." Boy, that has a nasty ring, doesn't it?' She hesitated. 'I didn't think things like this actually happened to people like me.'

'Jill, nothing *has* happened to you. At least, not so far. That's what you've got to keep in mind.'

'It's just been routine?'

'Pretty much.'

'Including my blouse in the dumpster?'

Even in the darkness she could see that he averted his eyes.

'We'll have to see about that. I'll check with Sievers first thing in the morning.'

'I'm trying not to be scared, Mitch.'

'Sleep will help.'

'I can't sleep. I'm going to get up and put on some coffee.' She closed her eyes momentarily. 'Tell me again not to be scared, Mitch.'

'Don't be scared.'

'I'm glad you came over tonight.'

'So am I. This'll all work out, Jill. I promise.'

'You and me or Eric's murder?'

'Both.'

'I wish I felt guiltier.'

'About Eric?'

'Uh-huh.'

'Sometimes you're numb for a while.'

'I guess I was that way about Peter. After the execution, I mean.'

'Try not to think about that tonight.'

'Blue skies and butterflies? You know how you say that's all I should worry about.'

'Blue skies and butterflies. That's all that should be in your head.'

'I really didn't kill him,' Jill said.

'I know.'

'Even if that was blood on my blouse.'

'I know.'

'Oh Mitch, I don't know how to deal with any of this at all. I can't keep second-guessing everything I say.'

'That's what lawyers are for.'

She laughed. 'I knew they served a purpose. So that's it, eh?'

'You know Deborah Douglas, right?'

'Did a portrait of her last year.'

'She's a very good criminal attorney. Call her in the morning.'

'Mitch?'

'Yes.'

'Do you think I can convince Sievers I'm innocent?'

'Absolutely.'

But the unspoken truth was that she didn't believe that, and Mitch probably didn't, either.

Then she set about the difficult task of filling her mind with blue skies and butterflies as she went into the kitchen and made coffee.

Chapter Forty-Seven

A city councilman had paid an early visit to Lieutenant Sievers and was discussing something at length inside the Lieutenant's office.

Mitch could see the two men sitting on either side of the desk, talking. Every few minutes, the councilman – Hank O'Mally was his name – would shove a document at the Lieutenant and then the Lieutenant would shove it right back.

'This could go on for a while,' one of the detectives said to Mitch. 'O'Mally's trying to get this constituent's charges dropped.'

'What'd he do?'

'Allegedly raped his fourteen-year-old babysitter. O'Mally comes up here every couple of days.' The detective winked at Mitch. 'The constituent must really have somethin' on O'Mally.'

Mitch smiled, nodded. This was a daily occurrence, somebody with power (real or imaginary) coming up here and trying, unsuccessfully, to get Lieutenant Sievers to drop some charge or other. Sievers was a great cop, liked and admired by all the men and women in the department. Wayne Sievers was middle-aged, a great racquetball player, and had lived for many years with a man who was obviously his lover. But that was nobody's business. Sievers didn't ask them about their sex-lives and they didn't ask him. He was a damned good cop and that was all that mattered.

Mitch watched the day begin as he sat nervously at his desk, waiting his chance with Sievers. Roll call over, the sixteen detectives filling the sixteen desks that were sprawled across the big dusty room now worked the phones, lining up witnesses and suspects to hit for information on their various cases.

O'Mally didn't wrap up for another twenty minutes.

When Lieutenant Sievers' door finally came open, O'Mally, a lean man in the expensive gray suit of a banker, was saying, 'He's done a lot for this community, Lieutenant and this girl— well, she isn't exactly from a real good family.'

'That's supposed to convince me she didn't get raped, is it – that she isn't from a real good family?'

'No, but it does bring her motives into question.'

'Oh yeah?'

O'Mally sighed, a thirtyish man with the faint air of weariness that touches all public officials after a few years. 'I think so. Here's a girl who hasn't had much in life. She sees the nice home he lives in, the nice car he drives her home in . . . and she gets resentful.'

'So she accuses him of rape?'

'That's how I see it.' O'Mally put out his hand. 'I hope you'll give it a little more thought.'

Lieutenant Sievers frowned. 'I just wish she'd gotten in here sooner. Too late for any kind of DNA evidence or anything like that.'

'I'm not even sure the DA'll want to press charges.'

'No?' Lieutenant Sievers said, irritated. 'You talk to him, did you?'

O'Mally's cheeks turned red. 'I just meant that he tends not to go ahead unless a case is very strong—'

Lieutenant Sievers was still angry. 'You leave the DA to me, all right, O'Mally?'

'Yessir.'

'Now get the hell out of here.'

O'Mally looked as if he wanted to protest at the Lieutenant's manner but then he thought better of it. He nodded to the Lieutenant and left.

'Jerk,' Sievers said to O'Mally's back. He was talking to Mitch. 'O'Mally wants me to drop the charges because this guy's a good friend of the Cardinal's and used to be some kind of Catholic Man of the Year.'

Then Sievers stood back, waved Mitch into his office, and closed the door behind them.

'You want the bad news first?' he said as he walked around behind his desk and sat down again. His desk was always orderly. He had his secretary come in twice a day and haul out all papers that weren't absolutely necessary.

'You seem eager to give it to me.'

'I'm not in the business of painting pretty pictures, Mitch. You came up here to find out how the Eric Brooks case was doing so I'm going to tell you how it's doing.'

'Fair enough.'

'Your friend Jill Coffey is starting to look awfully good for this.'

Mitch began to say something but Sievers raised his hand. 'I like you, Mitch. Believe me, I don't take any pleasure in telling you that your friend may be involved in a murder.'

'She didn't kill him.'

Lieutenant Sievers sat back. Shook his head. 'Mitch, this is an ongoing homicide investigation. I don't have to tell you that I don't want you interfering. Anyway, I can't afford to spare you – you've got to stay on the Allbright case sixteen hours a day.'

'I'm not interfering, Lieutenant, I'm just trying to help you get to know Jill the same way I do.'

'And she couldn't possibly kill anybody?'

'Right. Except maybe in self-defense.'

'Remember the Sister Rosemary case?'

'Oh God, Lieutenant, you always roll that one out.'

'You remember it or not?'

'Yes, I remember the Sister Rosemary case.'

'A nun for thirty-five years. A damned good one, too. When she wasn't working with orphans, she was helping feed the homeless. Who could ask for a better human being than that?'

'I know the punchline, Lieutenant.'

But the Lieutenant would not be rushed through the story. 'But one day we find this eighteen-year-old kid dead in the alley behind the school where Sister Rosemary teaches. And we find out that Sister Rosemary had just had a terrible argument with this kid because he wouldn't marry the nice little Catholic girl he'd just knocked up. Hit over the head with a brick, from behind. Skull crushed. And I say to my detectives – grown men who've had a lot of training and should be able to keep an open mind about things – I say, "Men, I kind've like this nun for the killer." And you know what my detectives said to me?'

Mitch grumpily played along. 'They said that a sweet old nun couldn't possibly pick up a brick and crush somebody's skull like that.'

'That's exactly what they said. Oh, and they said one other thing, too. They said: "Lieutenant, you always pick the first suspect you find. That's your fatal flaw, Lieutenant, always picking the first suspect." And you know what I told them?'

'You told them about your conviction rate.'

'Exactly, Mitch. I told them about my conviction rate. And what is that rate?'

'Over eighty per cent.'

'Wrong. These days, it's over eighty-five.'

'She didn't do it, Lieutenant.'

'Weren't you working for me back in the days of Sister Rosemary?'

'You know I was.'

'And weren't you one of the detectives who insisted that a sweet little old nun like Sister Rosemary couldn't possibly have—'

'She didn't do it, Lieutenant.'

'She certainly did, Mitch. In fact, she confessed.'

'Sister Rosemary confessed. Not Jill Coffey.'

'But Jill's going to confess, Mitch. Because I honestly believe that she's the killer.'

'There's no proof.'

Lieutenant Sievers opened the wide center drawer of his desk and took out three pages of a report. He dropped the report directly in front of Mitch.

'I need to go empty my bladder. You read through that while I'm gone.'

The Lieutenant was back in four minutes.

'You read it?' he said, sitting down again.

'Yes.'

'Would you say that was incriminating – her blood-soaked blouse and skirt found in a dumpster in the alley next to her place?'

'She didn't do it.'

'You ask me for evidence, I show you evidence, and all you can say is, "She didn't do it." Mitch, you've got to be a pro here. This is a murder investigation. We have to find out what happened and we can't let personal matters get in the way.'

The Lieutenant sat back, steepled his fingers. 'There's one more thing.'

'What?'

'The murder weapon.'

'Which is?'

'Which is a pair of scissors.'

'You found them at the scene?'

The Lieutenant nodded. 'Lots of prints on them, Mitch. Lots. I'm asking her to come in this afternoon to be printed.'

'You called her yet?'

'Not yet. But I will in the next half hour or so.'

'She'll be scared.'

'She can bring her lawyer if she wants to.'

'You sound as if you plan to charge her.'

'It's crossed my mind.'

'She didn't kill him.'

'I believe you told me that already.'

Mitch stood up. He felt a kind of panic, wanted to burst from this office, go for a long fast walk, or maybe even a run. He saw what was shaping up here – saw what was ahead for Jill – and he feared for her.

'I'd like to call you late this afternoon,' he said.

'About the fingerprints?'

'Yes.'

Lieutenant Sievers smiled sadly. 'I guess I could handle that all right.'

He stood up and came around the desk and put his hand on Mitch's shoulder. He was not a physical man, the Lieutenant, and so the gesture startled Mitch.

'I'm sorry, Mitch.'

'Thanks.'

'Maybe this'll have a happy ending yet.'

Now it was Mitch's turn to smile sadly. 'I sure hope so, Lieutenant. I sure hope so.'

Sievers nodded and slid his arm around Mitch's shoulder, walking the younger man out of the room. 'Just hang in there, Mitch. See how it goes.'

'Thanks. I appreciate it.'

He left.

Chapter Forty-Eight

This was the sort of day on which Marcy wanted to stay home in her little two-room apartment, clad only in her faded old red bathrobe. Watch the Sci-Fi Channel (they were doing a *Salute to Mutant Rodents* this week, including her all-time favorite *Them*, about these giant spiders), eat a little Orville Redenbacher Gourmet-Style popcorn, and wriggle her toes inside the bunny slippers (with bushy tails yet) she'd gotten for Christmas six years ago, and that still fit her.

These were her thoughts on waking. Unfortunately, Marcy had a hell of a lot to do today so, as usual, she hurried through her shower, hurried through her makeup and hair-brushing, and then set off for Hardee's in the massive black Ford pick-up truck, complete with glas-pak mufflers you could hear from a block away, that she'd borrowed from the used car lot down the street. She'd run down a few deadbeat customers for them (the car lot floated its own paper, meaning that they carried their own loans) and the owner was properly appreciative (plus he was always hitting on Marcy and probably figured loaning her the truck would bring him closer to her *boudoir*).

After breakfast, she drove the huge roaring beast of a truck over to a Volvo dealership on Dempster, where she asked one of the men on the floor if they had a brochure that showed various Volvo models for the last five, six years. The guy obviously thought this was kind of a weird request, but went along with it anyway. He left Marcy in his tiny cubbyhole of an office to look through brochures from the past eight years. The blue Volvo that had been at Jill's last night was a model from three years ago. She wrote it all down, thanked the salesman and left.

Her next stop was a computer outlet on West Belmont. On the way there, another truck pulled up alongside her. The driver, a guy who was doing his best to look like a pirate of the scurviest kind, right down to this really twinky eye-patch, obviously decided that here was some cute little chick with her big brother's wheels for the day. He was going to show her how to handle one of these babies. He ogled Marcy and then revved his engine.

Marcy blew him away. By the time the pirate was done peacocking around, the light had changed and Marcy was already through the intersection.

What a dip that guy was.

In the computer place, Marcy asked for a man named José and moments later a handsome Latino man appeared. He was in his forties, trim, wearing an inexpensive dark suit that gave him a funereal air contradicted by his merry dark eyes.

José Sanchez escorted her into his office, closed the door and said, 'It's illegal, isn't it?'

'Gee, José, you always make me feel like a criminal.'

He grinned. 'You are a criminal. And so am I.'

She grinned right back. 'Yeah, I guess we kind of are, at that.'

Technically they were, anyway. José always hacked into the state Driver's License Bureau computer for her. Marcy didn't know any cops who'd use the computer for her, so she had to turn to her former night-school computer instructor. José was very, very good as long as she stayed within his guidelines. He would only hack into public information. Nothing private, no violation of anybody's rights.

'How're the kids?'

'We bought Donna her first training bra.'

'Wow.'

'It depresses me.'

'How come?'

'All the boys I see around her. I know what they want.'

'You were probably one of those boys once.'

'I was. And that's why I'm so depressed.'

'Well, you turned out all right. Maybe these boys will, too.'

He nodded and sat back in his comfortable leather executive chair. His office was modestly appointed but neat in every respect. His father had been an illegal immigrant. José took great pride in how far he'd come. He was always pushing magazines of the conservative political persuasion at Marcy. José had grown up on welfare and knew how it strangled not only ambition but dignity as well. At this stage, his office furnishings were not the most expensive wood but someday, through his continued hard work, they would be the best cherry wood available. He had pride, and great drive. In addition to owning this small store, he still taught computer classes three nights a week.

'So what government computer are we going to rape today?' he enquired.

'The Driver's License Bureau.'

He grinned. 'Good. They will only give me twenty years in prison for that one.'

She handed him the particulars. 'Blue Volvo. Here's the year and the model. And here's a description of the guy.

See how many matches you can turn up.' Then she looked up at him from the notes she'd put on his desk. 'And this time, I'm going to pay you.'

'No, no. You were a pleasure to have as a student, and you're even more of a pleasure to have as a friend. Besides, we small-business people, we have to stick together.'

'José—'

'My word is final, Marcy. Final.'

She smiled and shook her head. 'You're crazy, you know that? But in a real nice way.'

She gave him a little kiss on the cheek before she left.

Then she went and got in the big black monster truck. She hoped she would run into that leering pirate again. This time she'd really humiliate him.

Chapter Forty-Nine

Jill worked in the darkroom all morning. Every twenty minutes or so, she'd call Mitch's phone and let it ring four times. Nobody ever answered. She'd hang up before the operator picked up. She didn't want to leave a message, didn't want Mitch to know how frantic she was getting. Did Lieutenant Sievers really have any hard evidence against her? Wouldn't he believe that somebody unknown had stolen her blouse and skirt and apparently soaked them in blood?

By two o'clock, Mitch still hadn't called.

Jill remained working in the darkroom, but now she was making some really stupid mistakes.

Really stupid mistakes.

Chapter Fifty

Cini's first stop was at Baskin-Robbins, where she bought one quart of French vanilla ice cream and one quart of Dutch chocolate.

Her second stop was at Dunkin' Donuts. She got a dozen assorted donuts and half a dozen filled cream puffs.

Forty-two minutes after leaving her apartment, she rolled into Fanny Farmer's in a strip mall on the way to O'Hare.

A bell tinkled above her as she walked in.

The place was tiny, with space for only three very small glass display cases and a nook for a cash register. Two prim elderly ladies with blue-tinted hair were at the register now. One of them paid the hefty, middle-aged, white-uniformed clerk with a trembling, liver-spotted hand. 'You know that Esther and I have been coming to Fanny Farmer ever since we were little girls?' The clerk resembled a *Woman in Prison* movie poster – with her cast in the role of sadistic guard.

Obviously, the elderly woman expected the clerk to make some sort of fuss.

The clerk just shrugged wide, sloping shoulders. 'Oh. That's nice.'

The old ladies exchanged glances of disappointment.

'Where's Molly today?' the second one said, obviously implying that Molly was more their type.

'She was awake all night pukin' her guts up,' the clerk informed them crudely. 'Musta picked up the flu. Anyway, they called me at home this morning at six-thirty, if you can believe it. My husband was really pissed. This is his day off.'

The prim ladies looked at each other again and sort of shook their heads.

'*Vulgar*,' Cini could hear them saying. '*So vulgar*.'

She felt sorry for the old ladies. The world was such a harsh place these days.

The ladies went out, the tinkling bell announcing their exit.

'I hope I never live to get all pruned-up like that. Yer skin hangin' down in bags 'n stuff. So how can I help you?'

Memories of the bad old days were coming back to Cini now. To an overeater, a Fanny Farmer store is just like a bar to an alcoholic.

She inhaled the various aromas of the rich, dark chocolates. Her eyes scanned row after row of chocolate delicacy.

'You hear me? I said so how can I help you?'

Cini said, 'I want two pounds of those and two pounds of those and two pounds of those.'

The woman whistled. 'You know how much that's gonna cost you? Especially the ones with the pecans?'

'I have plenty of money, if that's what you're worried about,' Cini said. Then, remembering how the clerk had treated the old ladies, she said, 'Anyway, my finances are none of your fucking business.'

The woman looked stunned.

A quiet upper-class girl like Cini, using language like that?

Cini had never spoken to anybody in her life like that. She knew she owed her mood to the terrible demands her body was putting on her.

She thought about apologizing but reminded herself of the bored and abusive tone the clerk had taken with the women.

'And I don't want to wait around all fucking day, either,' Cini said.

The clerk set immediately to work, seeming to be at least a trifle leery of Cini's mental state.

As well she should.

The parking lot was a drab wind tunnel. Cini made her way back to her car clutching the Fanny Farmer bag to her chest, the way she would carry something invaluable and holy.

When she got in the car and turned the key, the WGN news came on. The announcer said, 'Chicagoans are still expressing shock that one of their own most prominent advertising executives was stabbed to death in his Loop office sometime last night.'

She should go to the police.

She should tell them what she saw.

She should be a good citizen.

She put the car in gear and drove off.

In less than half a mile, she had eaten one third of the Fanny Farmer chocolate-covered turtles. The expensive ones with the pecans.

Chapter Fifty-One

'Mitch Ayers, please.'

'I'm sorry, miss. He's not in at the moment.'

'All right. Thank you.'

'Any message?'

'Just tell him to call Jill as soon as he hears anything.'

'Jill,' the detective repeated. 'Call ASAP when you hear anything. Got it.'

'Thank you.'

'My pleasure.'

Chapter Fifty-Two

An after-dinner speaker once noted that Arthur K. Halliwell was not 'a citizen of the United States, he is a citizen of Chicago.' The audience, knowing exactly what he meant, broke into both laughter and applause.

While other firms had opened branches in Washington, DC to take advantage of the national political set, and others still wanted New York with its international flavor, Halliwell had been content to rule Chicago. Though a patrician from a long line of patricians – the Wrigleys, the Palmers and the McCormicks had attended many of his birthday parties – Halliwell had always found the vulgarity of Chicago history heady and exhilarating.

And for this reason, many of the city's most powerful players trusted him in the way one would a father confessor. There was no problem Arthur K. Halliwell could not solve; no secret Arthur K. Halliwell would not keep. When a recent Mayor of this city found himself in trouble with a pregnant nineteen-year-old campaign worker who was thinking about going to the press, Arthur sent the young woman a copy of her father's police records on a morals charge (exposing himself to a twelve-year-old girl in 1967) on which he scrawled an anonymous note: '*Would you like to see this in the press?*' The young woman came to her senses. She aborted the child.

While the Arthur K. Halliwell law firm, which overlooked the city from its sixty-seventh-floor eyrie, ostensibly handled business and corporate matters for its clients, it was really a Big Brother program for the city's élite. Uncle Walter, as some chose to call him, was never more than a phone call away. As for Uncle Walter himself, he rather enjoyed playing God. He just wished that he were a little more powerful, as powerful as many of his clients imagined him to be – but that was probably a normal divine failing, wasn't it? Even gods wanted things a little nicer for themselves.

The offices reflected the firm's status of dignified wealth, with furnishings that lent the air of a sumptuous and elegant home. Beautiful as the secretaries were – Walter knew that both men *and* women appreciated beautiful, elegant women – they took care to dress as conservatively as the lawyers themselves, usually in corporate gray or blue. And as for the lawyers – no associate ever worked harder than at Uncle Walter's firm. The associate period generally lasted five years, and less than thirty per cent passed muster. Many simply collapsed from the exhaustion of constant eighteen-hour days and enough rules to make Marine boot camp look like Easy Street. If you complained, you always got the same time-honed anecdote about how Arthur K. Halliwell himself, who'd begun life as a trial lawyer, had lost his first fourteen cases and was dismissed by all the legal wags in the city as a lightweight. But he stayed the course and went on to win more than 1,100 cases in a row. Imagine the hours he'd put in. Imagine the sacrifices he'd made to family and frivolity. How could an associate demand any less of himself? In forty-three years, no associate had ever found a way to argue with that.

Halliwell thought of all this as he sat in his office that day. He did not usually engage in this kind of nostalgia – recalling his rise to prominence – but on mornings when his arthritis was acting up, he had no choice but to recall better days in order to get through the bad ones.

He paced the office now – everything cherry wood with leather, brass-studded furnishings that had clawed ball feet and carved legs – hobbled slightly by the arthritis that had lately inhibited his left knee, trying to appreciate his new framed map of the Old World (his taste in art came from his wife, to whom he had been unutterably faithful for fifty-one years), and his view of Lake Michigan. On a sunny day such as this one, he always wanted to start his life over, live it not in the hushed mahogany reverence of boardrooms but aboard the tramp steamers and dogsleds of the Jack London stories he'd enjoyed so much as a boy. So many years gone by so quickly . . .

As he paced, he also kept glancing at the phone.

What the hell had happened to Adam Morrow, anyway?

For the first time since losing those initial fourteen trials, Arthur K. Halliwell had the terrible feeling that he had perhaps gotten himself involved in something that was, in equal parts, foolish and self-destructive . . .

Had Uncle Walter at last come up against a problem he couldn't solve? Worse – a problem that had been of his own making.

He limped to the phone, arthritic fingers touching arthritic knee, a lion of an old man, silver-haired and handsome in a jowly, somewhat angry way – and dialed.

Dialed as he had every half hour for the past four days.

Just where in the hell was Adam Morrow?

The last Halliwell had heard from him was that frantic, furtive call a few days ago when he'd whispered that Rick Corday 'might be on' to them.

The phone rang several times. He waited for the answering machine to pick up, for Adam's deep voice to invite the caller to leave name and number and date of call.

But the phone machine didn't pick up.

Instead, somebody human did.

'Hello?' Arthur K. Halliwell said.

But the person who'd picked up said nothing. Simply listened.

'Hello?' Arthur K. Halliwell said again.

Breathing now.

'Adam, is that you?'

Breathing.

'Adam, are you all right?'

Breathing.

'This is Arthur K. Halliwell. I demand to speak to Adam Morrow.'

Now not even breathing. Just . . . silence.

'Damn you, I am Arthur K. Halliwell and I do not brook this kind of treatment!'

He laughed.

The bastard laughed.

Uncle Walter composed himself. 'Is this you, Rick?'

Silence again.

'Rick?'

The breathing.

'Rick?'

And then the person on the other phone hung up.

Uncle Walter slammed the receiver down.

Where the hell was Adam Morrow, anyway?

Chapter Fifty-Three

Lieutenant Sievers said, 'Mitch? I was waiting for your call.'

'How'd it go?'

'She came in just fine, no problem,' Sievers said.

'I mean matching the prints on the murder weapon with her prints.'

Lieutenant Sievers said, 'Mitch. They're a perfect match. I'm going to charge her with murder. I'm sorry.'

Part Three

Chapter Fifty-Four

One week later, it snowed in Chicago. Being the first really heavy snow of the season, everything – traffic on the expressways, schoolbuses picking up the kiddies, pushers going to meet their customers – got backed up a couple of hours. In Elmhurst, a man woke up in bed with a woman not his wife and realized that he'd passed out around midnight. He hurried out of his lover's arms so quickly that he tripped going down her icy front steps and broke his leg in two places. In Park Forest, a man who was planning to rob a bank that morning (he had pulled three successful bank robberies in the past two weeks and was beginning to believe this was one easy gig) started shoveling out his driveway and keeled over with a heart attack, dead by the time the wailing ambulance got there. In Lawndale, a hooker finished up the aerobics she always did to her old Jane Fonda videotape, and then went into the bathroom for a leisurely shower. She threw back her shower curtain and promptly screamed. There squatted a rat the size of a grown cat, all black and glistening and red-eyed. Then she remembered the gift her pimp had given her a few months ago. She fled into the bedroom, grabbed something from beneath her bed and returned to the bathroom, her pink fluffy mules going *clack clack clack* on the shiny hardwood floors as she ran. 'You little shit,' she said. And promptly pumped three armor-piercing rounds into the devil's hairy chest. The rat basically came apart in two big bloody chunks.

Nothing so exciting was going on with Marcy Browne. She was out near the suburb of Northbrook, parked an eighth of a mile from a large hip-roofed ranch house that had no close neighbors. Perfect for a guy who liked to do things he didn't want other people to know about.

She'd had to give up the black pick-up. Too obvious for this kind of work. Instead, she sat in a plain Chevrolet six-cylinder she'd rented for the week. The body shop said it'd take them a month to get her car fixed, what with ordering the parts and all, but that they could recommend a real good rental agency, leading suspicious Marcy to believe that body shop and rental agency were owned by the same people.

It was 7:35 a.m. and still snowing hard and there was virtually no music to be found on the radio. Everything was school closings and traffic reports and warnings to drive safely; everything was stay-tuned-for-further-traffic-and-weather-updates . . . all delivered in a tone that let you know that these radio station folks were virtual saints. *We love your collective asses off, folks. We really do. That's why we're giving you all these groovy facts about the blizzard.*

All Marcy wanted was a little music.

Well, and one more thing: she wanted the guy who came out of the ranch house to match the James Coburn lookalike on the photo that Jill had taken.

In the past week, José had been able to come up with forty-seven blue Volvos in the Illinois vehicle registration computer. By now, Marcy had visited thirty-nine of the owners. They had been fat, bald, black, crippled, red-haired, brown-haired and shaven-headed . . . but not one of them had been white-haired and not one of them had borne even a passing resemblance to James Coburn.

She only had eight to go.

Please God, make this the right one.

And please God, while You're at it, could You give us a little respite from traffic reports and all that stuff? You know I don't wake up in the morning unless I have three cups of steaming black coffee and a lot of really loud rock and roll.

The coffee she had. She'd filled a thermos at 7-Eleven.

It was the rock and roll she missed. Unlike her own car, this renter didn't have a tape deck.

She really needed some rock and roll.

Really really.

'Oh, God.'

'What?' Mitch said.

'The alarm. It didn't go off,' Jill said.

'It didn't? I thought you were going to pick up a new one yesterday.'

'I forgot.'

This time, Mitch said it: 'Oh, God.'

And then Mitch, in his subdued mint-green boxer shorts, and Jill in her pink silk pajamas, leapt from bed and got their respective mornings off to a heart-pounding start.

'You take the bathroom first,' Jill said. 'I'll start the coffee.'

'I'll be happy to start the coffee.'

She shook her head. 'I'm so groggy I need the caffeine even before I take a shower.'

Mitch padded into the bathroom and proceeded to perform a couple of really impressive (at least to him) stunts he'd picked up over the years. To wit: Mitch knew how to pee while brushing his teeth with his right hand and using his electric razor with his left.

He was performing this circus act when Jill knocked on the door and said, 'We should've looked out the window.'

Mitch took the toothbrush from his mouth. 'How come?'

'There's three feet of snow on the ground. We're having a blizzard.'

'Oh, God.'

'Everything and everybody's going to be late this morning. We can probably take our time a little more.'

'I'll call the Lieutenant and see how things are stacking up this morning. I still want to check out a few more bars.'

Five days ago, Jill had introduced Mitch to Marcy. They'd agreed that Mitch, with any time he could spare away from his socialite murder case, would check all the bars Eric Brooks had been known to hang out in. Mitch would look for the young woman who'd been in Eric's office. Jill had given him a detailed description of her. In the meantime, Marcy would go through the names and addresses of blue Volvo owners registered in and around Chicago.

During this same time, Jill had virtually shut down her business. The press made it impossible for her to work. Either they were calling her (and getting her answering machine) or they were banging on her door (and getting no reply). Some of the more industrious ones followed her to the supermarket and mall and post office, ambushing her when she emerged from these places.

They played just the angle she'd predicted they would:

EX-WIFE OF SERIAL KILLER A KILLER HERSELF?
Hints 'Mystery Woman' Can Prove Her Innocence

It didn't hurt (from their point of view) that she was

attractive, single, worked in what was considered a 'fashionable' occupation, and had once been associated with one of the state's wealthiest and most prominent families. All this made it easier to portray her as the *femme fatale*. They hinted darkly that Jill and Eric had been lovers as well as co-owners of the ad agency; and then there'd been a falling out, leading Jill to murder him. One TV station, in a news segment they called *You Be The Judge*, asked twenty-five people on the street if they thought that Jill had killed Eric. Twenty-three said yes; one said no; one wasn't sure. Jill had been convicted.

Jill had spent a good portion of each day at her lawyer's, going over and over her story of the night Eric had been murdered. She'd talked about the man in the blue Volvo who'd been watching her house, and she'd talked about the young woman in Eric's office. And she'd talked, over and over again, about how unreal all this seemed. She was plain old Jill Coffey. Anybody who knew her, was aware that she could never kill anybody. Not plain old Jill Coffey.

She eased the bathroom door open and waggled the front page of a morning newspaper at him. 'Guess who's on the front page again?'

He turned, still shaving, toothbrush still in his mouth – but finally done tinkling – and looked at the story in the upper right-hand section, complete with a close-up shot of Jill that had been taken one night when she was all dressed up for an AIDS fund-raising ball. She looked beautiful. The headline read:

BEAUTIFUL WOMEN WHO KILL

'They've got me in with some good company, anyway. A few actresses – remembering Andy Williams' wife who killed that skier she was having an affair with – and several prominent society matrons.'

'Those bastards.' He clicked off the shaver, set it down, took the toothbrush from his mouth, rinsed, spat and then walked over to her.

He pulled her to him.

She pushed him away. 'Oh God, no, Mitch. Morning mouth. Not fair. You've already brushed your teeth.'

'Then give me a hug.'

A hug she was willing to give him.

He knew she was trying to be tough about it all but he could gauge – by the slight frantic air of her derisive laughter as she'd shown him the newspaper – how the assault by the press was taking its toll on her.

They were convicting her long before she would ever come to trial, long before the police had a decent chance to find the real killer.

He hugged her. Tight. 'Have I told you how much I love you?'

She laughed. 'Not for five minutes.'

'Well then, I'm overdue.'

'Oh God, Mitch, I'd never make it through this without you. I really wouldn't.'

She put her face deep into his neck and after a moment he could feel her soft warm little-girl tears.

He held her more gently than he ever had before, trying to convey through the physical act of embracing all the tenderness and respect and abiding love he felt for her.

God granted one of Marcy's wishes, anyway.

She was able to find a rock and roll station that played, in order, *My Sharona*, *Love Shack* and *Give Me That Old-Time Rock And Roll*.

She was pounding the dash and having a great time.

The other wish He could have done a little better with, trying to match the James Coburn guy in the photo to the guy who lived in this house.

Not even close. He was fat, bald, old.

He came out of the side door of the house and ran with his head down against the whipping wind and slashing spiky snow toward the garage, where he emerged a few minutes later in his blue, four-door Volvo.

Marcy gave him a few minutes to leave then headed back to her office.

At least they kept on playing rock and roll.

On the scale this morning, Cini weighed nine pounds more than she had exactly one week ago today.

Didn't take her long to calculate that within two months, she'd be knocking on the door of the Whales Club and asking for re-admittance.

Nine pounds in seven days. My Lord.

She went out to the tiny kitchen and opened a box of powdered donuts and ate them.

Then she went to the refrigerator and took out the Snickers King-Size she'd been keeping in the freezer. They slowed you down, frozen like that; felt as if they were going to crack all your teeth they were so hard.

After that, she went into the living room and sat on the couch and bawled. 'Cried' was not the proper word, nor was 'sobbed' – what Cini did was bawl. Like a six-year-old trying to understand why her dog has been run over. Everything was just so effing incomprehensible sometimes. Why had she let herself please that scumbag Eric that way, just so she could please that cold-hearted ass-bandit Michael? And why, of all nights, did she have to please Eric on the night he was being murdered? And why did she have to go back up to his office at the exact moment the killer was stabbing away with his scissors?

Her life had actually been better when she'd been fat. She'd been an outcast, sure, but there were at least no terrible surprises in being an outcast. People smirked at you sometimes but mostly they left you alone. And your friends, unlike some worthless men she could name, never betrayed you or let you down. And inside your fortress of fat you felt safe and protected. Nobody could get to you. Not as long as you kept the walls of the fortress tall and deep.

She hadn't been to class for over a week now, having spent her time in the apartment reading romantic suspense novels in which most of the heroines seemed to be extremely horny TV reporters, and making a daily foray out for thirty, forty dollars' worth of goodies. She chose a different store each day. It was too humiliating to let the same clerk in on her awful secret.

Twice she'd forced herself to vomit, two days in a row she'd taken diuretics. But unlike bulimics, she did these things not so she could maintain her weight, she did them so that her stomach would have more capacity for food.

She lay on her side on the couch and looked out her front window. Even at 9 a.m. it was dark as dusk. She could hear the snowplow in the street below, its motor obstinately pushing against piles of the white stuff. She could even hear its two-way radio inside, crackling loud.

She kept thinking about last night.

She'd almost done it.

In fact, she'd gone as far as getting out of bed, putting on her robe, walking to the kitchen, picking up the wallphone and dialing the number of the nearest police station, which was on a sticker (along with ambulance and fire numbers) on the wall.

A lady cop had answered, asked if she could help.

And Cini almost said it.

Almost said, '*You know that woman you think killed Eric Brooks? Well, she didn't. I saw the real killer. My name is Cini and I'm coming in.*'

But then, just when she was about to get the words out, she imagined the press reports of what she'd been doing up in Eric's office.

All those horny women TV reporters in those trashy romance novels. They'd descend on her relentlessly.

'*Did you really – well, you know, have oral sex with Eric?*'

'*Do you usually have sex with men you don't know? Don't you ever worry about AIDS?*'

'*Were you always this promiscuous? Even when you were in high school?*'

And then the faces of her parents. God, that would be the worst thing of all. Something would die in their eyes – respect, maybe, or the hope of ever seeing their 'problem child' get her life straightened out. They would become old then, old of their humiliation, old of their despair, and they would open their arms to Death in hopes that there really was a better life beyond this one.

She just couldn't do it to them.

She felt sorry for Jill Coffey but she just couldn't do this to her parents.

After awhile, she got up from the couch and went out to the kitchen and took down a fresh package of Oreos.

And who could eat Oreos without a pint of French Vanilla Haagen Daz to go with them?

She sat at the kitchen table and utterly destroyed both Oreos and ice cream and then she went back to the living room and turned on an old *Perry Mason* show and tried to guess whodunnit.

A couple times more that morning, she thought again of calling the police, telling them the truth.

But whenever the urge came, she'd trot out and grab a quick candy bar. And then the urge went away.

Rick Corday was on the Stairmaster in the den when the call came. He'd been expecting it.

''lo.'

'Rick. You looked out the window yet?'

'I looked.'

'No way I can fly in today.'

'Convenient.'

'Oh shit, Rick, I don't need this. I really don't.'

'Poor baby.'

'Believe it or not, I'd like to be back there, sitting in our home – notice I said "our" home, Rick – having a nice sandwich and a glass of beer and watching one of those old sci-fi flicks you like so much. In fact, babe, why don't you go rent *This Island Earth* and we'll watch it tomorrow, when I get in?'

'I thought we had an understanding about "babe."'

'Did I say "babe"?'

'You said "babe."'

'When?'

'A little while back.'

'I apologize, Rick. I truly apologize.'

'That what you call all the guys you pick up in bars?'

'Could you have a little fucking compassion, Rick? I've had a tough week.'

'I bet.'

'How're things going with Jill Coffey?'

Rick said nothing. Scare the bastard a little.

'Rick?'

'They're going fine.'

'Man, you had me worried there for a minute.'

'I'll bet you really hate to see Chicago have a blizzard, don't you?'

'Rick, this isn't—'

'Have to stay in New York one more day and hit all the bars. Sounds like real tough duty.'

'I'm going now, Rick. I'd hoped we'd have a pleasant conversation.'

'We're going to have a real serious conversation when you get back here.'

'Yes we are, Rick. I want a real serious conversation just as much as you do.'

'Unless you die in an airplane crash or something.'

'Thanks, Rick. That's all I need. Somebody sending out that kind of karma.'

Rick slammed down the phone.

Arthur K. Halliwell came out of the bathroom feeling uncomfortable. Darned prostate gland, anyway. No matter how frequently you urinated, you never quite felt that you'd gotten it all – not when you had a chronic infection, you didn't.

He returned to his office just as his secretary buzzed him that his banker was on line two.

He picked up immediately.

'Hello, Walter, good to hear your voice,' James B. Roehler said after Halliwell had greeted him.

'Good to hear yours,' Halliwell said, unable to keep the note of irritation from his voice. This was no time for pleasantries. This was time for a simple yes or no.

'You met with the loan committee?'

'I did indeed, Walter.'

'And they said what exactly?'

'Walter, I'm afraid that—'

'Those bastards!'

'Walter—'

'I helped build that bank. Me and my clients!'

'Walter, please, listen—'

But Arthur K. Halliwell was in no mood to listen. None at all. He hung up.

He sat for several long moments, half-dazed, half-confused, feeling his age in a way that was almost horrific. How did a dashing, handsome man turn into a feeble old man who was deaf in his left ear, got gas whenever he drank milk, and was growing cataracts?

And who, even worse, was broke. Flat broke. Too many bad investments over the past ten years had done it. He was one of the few in his crowd to play all those late-eighties games and lose. All his other friends—

Now his arrangement with Adam Morrow was more important than ever.

He reached an arthritic hand out to the phone.

Felt the bloated bag of his prostate between his legs.

Heard his breath wheeze in his windpipe – and yet he'd never been a smoker.

He did not want to die in humiliation.

He needed money desperately.

He tried Morrow's number again.

All he got was that stupid answering machine.

He slammed the receiver down, not once but eight times, again and again and again, until his secretary came to the door and said, 'Is everything all right, sir?'

'Get out of here, you stupid bitch,' Arthur K. Halliwell snarled. 'Get out of here right now.'

Chapter Fifty-Five

The dermatome is his most specialized instrument, one used to take skin from one part of the body and graft it onto another part. The surgery has been going seven hours now, the dermatome in constant use for the past two; for the first time the surgeon is beginning to see his work start to take shape, the way a portrait artist first glimpses the face on his canvas. Blood, pus, urine, the stench of human flesh burning – these are some of the vulgar realities of the craft – but the art . . . The surgeon pauses a moment in his work to admire what he's accomplished.

STATEMENT

The bars used to get to me, the singles bars along the Strip especially, the rainy Wednesday night just starting to roll. The first exultant beat of the disco music summoning the dancers to the floor. The first roaring snort of coke shared in both the men's and women's bathrooms. The first inkling in the minds of otherwise faithful wives out with girlfriends that maybe . . . just maybe . . . well, who can be faithful forever, right? And over it all a kind of despair . . . everybody knowing that soon enough their looks will be gone and the dancefloor given over to younger and prettier people . . . and that life will be measured out in paychecks and annual health checkups and the ever-increasing number of funerals one attends as one gets older. But if the music is loud enough . . . if the drugs are spellbinding enough . . . if the sex is hard and fast and explosive enough . . . well, then all these terrible intimations of age and grief can be held at bay for one boozy night.

I was of them, the dancers, and yet not of them because I knew the secret: that it doesn't matter. *That you can go out and carve up as many people as you want because memory passes so quickly . . . collective memory . . . generation unto generation. All those people coming out of Loop office buildings today, soon enough they'll all be gone and gone utterly and gone for ever . . . in the dust and ash of relentless Time . . . the Time I'm always so aware of . . . the Death I see in the faces of infants . . . the Smile, there at the last, on the faces of the women, as if they're glad to finally have it over with.*

And so turn the music up louder; and take an extra hit of coke; and cut her up real good – butcher her, in fact – because in the end, despite all the bullshit the priests and the politicians try and fill us with, in the end, it doesn't matter.

It just doesn't matter at all.

Chapter Fifty-Six

Rick was back at Jill's place at 7 a.m. The media references to 'the mystery woman' and the inference that her former boyfriend Mitch was working on the case had made him curious. Was there really a 'mystery woman?' Could she truly prove Jill's innocence?

He decided to spend part of the morning following Mitch around, as he had the last two mornings.

Chapter Fifty-Seven

Mitch tended to remember neighborhoods by the murders that had been committed in them.

This one, where the young woman Cini lived, had been the site of three rather spectacular shootings a few years ago. A Yale man, no less, had been the shooter. He'd come to Northwestern to visit his fiancée and found that she'd fallen in with people he didn't care for, college theater people, a black, a gay male and a gay female – and one night during his four-night visit, the Yale man just went crazy and popped all three of them right in the living room.

The houses that lined the street ran to variations on Victorian. Most of them appeared to be forty, fifty years old, the kind of rental properties that investors were always looking for. You couldn't go wrong renting to college kids in an overcrowded market. They'd pay premium rates and they'd put up with just about anything you pushed their way.

The sun was out now and Mitch felt better. He'd read a piece in *Time* about the effects of cabin fever really being the result of lack of sunshine. He could believe it.

On his way up the steps he noticed a squat little snowman complete with an old watchplaid hunting cap, scarf and broom held in extended snow hand. And one more thing: in addition to the eyes and nose and mouth made of tiny sticks, the artist had also endowed the snowman with a penis. A large dirty carrot shot from his crotch.

There was probably some kind of city ordinance against this kind of thing, but what with the socialite murder still accounting for most of his time, Mitch figured he'd better not let Lieutenant Sievers find out he was busting snowmen.

Cini lived in a graying, two-story Victorian with a downslanting porch and several strips of masking tape on each window to cover cracks.

The vestibule smelled of dust, wet rubber snowshoes and cigarette smoke. He checked the mailbox then walked down a long dark narrow hallway toward a small window of light. Everything smelled old. You could smell the decades.

He stopped and knocked on 7A.

'Who is it?'

'I'm with the Chicago Police.'

'Right. Who is it, really?'

'My name is Mitch Ayers and I'm really a Chicago detective. I'd like to talk to you a minute.'

Long silence from inside.

'Do you have a badge?'

'Yes, I do.'

'I'm going to open the door on the chain and you show me your badge, all right?'

'Fine.'

The chain ticked back in its slot. The door opened three-quarters of an inch. Cini had an appealing, almost angelic face. And startling blue eyes. Very cute.

He held his badge up.

She said, 'How come you want to talk to me?' But she didn't open the door.

'I'd rather not explain out here in the hallway.'

Just then an explosion of sound came from the second floor. Reggae music.

'God, he drives me crazy,' Cini said. 'Upstairs, I mean.'

'How about letting me in?'

'Guess I sort of have to, don't I?' She smiled, but it wasn't a happy smile.

With sunlight streaming in through the dirty window, the spare little apartment looked habitable. All the furnishings – couch, armchair, recliner – were of another era, but in reasonably good condition.

The mess was what puzzled Mitch.

Here you had a very nice-looking young woman like Cini, and her entire front room was littered with half-consumed boxes, sacks and packages of junk food: potato chips, chocolate-covered graham crackers, macaroons, Twinkies, ginger snaps, mini-pies, bridge mix and something called 'Double Fudge Whammies.'

He sat on the edge of the armchair and looked at it all and then over at her again, and wondered how you could maintain this shapely a body when you gorged it on stuff like this.

Then he remembered the eighteen-year-old girl who'd killed both her parents. She'd weighed more than three hundred pounds. She'd told Mitch's partner that the only pleasure she'd ever had in her life was from a box of chocolates. 'People don't love me but food does,' she'd said.

Maybe he was looking at one of those people now. Who felt happy (and devoutly miserable) only when they ate.

She sat down across from him and said, 'I could probably dig up the receipt if I had to.'

'Receipt?'

'For the parking tickets.'

'I guess I don't know what you're talking about, Miss.'

'All those overdue parking tickets I ran up. That's why you're here, isn't it? Did the computer screw up and forget to mark me Paid?'

He decided to risk it. 'I'm here because I think you may know something about a murder.'

'I see.'

'Do you? A man named Eric Brooks?'

'No, I don't know anything about a murder and I've never heard of a man named Eric Brooks.'

'You were seen with him.'

'I was? By whom?'

'By a bartender named Ferguson.'

'I don't know a bartender named Ferguson.'

'He seems to know you.'

All he could think of was a lizard striking at prey, the way her hand lashed out and snatched a macaroon from the package. It was in her mouth and swallowed, in moments. Then she had another one. She was so cute. So slim. But there was something off-putting – almost inhuman – about the way she'd grabbed that cookie.

Then she took a third one. And held the package out to him. 'I'm being rude, sorry. Would you like one?'

'No, thanks.'

She indicated all the half-eaten packages and boxes. 'I was expecting the blizzard to last several days.' She shrugged, trying to be casual. Smiled. 'Guess I stocked up a little too much, didn't I?'

'I guess so.'

'I mean, I don't usually eat like this.'

'Be my guest.'

'You wouldn't mind if I had a piece of candy?'

'Not at all.'

It was then he noticed that her hands had begun to twitch and her eyes fill with tears. 'I really fucking resent this, you know.'

'Resent what?'

'You coming here and accusing me of something I don't know anything about.'

'I'm simply doing my job.'

'Right. Doing your job. You're accusing me of lying is what you're doing.'

'I'm not accusing you of anything.'

This time she was rewarded with two Double Fudge Whammies for her lizard-quickness.

She talked while her mouth was still full. It should have been funny. But it was sad.

'I'm sorry I said the "f" word.'

'I've been known to use it myself.'

'I've really never heard of Eric Brooks.'

'I see.'

'You still don't believe me, huh?'

'No, I'm afraid I don't.'

'Do you enjoy this?'

'Asking questions, you mean?'

'Bullying people. That's what you're doing, you know. Bullying me.' She took another Double Fudge Whammie. The package rattled with her ferocity.

'You know what I think I should do?' Mitch said.

'What?'

'I think I should leave my card and let you think about it for a while.'

'Think about what?'

'About telling me the truth.'

'I am telling you the truth.'

'Just think about it for a while, and if you change your mind then give me a call.'

'Eric Brooks is a name I'd never heard before you knocked on my door.'

Mitch stood up. The tiny apartment suddenly felt oppressive. All the years of this place, all the lives, crowding in on him ghost-like. He wanted cold dirty city air. Wanted it desperately.

He took his wallet from inside his tweed sport jacket. The white business card he extracted, he set on the edge of the couch, right on top of a potato chip bag.

'You're a very nice-looking young woman.'

'Are you coming on to me?'

'No, I'm just trying to tell you that you shouldn't put all that junk into your system.'

'You must be a part-time minister at night.'

He'd seen them before like this. So terrified of their situation that they became hard and angry. They wanted somebody to help them avoid their fate. But there was no escape from their fate. They knew something the police needed to know – and eventually they'd be forced to tell it.

He walked over to the door.

'My home number's on the card, too.'

'Fine. But I won't be needing it. I won't be calling.'

'Just in case.'

This time she extracted the Double Fudge Whammie with almost tender care. Held in such a way – almost like a priest holding the Communion host – that told him she wanted him to leave so she could get busy with the rest of the food.

'I'll be talking to you,' Mitch said.

'No, you won't.'

Mitch looked at her a long moment – she really did have a

perfect little face, the kind of innocent eroticism that middle-aged men found so devastating – and then opened the door and let himself out.

He had not gotten ten feet down the dark narrow hallway before he heard her break out in sobs.

She was the one, all right.

Jill spent two hours that morning with her attorney. It seemed more like ten hours.

Deborah's well-tailored tweed suit and white silk scarf gave her an elegance that belied her scrappy personality. She was almost belligerent in the way she questioned Jill sometimes, almost as if Jill were a hostile witness.

They went through Eric's initial phone call. 'Think carefully. Did he mention anybody who was with him in the office then?'

'I don't think so.'

'"Don't think so" isn't good enough, Jill. Think.'

'No, I'm sure he didn't mention anybody.'

'How about when you arrived there? Close your eyes and think back. You're walking in the lobby door. What do you see?'

Jill described what she'd seen.

'All right. You see the elevators. How many are there in that building?'

'Three.'

'All lined up?'

'Yes.'

'Now: do you see any of the doors opening?'

Jill thought a moment. 'Yes.'

'Which one?'

'The one in the middle.'

'Is anybody getting off that particular car?'

'No.'

'You're sure?'

'Yes.'

'You get on the car and you go up to Eric's office?'

'Right.'

'Does that car stop at any other floor first?'

'No.'

'You said that pretty fast. Think a moment.'

'It didn't stop at any other floor. I'm sure.'

'All right, the car stops on Eric's floor and the doors open and—' Deborah's intercom buzzed.

Jill opened her eyes to the nice new office, all glass and chrome and gray carpeting and dove-gray couches and matching chairs.

Deborah said, 'Yes?'

'There's a call for Jill. He says it's urgent.'

'Thank you.' Deborah nodded to the phone console on her desk.

Jill picked up.

Mitch said, 'I found her.'

'Really!'

'Really. Her name's Cini.'

'God, I can't believe it.'

'That's the good news.'

'There's bad news?'

'I'm afraid so. She doesn't want to cooperate. She won't admit anything.'

'But why?'

'I'm not sure.'

'God, what can we do?'

'If I don't hear from her by tomorrow, I'll run back out there and talk to her.'

'You're sure she's the right one?'

'You know that list of bar names I had where Eric hung out at various times? I found this bartender in number twenty-six who remembered seeing him in there the night he was murdered. He also happened to know who the girl was, this Cini. He thought she was maybe a Northwestern student and he was right. We lucked out.'

'Now if we can just get her to talk . . .'

'She'll talk. Eventually.'

'I can't wait to tell Deborah.'

'I'll see you tonight at your place.'

'Our place.'

'Our place, then. I didn't want to sound presumptuous.'

'That's not presumptuous at all.'

'See you tonight.'

'Dad?'

'Hi, honey.'

'Is it a bad time?'

'C'mon, now, where my little girl's concerned it's never a bad time.'

'She told you, huh? Mom, I mean.'

'She told me.'

'I'm sorry.'

'We're looking at it as only a temporary setback, Cini. And that's how you have to look at it, too.'

'I'm still eating.'

'You'll stop eventually. Then we'll deal with it again.'

'Dad, I didn't tell Mom everything.'

She heard a buzz. 'Could I put you on hold for a second, sweetheart?'

'Sure.'

She hated bugging him at work, knew how driven he was, but today she had no choice. Successful physician or not, he always managed to find time for his beloved daughter. She just wished she and her mom could get along this well. They could – but never for long.

'Sorry. Now you were saying that you didn't tell your mom everything.'

'No, I didn't. I mean, I told her I was overeating again but I didn't really say why.'

'Then you know why?'

She paused. 'Yes.'

'Cini, are you in some kind of trouble?'

'Yes, I am, Dad.'

'You want to talk about it?'

'Not on the phone.'

'I'll call your mother. She'll set your place for dinner.'

'No, Dad, I – I'd rather speak to you alone.'

Now her father paused. 'I wish you knew how much your mother loved you, sweetheart.'

'I know, Dad. But – but I'd rather talk to you about it. Alone. At least at first.'

'Is your car running in this weather?'

'I think so.'

'Why not come out to the office, then?' His clinic was near River Plaza. 'I'll be here all afternoon.'

'I'd really appreciate that, Dad.'

'You just hang in there, honey. Everything'll be fine. You'll see.'

'Oh Dad, I love you so much. Thanks.'

After hanging up, she sat there a moment, recalling the detective as he'd stood next to her door a few minutes ago. He had the same bearing as her father – imposing but not unkind.

But she was going to change her father, or at least change his perception of his one and only child. She was going to tell him what she'd done with Eric Brooks, and why, and then she would never again be the same girl in his eyes.

Never the same girl again.

* * *

Marcy spent the morning chasing down two more useless blue Volvo owners, not so easy to do with most parts of the city still a freezing mess from yesterday's blizzard. A couple of times she almost slid into people. She was not what you'd call incredibly deft at navigating icy streets.

The first owner turned out to be a wizened little guy with a glistening scalp and a cane to help him move his tiny arthritic body around.

By contrast, the second owner was a towering fat guy who wore an ascot tie and sunglasses and a cape. Marcy found out that he was a director in one of the local community theaters. She wondered if he ever wore spats.

Which left her with some guy – five more names to go – named Richard Corday, whom she chose on the basis of simple geography. He was the closest guy on the remaining list of names.

Marcy headed in his direction.

Here and there she saw cars that had run up into snowbanks. The wreckers hadn't gotten to them yet. The closer she came to the suburbs, the more snowmen and snow angels and snow forts she saw. All of which made her briefly nostalgic for her childhood. You'd come in at lunch all freezing and wet from rolling around in the snow and Mom had a nice big bowl of Campbell's tomato soup ready for you. She'd get you dry clothes and even wipe your runny nose for you. From Marcy's experience, adulthood wasn't anything like that at all. Especially if you tried to find somebody who'd wipe your nose.

Cini opened the door, ready to leave her apartment, and there he was in the gloom of her long dark hallway. Waiting.

Red-and-black checkered hunting hat with big checkered

ear-flaps; glasses so thick his blue eyes were grotesquely magnified; coat to match the hunting cap. Curly red hair tumbled out from beneath the cap.

'Are you Cini?'

'Yes, I am.'

'I have something for you.'

'A package, you mean?'

'No, this.'

Three things happened instantly: he brought up a nine-inch switchblade and snicked it open and put it right to her throat; he pushed her back into her apartment; and he grabbed her arm so tight, it hurt.

He closed the door and said, 'If you scream, I'll kill you right now.'

'Oh God, I don't even know who you are.' She was babbling.

He pushed her onto the couch. The tip of the shiny blade never left her throat.'

'The cop was here.'

'Please, please don't hurt me.'

'The cop was here.'

'Yes, he was.'

'What did you tell him?'

'I didn't tell him anything. Did you hear what I said? About not hurting me?'

'I heard you.'

He took off his cap. And then he took off his wig.

And then he took off the glasses.

She said, feeling sick and feeling faint, 'It's you. Oh my Lord.'

The killer in Eric Brooks' office removed the knife from her throat. He stood up straight and looked around.

'Where were you going just now?'

'To see my father.'

'Why?'

'H-he's my father.'

'That isn't an answer.'

'To talk to him.'

'About what?'

'Could I go to the bathroom? I have to go real bad. I really do. I've been sick. I've been – eating too much.'

'Just sit right there and tell me why you were going to see your father.'

'I needed to talk to him.'

'What about?'

'The detective who was here – he asked me questions.'

'Did you answer them?'

'No.'

He glanced around the room again, noticing the half-empty Fritos package (large size), the box of chocolate-covered graham crackers, the red and yellow and blue and green Tootsie-Pop wrappers that looked like dead flowers strewn across the coffee table; and the open half-gallon of ice cream that sat on a plate. Most of the ice cream had melted and formed a sticky pool around the box.

'You eat all this crap?'

'That's what I was telling you. I have an eating disorder.'

He seemed to lose interest quickly. 'Tell me exactly what you told the cop.'

She told him.

'Now tell me exactly what you told your father?'

She told him.

He sat down next to her. He put a hand on her breast and left it there a moment, daring her with his gaze to say anything. She said nothing. She was trembling and even twitching some.

He slashed her silk copper blouse with a single arc of the blade. He took the white strap of her bra and cut that, too.

He ripped blouse and bra away until one of her nicely-shaped breasts fell free.

He touched the tip of the blade to her sweet little nipple.

'Now you're going to tell me the truth.'

'Oh God, please, listen – listen to me, all right? I really don't want to get mixed up in this. I really don't. That's what I was going to tell my father when I went to see him. That I don't want to get mixed up in it. That I don't want to have anything to do with it at all.'

He was sitting there watching her, listening to her, when he could feel the first inkling of blackout coming over him. Distantly, somewhere inside him, he heard a voice – his own, yet not his own. What was the voice trying to tell him?

He said, pretending that nothing was wrong: 'Why do you eat all this crap?'

She was obviously confused, the way he kept jumping from one subject to another all the time.

'I – I have an illness. An eating disorder.'

'So you eat all this junk food?'

'Yes.'

'It's not good for you.'

'I know.'

God, he was so crazy.

'You're not telling me the truth, are you?'

'I am. Honest. Really, I am.'

She started to cry. She looked like a little girl. She looked so sad and helpless.

He kept the cold steel of the blade angled at her nipple. He could slice it away any time he wanted. He enjoyed that feeling.

'You know what I just did?' she said, crying even harder now.

'What?'

'I wet my pants. Just now. Because I'm so scared.'

'You really didn't tell anybody about seeing me that night in the office?'

'No. Honest, I didn't.'

'Good,' he said.

He grabbed her hair, threw her head back and slashed the knife across her throat in a single efficient motion.

She was a long time dying, gasping, choking, pleading for reprieve – and he enjoyed every moment of it.

Chapter Fifty-Eight

All her life, Doris' mother Evelyn had suffered from fits. There was no other way to describe them. She would awaken with a sense of dread virtually paralyzing her, certain that some terrible fate was about to take one or both of her children again.

Whoever could have predicted that a rattlesnake would climb into the playpen of her firstborn?

On these days, no matter what the season, no matter how much her children might want to play outside, Evelyn Daye Tappley made both Peter and Doris stay indoors. And she ordered the servants to keep all doors and windows bolted tight. And she herself looked in on her children every twenty minutes or so. You could never be sure . . .

Doris thought of this as she peered into the den and looked at her mother in the wingback chair. Evelyn had gotten smaller with the years – still formidable to be sure, especially when she was blustering about – but smaller nonetheless. She sat now reading the newspaper in a pair of black silk day pajamas, a small blanket thrown across her legs as her black slippered feet stretched to reach the ottoman.

Doris knew what she was reading: the latest installment of Jill Coffey's travails.

Doris also knew who had caused those travails . . . a man named Rick Corday . . . and her own mother.

Doris had already made up her mind about calling Jill this afternoon. She just wanted to make sure that her mother was safely ensconced in one place for a while. She didn't want Evelyn walking in on her phone call.

She stepped into the den and said, 'How're you feeling this morning, Mother?'

Evelyn glanced up from the newspaper. 'Feeling?'

'You said last night you had a scratchy throat.' That was another thing about her mother lately – she was forgetful.

'Oh, I'm fine.' Evelyn glanced at the front page with Jill's photo on it and said, 'She must be going through hell.'

'Yes, and I'm sure you feel terrible for her, don't you?'

'If I'd ever taken that tone with my mother, she would have sent me to my room.'

It worked, Evelyn's little attempt to shame Doris. It shouldn't have worked. But it did. Even after all these years. Even after all these times.

Doris walked over to her mother. 'I'm sorry, Mother.'

'I admit I don't care for Jill, of course, but I certainly wouldn't wish this on her.'

'Of course not. I shouldn't have said it.'

Doris bent and kissed her mother on the cheek. The flesh was so loose now. There was a sad mortal feel to it. She hated this woman and yet loved her; cursed her for what she'd done to poor Jill and yet had at least an inkling of why she'd done it.

'I think I'll go lie down, Mother.'

Evelyn patted her daughter's hand. 'A nap? Maybe you're coming down with something. You never take naps.'

Doris tried not to look at Jill's photograph on the front page. She hated to think her ex-sister-in-law was having to deal with the nightmare of publicity all over again. It was easy to sit in your living room and gloat over the grief of others. It was another matter to endure those griefs.

'I'll probably be down in an hour or so.'

'Maybe you should take an aspirin or something.'

'I'll be fine,' Doris said, glancing out the mullioned window at the snowy pines and the white hills beyond them. She could see herself and Peter sliding down those hills on their sleds many, many years ago.

Her mother always went with them, of course, petrified they'd break their necks.

Poor Mother, she thought, loving and hating her, hating and loving her, as she had all her life.

'See you in a while.'

'Yes, dear,' Evelyn said.

Mr Corday lived in a hip-roofed ranch house that had no neighbors close by. Despite the sun and the blue sky, the wind was whipping up the snow into duststorms of sparkling diamonds.

Marcy drove by once and noticed that there was a two-stall garage to the right of the house. The overhead door was open and she could see the tail end of a blue Volvo. Then she got a glimpse of a tall man in a dark topcoat and a merry red scarf emerging from the house and walking to the garage. The man had white hair and looked like James Coburn. He was the man in Jill's photograph.

Just as she reached the corner, Marcy turned right and drove down half a block. She turned into a driveway and then backed out quickly. At the head of the block she pulled into the curb.

A few minutes later, Corday drove by. He was headed east. He gave no sign that he'd noticed her.

She gave him a full five minutes, just in case he had noticed her and was going to try something fancy.

She then took a left and drove back past his house. She continued a quarter mile down the road. The snow was a whirling dervish, blinding her momentarily.

She found a DX station, one of those that likely got abandoned during the last recession when all the big oil companies were finding direct sales unprofitable, parked on the snow-covered drive and started her trek back to Corday's house.

The headwinds were a bitch. She kept her head down. Her cheeks froze into numbness almost immediately. The Midwestern countryside was diabolically pretty on a day like this. It could kill you through exposure, but at least you'd die looking at beautiful scenery.

She hoped that she wouldn't find anybody home at Corday's place. That was the first universal rule of the private eye: Never illegally enter a house that is occupied.

It's a fast way to get yourself killed.

Jill had just gotten back from her lawyer's – was just unwinding her scarf and slipping off her western boots – when the phone rang.

She hobbled across the floor with a single boot on.

'Hello?'

'Jill, it's Doris.'

'It's nice to hear your voice.'

'Nice to hear yours, too. But right now—' She was silent a moment, and spoke in a much lower voice when she resumed speaking. 'I thought I heard somebody at the door.'

'Are you at home?'

'Yes. And I'm sure you remember how Mother is.' She tried to sound sardonic but a certain bitterness was there, too. 'I'd like to set up a lunch for tomorrow.'

'I'd like that.'

'Then you're free?'

'Even if I wasn't, I'd make time.'

The pause again. 'Jill, I'm sorry for what you've been going through.'

Jill thought of what her lawyer Deborah had suggested during many of their conversations. Couldn't a bitter old woman with millions and millions of dollars have engineered this murder – and made it look as if Jill were guilty?

'I appreciate you saying that.'

'Well, I have my reasons, believe me. That's why I want to have lunch. Just a minute.'

Silence.

Much lower speaking voice when she came back. 'Now I'm sure I heard somebody in the hall. I'd better go.' She named a place for lunch. 'Around noon?'

'That'd be great. It's so good hearing from you, Doris. It really is.'

'We'll have a lot of things to discuss tomorrow.'

'See you then.'

As she hung up the telephone, Jill replayed Doris' whispers. The poor woman. Still having to sneak around so her mother didn't know what she was up to. Jill even felt an errant wisp of pity for Evelyn. Her infant had been killed in one of the most unlikely ways anybody had ever heard of. Easy to understand why Evelyn had turned into a paranoid, over-controlling old witch. But she couldn't be forgiven for what she'd done to Peter and Doris. Not ever.

Jill had just gotten her second boot off when the phone rang again.

This time it was Kate.

Jill, exuberantly, told her all about Mitch tracking down Cini.

The lock took less than five minutes to pick.

Six months ago, Marcy had tailed an unfaithful wife for a husband who didn't have much money. But what he did have, as a graduate of Illinois State Prison, was a nice new set of burglar tools, the kind you just couldn't find at Sears.

Marcy swapped him pictures of his wife entering a place that said M TEL where she was trysting that afternoon with this kind of dorky-looking white guy who sold appliances out to Best Buys.

The client, black, had gotten very angry. 'He's white? She's makin' it with some white guy? White people don't know shit about sex! Nothin' personal, you understand.'

'Right. Now how about those burglary tools?'

This was Marcy's first opportunity to use them, standing in the wind-whipped side door of Rick Corday's house, her face a frozen mask from the biting snow dervishes, her hands a chafed red though they'd been gloveless less than a minute.

The first three picks were wrong.

The fourth one got the lock tumblers to move a millionth of an inch or so.

The fifth one opened the door instantly.

The smell. That was the first thing she noticed, even though she wasn't all the way inside yet. The smell. She wasn't sure she knew what it was. She wasn't sure she wanted to know.

She went in, closed the door.

Appliances thrummed; a grandfather clock tocked out eternity. A built-in dishwasher had reached rinse cycle.

The smell wasn't as acrid here as it had been on the landing leading to the basement. Spices – cinnamon, paprika, oregano – scented the kitchen pleasantly. The room was done in contrasting yellows. The cabinets new built-ins, the refrigerator a mammoth sunny yellow machine that had an ice-maker set into one of the two front doors.

As soon as she left the kitchen, she picked up the odor again. What was it, anyway?

The living room was a modern blend of natural fabrics and decorative accents – very feminine but not effeminate – a stylish cream-colored button-arm sofa with button-arm chairs in a dark brown and a glass-top coffee table in the center of the ensemble.

Nice. Comfortable. Homey.

Except for the smell.

'Gag me with a spoon,' as she used to say back in the misty days of eight years ago when she'd been in high school.

To the left was a hallway. She took it. The smell faded considerably back here. Wind caught in the chimney and let out a mournful whistle. She felt weird being here. She would be glad to get out. But what kind of self-respecting private investigator would go to all the trouble of breaking into somebody's house and then not go searching through his secret stuff?

The first bedroom was curious indeed for a man, with its rice carved bed with flowery spread. A highboy sat next to the bed, which was supported on a huge platform that lifted it several feet into the air. There was a trellis chainstitch rug and a cheval mirror and a massive burgundy lamp on the night-stand. It was all a little too decorative for her; a little too cloying.

The bureau was pushed against the back wall, next to a bookcase snug with bestsellers that ran to books intent on building your self-esteem. From what Marcy could gather about these books, the only people whose self-esteem they helped was the authors'. They felt just dandy about taking all that money from idiots.

Inside the bureau drawer, she found a tidy array of socks, underwear and T-shirts. Rick Corday was a neat freak. Everything was lined up just so, displayed just so. She hated neat freaks. Life was too short for all that anal-retentive stuff.

She tried the second drawer.

You might call this one The Wonderful World of Sweaters. V-necks, turtle-necks, crew-necks. Red, yellow, blue, green.

She was just opening the third drawer when somebody behind her said, 'Walk away from the bureau and put your hands up. And then turn around and face me. Just like TV.'

She put her hands up.

And turned around real nice and slow as if she were back in ballet class working on her pirouette.

And then she gazed up at the James Coburn-like countenance of Rick Corday standing in the doorway.

He had a .45 straight out of a Bogart movie in his right hand.

He smiled. 'I knew I faked you out.'

'Huh?'

'When you were parked down at the corner there, waiting for me to drive past. I knew I faked you out.'

'You knew I was there?'

'Sure. I got curious the second time you drove by my house. We don't get a lot of that out here.'

'You're Rick Corday.'

'Right.'

'I can explain this, Mr Corday.'

'Sure you can.'

'What're you going to do to me?'

He didn't hesitate. 'Jeeze, kid, you should've figured that out by now. I'm going to kill you.'

'Ma'am.'

One thing servants in the Tappley house learned immediately: You were to report any suspicious activity to Mrs Tappley or risk losing your job. To keep her happy was to keep her informed, and so the maids tended to eavesdrop on any conversations that the children had – when they were growing up – or that Doris had now.

The upstairs maid had listened at the door as Doris spoke to Jill.

She went downstairs, saw Mrs Tappley in the cozy warmth of the den, and said, 'Excuse me, ma'am.'

Mrs Tappley sighed. She was at a particularly exciting place in her Barbara Cartland novel. 'What is it, Jess?'

'I'm sorry to interrupt.'

'I didn't ask you to grovel. I asked you to tell me what you wanted.'

'Yes'm.'

'Well?'

'Doris was on the phone.'

Interest flickered in Evelyn's eyes. 'Oh?'

'Yes'm. For almost ten minutes.'

'I see.'

'And she was talking to your former daughter-in-law.'

Evelyn sat up in her wingchair and put the book face down on her lap. 'She was talking to Jill?'

'Yes'm.'

'You're positive? Jill?'

'She said her name two or three times. That's what I thought was so funny, ma'am, her talking to her.'

'I appreciate you telling me this, Jess.'

'Yes'm.'

'I'll speak with you later.'

Jess nodded and left.

Evelyn didn't go back to her Barbara Cartland. Instead, she began thinking of her medicine cabinet, and something Dr Steiner had given her for when she felt a nervous attack coming on . . .

Mitch spent the early afternoon forcing himself to smile and pretend that he really enjoyed being called a moron.

The man doing the calling was a dapper yuppie from the DA's office named Fitzsimmons. Twice in the conversation he managed to sneak in the fact that he was a Yale alumnus, and three times he mentioned that he'd been on a Barbara Walters Special about crime prevention in the United States.

Nobody on the planet was half as cool as Robert D. Fitzsimmons imagined himself to be.

'I belong to the same club,' he said toward the end of the conversation.

'Club?' Mitch said.

'Country club.'

'Ah.'

Fitzsimmons studied him a moment, looking for any signs of irony in Mitch's face. He then glanced at Lieutenant Sievers as if he expected Sievers to reprimand Mitch in some way. They were in Sievers' office and had been for better than an hour.

'What I'm saying,' Fitzsimmons said, hooking his thumbs in the pockets of his vest and strutting around the office as if he were presenting a case to a jury, 'is that this should be your one and only case, Mitch. No other cases until this one is solved. I thought we had an understanding.'

'I'm not working on any other cases.'

'Of course you are.' He shook his head. 'I have my spies in the department, Mitch. I know what's going on. You're concerned about your lady friend.'

'I don't know why I would be,' Mitch said, letting a nasty edge come into his voice. 'She's only being charged with murder.'

Fitzsimmons of the seventy-five-dollar haircut addressed Sievers directly. 'I see two things wrong with Mitch working on his lady friend's case.'

'I'd appreciate it if you wouldn't call her my "lady friend." Her name is Jill.'

Fitzsimmons paused a moment and pursed his lips, as if pondering a vast and deep philosophical issue.

'All right, then. Jill it is.'

He still looked directly at Sievers. 'There are two things wrong with Mitch working on Jill's case. One, it takes him away from the case we want him working on; and two, it's hardly professional for a detective to work on a case involving somebody he's in love with.'

Sievers said, 'He isn't spending much time on it, Bob. Just an odd hour here and there. Most of the time he's working on your case.'

Fitzsimmons burst into rage, slamming his fist on the desk and spearing a long finger in Sievers' face. 'I told you I don't want him working on anything except my case! Do we understand each other!'

He had shouted so loudly that the cops outside the glass-walled office looked in.

Sievers sat there, eyes downcast, humiliated.

Mitch wanted to grab this candy-ass by the throat and throw him out the fourth-floor window.

'We understand each other,' Sievers said meekly. 'Mitch works on your case.'

'And I'm holding you personally responsible, Lieutenant, to see that he does.'

He was still angry. His neck was red behind his white collar. Spittle covered his lower lip. His parents had perhaps given him a little too much self-esteem.

He picked up his topcoat, which he'd laid neatly across the back of a chair, and his briefcase, which appeared to have cost about as much as Sievers made in a week.

'I don't like pulling rank but sometimes it's necessary,' he said.

Mitch wondered if this was a clumsy attempt at apologizing. Not that it would change his opinion of this jerk, even if it were.

Fitzsimmons walked to the door, opened it slightly. The collective noise of phones, computers, faxes and voices invaded Sievers' tiny domain.

Sievers still looked humiliated and whipped. When somebody this rich was murdered, there was always a lot of heat, especially when the DA put a country-clubber like Fitzsimmons in charge of the case.

Fitzsimmons said, 'I'm going to trust you'll do your job as I've outlined it, Lieutenant.'

He still wasn't favoring Mitch with any eye contact.

He left.

The asshole.

Mitch said, 'You OK?'

Sievers smiled sadly. 'You ever see that John Wayne picture *She Wore A Yellow Ribbon*?'

'Sure. It's one of my favorites.'

'You know how Wayne had this big calendar hanging on his wall and he checked off every day till he retired?' He smiled. Sievers was always good at bouncing back. 'I think I'm going to get myself a calendar. And meanwhile, go call that Cini girl. Keep the heat on her.'

'What about Fitzsimmons?'

'Screw him.'

'Thanks, Lieutenant. I appreciate it.'

Mitch went back to his desk.

Doris slept.

Just as she was drifting off, she realized how odd this was. She'd never been able to nap, not even as a small child.

But today – possibly because of her anxiety over meeting Jill tomorrow – she fell into a fast and deep slumber.

So she was not aware when her door crept open—

Not aware when her mother entered the room bearing a needle and syringe—

Not aware when Evelyn sat down next to her on the bed and pulled up the hem of her dress so she could find a good and true place to administer the shot—

Not aware—

But then she *was* aware.

Mother. Needle in her hand. Injecting the fluid into Doris' thigh. Pain.

'Don't worry, dear. This is just the sedative Dr Steiner has me give myself. I'm letting you have a triple dose, is all.'

Shrieking, grabbing her mother. 'Why are you doing this?'

'I want you to be sensible about Jill, dear, that's all. I want you to see that you shouldn't be talking to anybody who betrayed our trust and our family the way she did.'

Triple dose. Feeling the effects already. A darkness pulling her downward . . .

'You shouldn't talk to her, dear. Not ever.'

Her mother's face blurring. Her voice faint.

'She betrayed our family, dear. Every one of us. I'm just trying to protect you from doing something you'll regret.'

The darkness pulling Doris down . . .

Down . . .

Marcy had to give Rick Corday one thing: he was real good at tying people up. He was also good at taking their clothes off.

Marcy lay naked and trussed on a dusty single bed in the east corner of the very cold basement. Rick Corday's basement. She was already sneezing. And her throat was already raw.

Actually, she tried not to think about her throat.

Before he'd left this morning – right before, at the last moment, almost as an afterthought, he'd tied a gag across her mouth – he took his axe and he gave Marcy a little demonstration.

It had been truly weird. Rick brought out this simple wooden X made of two-by-fours. He'd set the log in the crook of the X and then chop away.

He could cut a log in violent half with a single swing.

Impressive.

She tried real hard not to think of what would happen to her head if he ever rested her neck on the log-holder.

But that wasn't the weird part.

All the time he split logs – and he must have split around thirty of them – he told her about axes.

It was as if he were doing a TV infommercial and she was the audience at home.

'Don't buy a long handle just because it looks more powerful. Always get a handle you feel comfortable with.'

And then he'd rend another log in two.

'Always treat your axe like your best friend. If it's been

stored away for some time and the socket at the head of the handle isn't snug around the axe, soak the handle in water and then later on treat it with linseed oil.'

Another log would shatter.

'Be sure to be careful in winter weather, especially when you're outside. Axes can break sometimes. It's a good practice to warm the axe first over a stove or fire.'

'*Enough already!*' she was shouting inside her mind. Too bad she couldn't shout it out loud. Maybe then he'd take the hint.

She tried for a time to will herself out of this basement. She'd read somewhere that during great periods of stress in World War Two some soldiers had been able to will themselves out of their bodies.

But it proved impossible to do this feat with a four-inch-thick piece of wood clattering to the concrete floor every few minutes. Sawdust and chips and chunks of bark littered the floor around the X.

'So what's the best axe-head for you?'

She forced herself not to listen anymore.

There was only one thing she knew about Rick Corday. He was clinical. Real clinical. One of her Crim courses had included some profiles of criminally insane people, and Rick here certainly fit the profile.

Especially since his voice kept changing every five minutes or so. He was, from what she could see, at least two different people – and both of them were insane.

He finished with the axe and then walked over to her.

'I'm going to go get my friend and bring him back here and then the three of us are going to have a good time.'

She just stared up at him. She felt very self-conscious about being naked – and very scared of what he might be suggesting here – but she wasn't going to give him the satisfaction of letting him see this.

'Did I mention that you've got a nice little body? You've got a very nice little body. And I'm going to capture it for posterity on my videocam.' He smiled his fruitcake smile. 'That'll be fun, won't it?'

'*Oh yeah*,' she wanted to say. '*Yeah, that'll be a whole lot of fun*.'

Rick left then, clomp clomp clomp up the basement stairs, clomp clomp clomp across the kitchen and out the back door.

Then she was alone, utterly alone, and terrified.

O'Hare was always a pain in the ass and never more so than when flights were delayed because of bad weather. Even though the plows had been out and the runways were clear, flights had piled up from yesterday and many people were still waiting to get flown out of here.

The place looked like a refugee camp as Adam made his way to the public phones. Some people had slept in their seats all night and looked like it, rumpled, glassy-eyed, vaguely dirty. Little kids ran around screaming while sleepy parents snapped at them. College students tried hard to concentrate on Sartre just as housewives tried hard to concentrate on Danielle Steel. The masses – in the abstract they weren't a bad idea. It was just when you got up close to them.

When Adam reached the phone, he took his wallet from his topcoat and ran a finger down a list of names and phone numbers. He called the office of Arthur K. Halliwell and when the receptionist asked who was calling, Adam gave a false name that Halliwell alone would recognize.

Halliwell came on. 'Do you know how many days I've been trying to reach you?'

'I went to New York on business. I wish to hell you'd relax.'

'He's going to get us in trouble. He's a loose cannon. I take it you know by now that he killed Eric Brooks?'

'Yes, he told me.'

Halliwell sighed. 'I need to approach Evelyn today. I need the money.'

It was all going to be so simple, Adam thought. Several years ago, just after Adam had gotten to know him, Rick had told him a strange story – that he had once been a young man named Peter Tappley supposedly put to death in the electric chair for killing several young women. But he'd made a deal with the family lawyer to give him his entire part of the Tappley estate if Halliwell could arrange for the execution to be faked. This meant bribing, for a great deal of money, the man in charge of the execution, the attending physician, the County Coroner and the funeral home director in charge of the corpse. Evelyn Tappley knew nothing about any of this, as Peter wanted to escape her power and influence. He'd gotten extensive plastic surgery in readiness to start a new life. He was sentimental about the Chicago area so the two men lived there. The first year or so was fine, Adam showing him how paid assassins went about their work, Peter being a willing and eager student. Then the change started. Adam first noted the symptoms in Rick: the mood swings, the depression, the blinding headaches, even the change in voice. There seemed to be another person inside of Peter struggling to get out. Then the more frightening symptoms began: periods of amnesia, sleepwalking, terrifying hours of dazedness . . . and then insane fits of jealousy. Where had Adam been? How could he betray Rick this way? Didn't he know that someday he'd be sorry? Adam was unfaithful, true; but not *that* unfaithful. Adam called Halliwell and introduced himself. Both were afraid that Rick would crack and end up in a hospital and tell his doctors all about how Halliwell had faked Peter's execution and how Adam was a hit man. Peter had become somebody else completely, somebody Adam neither recognized nor controlled. One day, Adam had shown Rick some pictures of Peter Tappley as a boy – and newspaper clippings of his execution – but Rick had shown no recognition whatsoever. Then Evelyn called one day and asked Halliwell to arrange a murder for which her former daughter-in-law Jill Coffey would be blamed. Halliwell said yes. He was virtually bankrupt. He needed money desperately and Evelyn was offering half a million. Then Halliwell got a better idea. After Jill was framed, he'd go to Evelyn and tell her that he'd just learned that Peter was alive. Naturally, she'd be desperate to see him. He would say that his source wanted one million dollars for the rest of the information. Evelyn would pay it without question. They would set up a meeting for mother and son, but just before it took place, Adam would kill Peter, for which he would be paid one hundred thousand dollars. Adam would then leave town. By now, both men were seriously worried about Peter. What if he did something really crazy before they got their million from Evelyn?

'I wish we could just kill him now,' Halliwell said, 'but we can't. In order to convince Evelyn that he's alive, we'll have to have him say hello to her.'

That was the only reason they wanted Rick alive now. They'd have him call this woman and say hello to her – they'd force him at gunpoint, if necessary. She'd recognize the voice – there wasn't anything the plastic surgeons could do to alter a voice in any significant way – she'd recognize the voice and pay Halliwell the million dollars.

'Just hope he doesn't run amuck somewhere and take us all down with him,' Halliwell said.

Adam checked his watch. 'I'll keep a close eye on him,

Arthur. Relax. This'll work out fine. I can control him. I really can.'

'I'm not sure you can these days, Adam. He's different now. Truly psychotic.'

Adam heard several flights being announced. 'I'd better go. He's waiting out there to pick me up.'

'Call me and let me know how things are going.'

'Just relax, Arthur. Relax.'

He hung up and walked out to find Rick.

Chapter Fifty-Nine

The final work consists of inserting the plastic to reshape cheeks and chin. It is here that the surgeon's craft becomes his art. It is here that most surgeons reveal themselves to be mediocrities. He is different, of course. From Buenos Aires to Geneva; from Paris to Washington, DC, he is known as indisputably the best. And now, as he finishes his molding with the plastic, looking at the finished product, he can agree with them. He is indeed no mere journeyman; he is an artist of the first rank.

Chapter Sixty

Adam scared him. He hated to admit it but it was true. This incredible power Adam had over him to hurt his feelings, to make him feel less than he really was—

'Everything go all right?' Adam asked when they were in the car and on the way home.

'Went fine.'

'No trouble, then?'

'You were expecting trouble, Adam?'

'I was asking a civil question, Rick.'

'No, you weren't. You were implying that I couldn't pull anything off without you.'

Adam, blond Adam, shook his head and looked out the window at the fine autumn day. 'I'm really not up for this crap, Rick. I mean it.' He didn't look at Rick. Continued to stare out the driver's window.

'Meet anybody interesting in New York?' Rick said. He knew he shouldn't have said it but couldn't help himself.

'I'm not even going to answer that.'

'Maybe I'll find another note on the floor.'

Adam looked at him. 'Maybe you will. And you know what, Rick? I don't give a damn if you do.'

Scared, that's what Rick was. Scared that Adam was

going to say goodbye to him. So what does he do? *Pushes* Adam into saying goodbye to him. Go figure.

'Maybe we should give it a rest, Rick, you ever think about that?'

'Meaning what – you met somebody here in Chicago, too?'

Very dramatic sigh. 'Meaning that I'm not in the car two minutes before you're on my case. Meaning that we should be talking about how it went with Jill Coffey and instead we're arguing about some imaginary lover.'

'Imaginary. Right, Adam. Was that note I found imaginary?'

'One note. Not exactly the end of the world, Rick.'

'Maybe not for somebody who doesn't care about being true and loyal.'

Another sigh. 'The subject, Rick, is Jill Coffey.'

Rick's jaw clenched. He wanted to keep on talking about what an utter bastard Adam was – just the sight of him had made Rick insane with anger – but he supposed he'd have to let Adam shame him into talking about Jill Coffey.

'Everything went fine.'

'You were able to get some of her clothes?'

'No problem.'

'And Eric Brooks has been found by now, I take it?'

'Two hours after I killed him. It's all over TV and the papers.'

'You know what our good friend the lawyer told us – Mrs Tappley plans a very big bonus if things go right.'

'You trust him?'

'Who?'

'Halliwell. Arthur K. Halliwell. I don't trust him.'

'Rick, you say that about half the people we work with. You ever think of seeing a shrink about your paranoia?'

'What's that supposed to mean?'

'What's what supposed to mean?'

'About me seeing a shrink. You think I'm losing it or something?'

Yet another sigh. 'Rick, you're all the time talking about how we can't trust this guy or can't trust that guy. I mean, it gets a little crazy after a while.'

'So that's it.'

'What's it?'

'Crazy. I figured you'd get around to using that word eventually.'

'Rick.'

'What?'

'Shut the hell up, will you? I'm half an hour off the plane and I'm already ass-deep into one of these *things* you insist on us having.'

And then Rick reached inside his sport jacket, felt for his shirt pocket and took out the photo, the lone photo he'd kept from the envelope in Adam's bottom drawer.

'Where the hell did you get that?'

'Where do you think, Adam?'

'That cuts it, pal. That cuts it clean. Once we start snooping in each other's private business . . .'

Rick tried not to smile. He was enjoying himself. Something about the photo of fifteen-year-old Peter Tappley had alarmed Adam greatly.

They reached the Dan Ryan.

'Adam?'

'God, Rick. You don't get it, do you?'

'Get what?'

'Who you are.'

'What the hell's that supposed to mean?'

'God,' Adam said. 'That you – that you're Peter Tappley.'

'What the hell are you talking about?' Rick said.

'The headaches, Rick, and the blackouts. They're part of the multiple personality thing. I did some reading about them.'

'You're saying I have this multiple personality thing?'

Adam looked at him and shook his head. Crazy sonofabitch. Pitiful crazy sonofabitch. That's what Rick was.

'Just drive,' Adam said. 'Just goddamm drive.'

Chapter Sixty-One

Evelyn sat in her den, looking out the mullioned windows at the fading day. November always depressed her, land and sky blanched of all color, nights when the winds howled out here on the plains like the cries of some animal dying.

She tried not to think of her daughter Doris.

Of how her daughter Doris had been about to betray her.

Of how her daughter Doris preferred the esteem of Jill Coffey to her own mother.

Of how her daughter Doris would set her own mother in jeopardy with the law.

A knock.

'Ma'am?'

'Yes.'

'Would you like a lamb chop for dinner?'

'There'll be no dinner tonight.'

'No dinner?'

'Are you deaf, girl? I said no dinner.'

'Yes, ma'am.'

'Now go find something useful to do. And don't sit in the bathroom so long. I'm well aware that you sit in there and read magazines.'

'Yes, ma'am.'

Evelyn went back to her thoughts.

On such a dusk as this, she felt old far beyond her years. There was no one to comfort her. Nobody ever pitied – or tried to understand – the truly wealthy. All the prattle today about minorities who weren't treated well, from blacks to gays. Well, in many respects, the minority of rich people were treated far worse than all the other minorities put together. When a rich person got very ill, the masses were spiteful: '*He deserves it, the rich old bastard.*' When the congress decided it needed money, to whom did it always turn? '*Rich people, let's tax rich people.*' And when a rich person's son got in trouble with the law . . . Well, if Peter had been the son of a black man who lived in inner-city Chicago, the press would hardly have paid attention at all. Certainly, no army of press would have besieged his trial, his prison years and his execution. But no . . . rich people were always fair game for the press. And so she'd had to endure the media circus all those years. They'd even taken to helicopters so they could get video film of her playing croquet on sunny Sunday afternoons . . .

But on this dusk, Evelyn knew an even deeper bitterness than being held up to public scrutiny and spectacle. She had lost her children.

Maybe, she sometimes thought, maybe she'd been lucky to lose the first one to the rattlesnake and the vaccine. She did not have to watch as he grew up and turned against her . . . the way Peter and Doris had.

Peter . . . dragging Jill Coffey into this place to live. Jill, who could barely contain her contempt for Evelyn and all she stood for. Who silently accused Evelyn of having over-protected her children. Who wanted to smirk every time Evelyn asked her to give up her photography career and live here with Peter and Doris. If she hadn't gone back to taking her inane pictures then Peter would never have been driven to killing those women.

And now Doris . . .

In the end, you were left alone, utterly alone, to face your own death and extinction.

For years, Evelyn had felt that Doris would be there to comfort her, help her.

But now she knew better . . .

Well, when Doris came out of the sedative, Evelyn was going to have a little talk with her, remind Doris that she had better not take for granted that she was going to be part of Evelyn's will. A simple phone call to Arthur K. Halliwell could change all that.

Evelyn amused herself with images of Doris trying to make her way in the world. There was nothing the girl could do to support herself; absolutely nothing.

Knock.

'Ma'am?'

'I told you not to interrupt me.'

'It's Doris, ma'am.'

'What about her?'

'I was walking by her room – I think she might be waking up.'

'Impossible. I gave her a triple dosage.'

'Maybe you'd better check, ma'am.'

'I can't even have a few minutes peace, can I?'

'No, ma'am.'

'I've worked so hard all my life and I can't even have a few minutes peace.'

'No, ma'am. I'm sorry, ma'am.'

'She'd damned well better be waking up or you're going to answer to me, girl.'

'Yes, ma'am. I just thought—'

'Just get out of here and quit pestering me.'

'Yes, ma'am.'

Evelyn stood up, brittle bones hard at work beneath aged flesh.

Oh yes, she'd have a few unpleasant surprises for Doris the next time they had a long conversation.

She'd tell Doris to imagine herself in a McDonald's uniform asking some sweat-reeking black man if he'd like fries with his Big Mac . . .

Let's just see how Doris likes that.

The very first thing Rick did once they were inside the house, not more than three steps inside the house, was to take his .45 from his topcoat pocket and bring it down across the back of Adam's head.

Adam always boasted how tough he was. Sure. As soon as the butt of the gun struck his head, he made a whimpering sound, tried to turn around to grab Rick, and then collapsed on the floor of the kitchen.

Rick had hit him good and hard.

Just the way he deserved, the unfaithful bastard.

Rick reached down to take him by the collar of his coat. He was going to drag him downstairs. Wouldn't be any trouble carrying him – Rick was actually quite strong – but Adam would get nice and bruised (maybe even a little bloody) bumping down the stairs.

And then the blackness overwhelmed him once again, this time with no warning, and then came the headache, like a broadsword cleaving his skull.

Then the voice.

The voice that was always inside him, lurking.

He could never quite tell what the voice was saying. It spoke in this faint whisper. But whatever it said always upset Rick. And he wasn't even sure why.

For some reason, he tried real hard not to think of what Adam had said – that Rick was really this Peter Tappley.

How could you be two people? Rick was Rick and Peter Tappley was Peter Tappley. Right?

The headache got so bad that Peter gripped his head in his hands and staggered over to the shiny twin sinks and turned the cold water on full force.

He put his head beneath the fall and began to massage the water into his head.

He screamed.

He could hear himself scream.

That should shake up the little guy sitting inside his mind, the way he'd just screamed. Between the cold cold water and the scream, the little guy didn't have a chance.

He'd never whisper to Rick again.

Never.

He whispered to Rick.

He was still in there.

Rick, enraged, slammed his head against the edge of the sink hard enough that he left a small dent.

But he didn't even feel it, he was so intent on getting rid of the little man who whispered to him all the time.

Bastard.

Little bastard.

I'll show you.

And then the darkness was gone. And the headache.

And he was left to feel the pain he had inflicted on himself when he'd slammed his head against the edge of the sink.

He laughed about it. 'Real bright, Rick. Why don't you stick your tongue in an electrical outlet next time?'

He was all right now. Just fine. He needed a couple aspirins, was all.

—And how did you get your headache, Mr Corday?

—Well, I pounded my head against the edge of the sink.

—I see, Mr Corday. Why don't you not *do that for a few days and see if the headache goes away?*

It really was pretty funny.

He stepped over the unconscious form of Adam Morrow and walked into the bathroom and got himself two buffered aspirin. The regular kind always gave him heartburn.

He swallowed the aspirins and then walked back to the kitchen.

All he thought about now was how sweet that axe-handle was going to feel in his hands.

Yes indeedy.

Daniel Ransom was a thing of beauty, scrubbed, shined, moussed, teased and polished to perfection. He was Hunk Among Hunks of the local news-teams and he was best buds with a certain Fitzsimmons in the DA's office and Mitch had no doubt that it was that same Mr Fitzsimmons who had sicced Ransom on Mitch this late cold November afternoon.

They were on the elevator, Ransom and his cameraman, and they were taping and Ransom, in his white trenchcoat with the collar up and his dark locks fashionably askew, said: 'You sound a little cavalier to me, if you'll forgive me saying so, Inspector.'

'There were two little black girls killed in front of a school last week. Why aren't you asking me about them?'

Daniel Ransom was programmed to look gorgeous, he was not programmed to think quickly. 'Well, you know—'

'Sure, I know, pretty-boy. Because those two little black girls don't matter to you or your moron station manager or all those stupid whores who peddle time for your station.

You can't sell much advertising when two little black girls die. But let a rich white socialite die and you get all worked up.' He made a big thing of peering closely at Ransom's face. 'Your lipstick is crooked, you know that?'

'Turn that fucking camera off!' Ransom snapped.

'Hey, you asked me to say something on camera, and I did. So what're you so steamed up about?'

'You could always lose your job, you know.'

'So could you, sweetheart, if they ever make reporters take an IQ test.'

They rode the rest of the floors in silence.

When he stepped off the elevator, Mitch made sure that he trod painfully on the instep of the Hunk of Hunks.

Cheating was what she was doing. If you were going to make cookies you should go out and get all the makings – the flour, the brown sugar, the chocolate chips – you should not buy one of those frozen dough dealies and slice it all up and pop it in the oven and pretend that you were making homemade cookies.

But the smells were good and that's all that mattered this late and gloomy afternoon.

Maybe they weren't as good as the smells of her mother's old kitchen but, Jill thought, they were close enough.

She got out a festively-colored heating glove and extracted the cookie sheet from the oven.

She set them on the stove and stood there with her eyes closed, imagining herself eight or nine again, and her mother inviting her into the kitchen to clean out the bowl with a big spoon. Jill had loved the taste of the uncooked cookie dough. Childhood was so sweet; you had no idea how sweet until you were in your thirties.

She thought of Mitch and of how things were going to go well. She was sure of it now.

It was all like one of those improbable romance movies of her youth. Cini coming forward, clearing Jill's name. Mitch and Jill marrying, say a year later. A kitchen very much like her mother's a few years later still – and Jill's own daughter sampling some of the cookies Jill had made. It was all going to be so good, so very good.

She wished Mitch were here now, holding her . . .

Marcy wondered how long she could survive this way, naked, trussed, shivering in the cold of the basement.

For the first hour or so, she'd been able to amuse herself with thoughts of all the great publicity this little turn of events would bring her.

WOMAN PI FOILS KILLER

That's how it would read in the respectable press, anyway. In the disreputable press it would probably be:

NAKED GAL PI LURES KILLER

The naked part would really freak her dad out, even though it hadn't been her fault.

'*A daughter of mine naked in some stranger's basement!*' Imagine.

But after several hours she quit thinking about publicity and her dad and started thinking about herself. For one thing, she was really getting cold. She was sneezing all the time now. And her throat was definitely raw. And she couldn't quit shivering.

For another thing, the bare mattress on which she lay was starting to chafe her skin. No matter which way she moved, it scratched at her like a thousand tiny invisible fingers.

She had wet herself twice. The first time she'd been ashamed and self-conscious. God, couldn't she hold it any longer than this?

But the second time she made telepathic contact with her bladder and simply opened the floodgates.

The only problem now was the smell.

Pretty darn bad.

But not bad enough, unfortunately, to cover up the other smell she'd noticed when she'd first stepped inside the house upstairs.

By now, she knew that the stench emanated from the square wooden room at the far end of the basement. The door was ajar. The odor, even from here, was almost suffocating.

By now, she also had a pretty good guess of what the smell was, too. She remembered reading something in her Crim courses about how human blood has this tart, steely smell even after you've tried to scrub it away.

Blood. That was the smell. Whatever this Rick guy did with his victims, he did it in that room down there.

The basement door at the top of the stairs opened.

Rick came down but he wasn't alone.

He was carrying somebody in his arms. This well-dressed, handsome guy. Rick wasn't even panting. He must be very strong, she thought.

Rick looked over at her and said, 'Dammit, I forgot to get you a blanket. You're probably freezing, aren't you?'

It was kind of strange, him being so solicitous and all, with an unconscious guy in his arms.

'I'll take care of Adam here and then be right back.' He sounded like her next-door neighbor kibitzing over the backyard fence.

Rick hefted Adam a little and started walking to the room at the other end of the basement.

He eased the door open with his foot and then carried Adam inside.

He was in there for maybe five minutes. Adam must have awakened because he started screaming. 'Help! Help!'

'Shut up, you pussy! You wouldn't want all your little boyfriends to hear you yell like that, would you?'

Then Adam was pleading. It was kind of sickening, actually, hearing somebody beg like that. 'Listen, Rick. Listen – I'm sorry for how I've been lately. Listen to me, Rick – *listen to me!* You're not well. You need to see Dr Milligan again. He'll tell you the truth about yourself, Rick. You're really Peter Tappley. You really are. Peter – it used to be he couldn't kill anybody – so he became Rick. Don't you understand that? But now it doesn't seem to matter. Both Rick and Peter can kill people.'

Peter Tappley, she thought. Wasn't that the name of Jill Coffey's husband?

But hadn't Peter Tappley been executed?

Adam tried saying more but then she could hear him struggling against a gag being put over his mouth. Rick, or Peter, or whoever he was, had probably already tied his hands.

'You've had this coming for a long time, Adam. A long, long time.'

Then there were just the sounds of the basement. The relative silence was even weirder than the shouting had been.

She wondered what Rick was doing.

And then he was there, striding out of the room to say, 'I'll get you that blanket in a few minutes.'

But she didn't pay much attention to his words.

She was more interested in the long-handled axe he held casually in his right hand.

Blood had splashed and splattered and spattered all over the axe-head and halfway up the handle.

'I need to take care of Adam first.' He shook his head. 'He really has treated me like shit. I mean, if he'd been any kind of friend at all, I wouldn't be doing this. Did you ever have an unfaithful lover? It's real hard to deal with, believe me.' He shook his head again. 'I've lost fourteen pounds in the last month. I can't eat, I can't sleep. This is the only way left to deal with it.'

Insane, she thought.

Totally clinical.

Did he expect her to respond to his monologue, or hadn't he noticed that she was gagged?

'This won't take long.'

He went back into the room, leaving the door ajar again.

There was a scraping sound, as if Rick was moving stuff around, and then there were the faint useless sounds Adam made screaming into his gag.

'I gave you every chance,' Rick said, sounding sad. 'If you'd been even a little bit honest with me—'

More frantic screaming from Adam.

By now, Rick was muttering. She couldn't make out his exact words.

She tried not to think about the axe. How it would look as Rick held it over his head. Brought it downward. Sliced it into Adam's neck.

A terrible sharp sound filled the basement.

Edge of axe connecting with human neck.

She thought of her grandpa beheading chickens back on the farm.

Then Adam's head came rolling out through the open space between the door and the threshold.

It was almost like an optical illusion. Human heads didn't really roll . . .

But this one had.

Rolled away from the chopping block and right out the door.

Even in death, Adam was pretty good-looking. Except for the eyes, that is. The expression in the blue eyes conveyed all the terror and horror of his last moments.

Adam's head sat there staring at her as if to say: '*Don't be so smug. You're next.*'

A white hand reached out and lifted Adam up by the hair. Blood and gore dripped from his cleaved neck, puddling on the floor below.

'You can't even be faithful to your own body,' Rick said from behind the door.

Silence again. Awareness of the scratchy mattress again (maybe it had bedbugs). The need to urinate again.

What was Rick doing in there, anyway?

Marcy sure wouldn't want to spend any more time with a beheaded corpse than she had to.

But then, Marcy was Marcy and Rick was Rick.

And then the scream came and she couldn't ever recall hearing a scream to match it. It came not just from the lungs and chest and throat of somebody; it came from his very essence, his soul, his entire being.

She closed her eyes, hoping he would not scream again.

The scream was worse than the sound of the axe severing the head.

Please don't scream again, Rick. Please.

He was down on his knees and he was gripping his head vise-like and he was Peter Tappley.

i

am

peter

tappley
i
am
not
rick
corday
i
am

He opened his eyes.

Basement.

Cold concrete floor.

Stench: blood and feces and urine.

Man, handsome man, blond handsome man.

Adam.

In one corner sat Adam's head.

His torso lay sprawled on the cold concrete floor, blood running from the shoulders into the drain.

Blood feces urine.

Adam's eyes watching him.

i
am
peter
tappley

Then: *mother*.

Then: *execution*.

Then: *Arthur K. Halliwell*.

Then: *escape to Europe. Endless plastic surgery. Freedom*.

Then: *darkness . . . and deep within him . . . a voice:*

i
am
rick
corday

Then: Adam explaining this to him.

How sometimes he (Peter) was Rick . . . and how sometimes he (Rick) was Peter.

Basement – cold – odors

Then: *mother*

mothermothermothermother

MOTHER.

Peter Tappley (or Rick – Marcy wasn't sure now which to call him) came out carrying the axe.

The axe dripped blood, the same blood that was all over Peter's hands and face.

The blood of his friend Adam.

She sat cowering on the mattress, trembling even more from her fear than from the cold.

He was going to cut off her head, too.

She closed her eyes.

Sure, she was nothing but a big fraidy cat but she just couldn't deal with it.

If he wanted to cut her head off, she wasn't going to give him the satisfaction of watching him.

Oh no.

She was going to keep her eyes closed.

His soles squeaked on the concrete floor because they were soaked in blood.

Squeak squeak squeak.

Coming closer.

With his axe.

Then the squeaking grew fainter.

Fainter.

She opened her eyes.

All she could see was from the backs of his knees down to his bloody shoes.

He was going up the basement stairs.

Opening the door.

Closing the door.

He hadn't paid any attention to her whatsoever.

Hadn't even slowed down.

Just gone straight up the stairs.

With his axe.

She started crying. It was crazy, she knew. She should be trying to whoop and yelp her good fortune but probably because she'd been scared so hard for so long she had to cry it out of her system.

But it was a good cry.

A positive cry.

The kind of cry that—

The basement door at the top of the stairs opened.

Then – nothing.

She couldn't hear anybody.

She could just look up the shadowy steps and see that the door was open a little bit.

Who was up there?

Why wasn't he coming down?

A trouser leg appeared. Then another one.

It was Peter.

He started walking down the stairs, carrying his axe.

At this point that's all she could see – the shoes, the trouser legs from the knees down, the axe.

The bloody bloody axe.

Then Peter came the rest of the way down the stairs and stood looking at her.

She had promised herself one and no more – well, maybe two, but certainly not anymore than that. Well, an absolute stratospheric max of three . . .

So far, in twenty-five minutes, Jill Coffey had eaten four of her semi-homemade cookies and was contemplating a fifth when somebody knocked on the downstairs door.

Reporters.

These days, that was always her first thought whenever a knock sounded or the phone rang.

Reporters.

But then came the code – three-pause-two-pause-one.

Mitch was here.

She felt as exuberant as a little girl going down the stairs, trying to imagine his surprise as she opened the door and he smelled the tangy odor of the semi-homemade cookies.

'Wow,' Mitch said. 'What smells so good?'

She let him in, glimpsing the chill dusk, the coral-color sky, the quarter-moon above the snow-covered rooftops, the chink-chink-chink of tire chains on a big city sand truck just now passing by.

She led him upstairs by the hand.

Halfway up, he said, 'Would you explain something to me?'

'What?'

'What exactly is a "semi"-homemade cookie?'

She explained.

'God, they smell great.'

'Wait till you taste one. I added some chocolate chips. And there's also fresh coffee.'

'Is this a glimpse of married life with my future bride?'

'If I say yes, will that mean that we get married soon?'

He laughed. 'Very soon.'

She set a place for him at the table and made him sit down and take off his hat, which he sometimes forgot to do, and then she brought over the cookies and the coffee.

'These are fantastic,' he said after a sizeable bite.

She smiled. 'Well, I don't know if I'd go that far.'

'They are. Truly. If I didn't know the difference, I'd say these weren't "semi"-homemade at all.' He laughed. 'Now, do I get the part in this commercial or don't I?'

'I've had four.'

'Really? Four?'

'Actually, five.'

'*Five?* You ate five cookies? I didn't know there was such a self-indulgent side to my future bride.'

'Fortunately, not with alcohol or drugs or sticking up convenience stores. Only with semi-homemade cookies.'

He watched her with overwhelming affection. 'God, I love you, Jill.'

'Ditto,' she said, and leaned over and kissed the cookie crumbs from his mouth.

In all, he ate three cookies, which he was quick to point out was several less – well, he tried to get away with the word 'several' but she scolded him and changed the word to 'two' – than she'd had.

And then she said, knowing this was going to puncture the pretty pink party balloon they'd made for themselves: 'What if she decides not to help us?'

'Cini, you mean?'

'Right.'

'She will. I'm sure of it.'

Jill sighed. Up and down, that's how her moods ran. Up and down. She was in a downswing now. 'Maybe I should talk to her.'

He shook his head. 'Your lawyer Deborah would go ballistic if you did. No, I'll talk to her.' He checked his watch. 'In fact, I was thinking of running over there about now. Remind her that I'm still around. See if there's any way I can help her – see what she's afraid of, is what I'm really saying. There's something holding her back and maybe I can get her to tell me.'

Jill glanced around the apartment. 'Boy, it was so nice watching you eating those cookies.'

'There's nothing like semi-homemades.'

'For a couple of minutes there, I absolutely forgot everything except you and me.'

He took her hand, held it tenderly. 'I know. I was feeling the same way.'

'I'm getting scared again.'

'She'll help us, Jill. I know she will. Maybe not tonight – but soon. I can feel it. I really can.'

She got up and walked over to the window and he joined her. They looked out at the city beneath its white winter wrappings. The snow was the beautiful soft blue of the sky with the golden highlights of the moonglow. Snow masked so much of the city's ugliness and harshness.

'You just start planning our wedding,' he said, sliding his arm around her shoulder. 'That's all you need to worry about.'

'Are you really going over to see her?'

'Soon as I get done with a stop for the socialite case. One of her tennis-playing lovers just got back into the city and I need to ask him some questions. Then I'm going over to see Cini.'

'Then you're coming back here?'

'I sure am. And I can't wait till it's time.'

He kissed her several times, and she clung to him with a little more desperation than she wanted to show, and then he left.

She watched him in the winter night, so small and vulnerable-looking against the white snowbanks, and then he was in his car, headlights lancing the darkness, and gone.

Peter stood looking at Marcy for a moment but he didn't really see her. She could tell that. His mind was so preoccupied with something else that she didn't register on his consciousness at all. She was just part of the furniture.

He turned away from the bed and walked to the far end of the basement, to the room where he'd killed his friend Adam.

The blood-splashed axe still dangled from his left hand.

God, what was he going to do now?

She heard him making some noises in the room but she couldn't tell what he was up to.

A long silence.

Then she heard him walking again, his shoes squishing with the blood that had soaked them.

He came walking out with Adam's head tucked into his arm, as if he were carrying something home from the supermarket.

Adam's blue eyes were forever fixed in utter horror and his handsome face was splotched with blood.

Peter carried the axe in the other hand.

He walked past her very slowly, not even glancing in her direction, and reached the stairs and started climbing them.

Squish squish squish went his bloody shoes all the way up.

Squish squish squish.

When he reached the top of the stairs, he opened and closed the door very quietly.

A few minutes later, she heard his car engine start up, hesitant at first in the near-zero temperature.

Then he backed out of the driveway and was gone.

Chapter Sixty-Two

The tennis player's name was Randy Dupree and he would have been a much happier young man if he'd been born thirty years earlier, before tennis went all democratic and started letting in blacks and kids who'd learned on public courts and girls who would not grow up to be princesses.

He said, very spiffy in his dark blue Calvin Klein V-neck sweater and his pressed wheat-colored jeans, 'I can make this fast.'

'All right, make it fast.'

'Would you like a drink?'

'No, thanks.'

'Will you think I'm nervous if I fix myself one?'

'Not at all. I'll just think you want a drink.'

'Good. Because, as I said, I'm going to make this fast.'

Mitch wanted to dislike him but he couldn't quite. Sure, Randy looked like a spoiled twenty-five-year-old rich boy. And sure, he lived in this beautifully-appointed Lake Shore drive condo. And true there was an ever-so-slight look of derision in his eyes whenever he chose to focus on Mitch . . . but still . . . he wasn't a jerk.

He made himself a martini at the dry bar – the martini surprising Mitch, who'd never thought of jock-types also being martini-types – and then he sat down in the living room and said, 'Nice view, huh?'

Nice and expensive, Mitch thought. But he was impressed despite himself. There was an almost other-worldly aspect to Chicago from this height and vantage point, a different planet, especially with the snow covering everything. No homeless. No drug dealers. No abused wives. No little kids grubbing up the money their parents couldn't afford to give them.

'Do you think I killed her?' Randy said.

Mitch turned around and faced him. 'Yes, I do.'

'I see. Did your friend Unzak tell you about my alibi?'

'Is that how you're going to make this fast? By telling me about that former girlfriend of yours, the one who'll swear you were with her all night?'

The lights were on in the dining room. The living room was in shadow.

Randy Dupree said, 'No, I was going to make this fast another way.'

'And what way is that?'

'By telling you that I killed her.'

Mitch hoped his small gasp wasn't audible. 'I see.'

'You sound shocked.'

'I guess I am.'

'Because I just said it right out.'

'Uh-huh. And because you didn't even give me a chance to read you your rights. It's not as simple as it is on TV, you know.'

'I don't give a shit about my rights. Or a lawyer. Right now I don't give a shit about anything.'

He started sobbing.

He let the martini glass fall, nearly full, to the floor and he put his face in his hands like a little boy and began weeping.

'I didn't mean to kill her. I was just – angry. She'd been so goddammed unfaithful.'

And then he was sobbing again.

Mitch thought of his own wife. And how he'd felt – the terrible agony of someone whose mate is unfaithful – and he said a silent prayer of thanks for Jill.

He went over to Randy and put a paternal hand on his shoulder. 'I'm sorry, Randy. I'm sorry.'

Then he went to the phone.

Now, finally, he'd be able to spend a decent amount of time helping Jill.

He called the station and asked for Sievers and when Sievers came on he told him what Randy had just told him.

Sievers said he'd be right over.

Right over.

Rick had some trouble at the gates.

He said, 'I'd like to see Mrs Tappley.'

'May I ask what about?' asked the maid.

'Is Robert there?'

'I'm afraid not. This is his night off. May I have your name, please?'

He hesitated. 'Rick Corday.'

It was full night now, and the snow glistened in the moonlight, and sitting here shouting into a speaker concealed in the stone face of the fence made him self-conscious.

'Tell her I want to speak to her about her son.'

This time, it was the maid who hesitated. 'Her son? You mean Peter?'

'I mean Peter.'

The maid grew suddenly hostile. 'I think you'd better drive on before I call the police.'

'Look, you bitch, go and tell Mrs Tappley that I'm out here. Let her decide if I get in or not.'

She was thinking it over, that he could tell. But there was still the chance that she'd bypass Mrs Tappley completely and phone straight to the police.

Then what would he do?

'I'll tell you something. Mrs Tappley's going to be damned mad at you if you don't tell her I'm here, I can promise you that.'

His mother hired the kind of people she could easily bully. So now that he'd raised the specter of displeasing Mrs Tappley, the maid was more likely to help him out.

'I'll be right back,' she said.

Inside the car, the heater kept things warm. Too warm. That's why he kept the window rolled down. The cold night air felt good and clean. He remembered building a snowman not far from these gates. The snowman had a top hat and a merry red woolen scarf and a cane such as a vaudevillian would use. Doris hung a sign on him, WELCOME EVERYONE, a sign her mother soon ripped away. Did Doris want the riffraff of the entire Chicago area crowding around their gates?

'Yes?' The voice, even after all these years, had lost none of its imperious edge.

'Mrs Tappley, listen closely and maybe you'll recognize my voice.'

She listened. She said to the maid, 'Please leave now, *immediately*. Go upstairs and dust the library.'

After the door closed, Evelyn Daye Tappley said, 'When I find out who you are, I'm going to see to it that you spend the rest of your life behind bars.'

'Don't you really believe it's me, Mother?'

Obviously, the woman wanted to break off the connection but she was too snake-charmed to act so hastily.

'It's really me, Mother. Back from the dead.'

'This isn't funny at all.'

'In 1956 you took me to a resort in Wisconsin and I found a turtle on the shore and brought him home and named him Daniel Boone because of the TV show at that time.'

'You could've found that out.'

'How?'

'I—' She paused. Some of the imperiousness had gone from her voice. Evelyn Daye Tappley, believe it or not, had begun to sound downright vulnerable and sad. 'My son had a favorite model airplane in his room.'

'A blue Cessna. Just like the one my father owned.'

'And in the basement he had a favorite game he played—'

'Bean bags. I never got tired of throwing bean bags through the clown's face.'

A long pause. 'I don't want to be a foolish old woman. I could stand anything but being a foolish old woman – being tricked into some pathetic, impossible belief.' Another pause. He could feel her reluctantly beginning to believe him. 'My son died in the electric chair.'

'Arthur fixed things for me.'

'Arthur?'

'Arthur Halliwell. Your lawyer.'

'Fixed things? I don't understand.'

So he told her. Arthur had gone to a prominent physician, sworn him to silence, paid him a great deal of money, and then had the physician plot out the way that an execution could be faked – that the prisoner would appear to die and be taken from the stretcher in a hearse and then put through all the legalities of being prepared for burial. Two different drugs had to be used to simulate death, Peter had to be coached at length, the executioner, the Coroner and the funeral home director all had to be bribed, and then the sham burial performed. Then Peter went to Europe for an extended stay.

'You won't recognize me now, Mother.'

'Y-you're really my son?'

'I am, Mother.'

She began to weep.

'Please open the gates, Mother. Now.'

The gates opened at once.

He felt a kind of triumph driving up toward the mansion again, the snow so moon-kissed beautiful, the mullioned windows of the great house so gently illumined, as if by candlelight. While the estate had always been his prison, it had also been his retreat for many years. Not for him the concerns and cares that daily beleaguered the average citizen. Here he'd been able to devote himself to doing exactly what he wanted to do . . . as long as it met with Mother's approval. He felt almost sentimental about the place and even, in a strange melancholy way, about her – even though one of the reasons he'd forbidden Halliwell to tell her about her son, was so she could no longer shape and dominate his life.

He pulled up in front of the massive house, stopping the car and picking up his topcoat. He was still bloody, even more so since carrying Adam's head from the basement. But there was no time to clean up. There was only time to—

She stood silhouetted in the open doorway. In memory, she was always this huge and formidable woman, but in reality she was a small and fine-boned lady who had shrunk even more with old age.

He saw the shocked look on her face as he walked across the threshold and into the house. But it, too, had shrunk from its remembered size. What had been vast and unimaginable as a Disney castle was now a luxurious but not overwhelming house of large dimensions and priceless furnishings.

'You're not Peter.'

He stopped so she could get a better look at him. 'They did a good job.'

'They?'

'The doctors in Europe. Plastic surgery.'

'But your hair – it's white! And your features—'

He laughed. 'I've had a difficult life, Mother. Not many men survive their own execution.'

'But you can't be Peter. You can't be!'

'But I am.'

He had been carrying his overcoat rolled up. He sat it on the edge of a chair. He pulled up the cuff of his suitjacket and his shirt.

He showed her the pear-shaped brown birthmark on the lower inside of his forearm.

'Unlikely they could fake that.'

But she still stared at him open-mouthed, disbelieving. How could this possibly be—

'I need a drink of brandy,' she said, almost to herself.

Grabbing his topcoat, he followed her into the den. He'd forgotten how much he'd enjoyed this room. The authentic coat of arms on the wall above the fireplace. The Robert Louis Stevenson collected in leatherbound editions, all signed by the author a hundred or more years ago. The dry bar with its impressive array of cut-glass wine snifters.

Evelyn had brandy and so did Peter.

She sat behind her writing desk, sipping brandy, still staring at him.

'You had no right to deceive me that way.'

He sat in a deep leather armchair directly across from the

desk. His topcoat was on his lap. He smiled. 'You sound just the same as you always did when you chastised me, Mother.'

'I'm very serious. All these years I've mourned the loss of my second son—'

'And all these years I've been free of you, Mother.' He laughed. 'I wouldn't trade them.'

He heard the bitterness in his voice but felt no shame or regret. It was high time she heard what he really thought of her.

'All those years you choked the life out of me—'

She slammed her brandy glass on the desk. 'Is that why you came back, after all these years? To tell me how terrible a person I am?'

'It's one of the reasons. I also want to see my sister.'

Her anger was gone suddenly. She slumped in her chair. In the past few minutes, she'd aged another few years. 'You haven't even given me a hug.'

'I don't want to hug you. I don't want to touch you in any way.'

'I'm your mother.'

'Yes, you are. Yes, I could never forget that.'

'I can't believe you hate me this much.'

'I want to see Doris. Where is she?'

She got up from the desk unsteadily and started to walk around the desk. 'Peter, I want to hold you. You're my own flesh and blood.'

'Not anymore I'm not, Mother. I'm somebody else now. Even you didn't recognize me.'

She leaned over to slide her arms around him but he pushed her away so hard she fell back against her desk.

'I want to see my sister. That's why I came here.'

'Your sister,' she said. 'Your sister didn't raise you, I did. Your sister didn't take care of you when you were sick, or worry about you when you were playing outdoors, or hire bodyguards to watch you night and day.'

He stood up, clutching his topcoat to him. 'Where is she?'

'She's upstairs, if you really want to know. I forced a sedative on her because she was going to tell that bitch you married what Arthur and I did to her. Your sister! She's not any more grateful to me than you are!'

She started crying, a crazed old woman's tears. He saw now that she was broken and alone and he thought: '*It'll be a mercy, what I'm going to do. A mercy for me – and a mercy for her*.'

She looked up at him and held her arms out and said, 'Can't I just hold you for a little while? Do you hate me that much, Peter?'

He moved quickly then.

He didn't want to change his mind.

The topcoat fell away from his arm, leaving behind the bloody axe it had been covering.

When she saw it, she screamed, knowing instantly what he was going to do.

A maid appeared in the doorway suddenly – probably the same bitch who'd hassled him over the gate speaker – and so he reached calmly into the pocket of his suitjacket and pulled out his .45 and shot her in the middle of the forehead.

'Oh my God, Peter, you don't know what you're doing. You need to calm yourself down. You need to talk to – somebody. Get some help. You really do.' She was gibbering. 'I can see that now. I should've gotten you help years ago; years ago. I'm sorry I didn't, Peter. I really should have.'

All this time she was backing up, first toward the fireplace then toward the built-in bookcases.

But she couldn't find any place to hide from Peter and his axe.

There wasn't any place to hide.

'All those years you kept me a prisoner here, Mother,' he said over and over again, until the mere sound of his own voice sickened him. 'All those years.'

'Peter, you can go away again – back to Europe. I won't tell anybody. I won't. I promise.' She looked frantically to the door where the maid sprawled on the floor. 'We can bury her down by the river. Nobody'll ever find her. Not ever. You'll be free, Peter. You really will.'

The first time he swung the axe, she was quick enough to duck and so all he was able to catch was a brass candlestick lamp. The entire thing flew apart in large chunks. Evelyn screamed again and ran to the other side of the room. She kept looking for a way to get around him, to make it to the door.

But he was not going to let that happen.

The second time, his blade caught a mirror of beautiful glass and even more beautiful fretwork. The glass shattered in large dagger-like shards and fell to the floor.

This time she covered her ears and closed her eyes, as if she were trying to will him out of existence.

And that made it easy for him.

'Mother.'

He knew she heard him but wouldn't open her eyes.

'Mother.'

Eyes closed; ears covered.

'Mother.' Then: 'Goodbye, Mother.'

He got her neck clean. At the last moment, curious to see what he was doing, she opened her eyes and dropped her hands from her ears and—

—and that was when the axe came angling through the air right at her neck.

It was a clean cut. Her head wobbled leftward then rightward then rolled down her back to the floor.

Blood was geysering from the enormous wound just as the body was falling to the floor.

He walked around the body that was violently spasming to some rhythm only the dead could possibly appreciate . . . all the way around to where her head had rolled over in front of the fireplace.

The head was on its side. Clean as the cut had been, there was an awful lot of gore dripping now from the neck.

She was a mess.

He was happy.

He went to find his sister.

Fitzsimmons from the DA's office arrived shortly after the boys and girls from the crime lab.

He came over to Mitch. 'I suppose you expect me to tell you what a good job you did. Getting a confession and all.'

'First of all, I didn't "get" the confession. He told me willingly. Second of all, I wouldn't want a compliment from you. It would spoil your track record.'

'I suppose I was kind of a jerk this afternoon.'

'This afternoon? Fitzsimmons, you've been a jerk all your life. And someday somebody's going to wipe that smirk off your face.'

'I take it you'd like that privilege?'

But Mitch was sick of him. Fitzsimmons already had the aura of celebrity about him. Somehow he'd manage to take credit for solving the case – at the very least he'd take credit for pushing the police department so hard – and then he'd find a reason to hold seven or eight press conferences over the next week or so. Everybody knew by now that Fitzsimmons wanted to be Governor in the next two or three terms.

Mitch went in to see Sievers.

Just as he arrived, Randy Dupree went into the bathroom. Closed the door. You could hear him barfing.

Sievers shrugged. 'Second degree, maybe even manslaughter. He pushed her, she fell. There won't be much to contradict that from the lab boys.'

'Yeah, but Fitzsimmons'll be able to ride it all the way to the state capitol. Wonder how he'll like prosecuting somebody from his own class.'

Sievers laughed. 'I could promote one hell of a boxing match between you two.'

Mitch nodded. 'Yeah, I guess I do sound pretty childish.'

'Fitzsimmons is a spoiled, arrogant prick. But there are a lot worse people in this world, Mitch. There really are.'

Randy Dupree came back. He looked pale and shaken. He sat down and stared at the floor. Mitch felt sorry for him but he also felt sorry for the victim. She was already forgotten and depersonalized – 'victim' – no name, just 'victim.' She'd had a long life ahead of her.

'I guess I'll go see that girl I was telling you about,' Mitch said quietly to Sievers.

'That Cini?'

'Yeah.'

'Well, you can spend a little more time on that case now.'

'Yeah.'

'But not full-time, Mitch. We're up to our elbows in work so I'm going to need you.'

'I understand.'

He nodded to Sievers, glanced at Dupree again, and left.

The call came just when Jill was putting her eighth cookie to her mouth.

She was thankful for the phone call. It gave her an excuse to put the cookie down.

'Hello.'

'Jill.'

Didn't recognize the voice.

'Jill, this is Doris.'

'Doris? Are you all right? You sound kind of—'

'I just woke up. I was taking a nap.' Pause. 'I'm sorry but I won't be able to keep our lunch date tomorrow.'

Jill had been looking forward to seeing Doris again. She'd also suspected that Doris had been going to tell her something about Eric Brooks' murder.

'Did something happen, Doris?'

'No. But I was wondering if you could come out here tonight.'

'Out there? But—'

'Don't worry about Mother. She's gone out to one of her board meetings and she won't be back till late. They've just bought a new company in Argentina.'

'I'd feel uncomfortable, Doris. Going out there, I mean.'

'It'd just be us, Jill. Just the two of us.'

'Well—'

There was a pause. 'I need to talk to you about Eric Brooks, Jill.'

'Can't we talk now?'

'Not over the phone. I – well, you know how paranoid Mother is. I guess I got that from her. I never discuss anything personal over the phone.'

Unthinkable, really. Driving out there. Entering into the shadows and gloom of Evelyn's prison.

But Doris really did seem to know something about Eric Brooks' death.

She spoke without thinking: 'It'll probably take me a little while to get there.'

'There's no hurry.'

'You're sure everything's all right?'

'Everything's fine, Jill. I just woke up, that's all. Sort of muzzy, I guess.'

'I guess I'll come out, then.'

'I'm looking forward to it. See you in awhile.'

Jill hung up slowly. The receiver hadn't been cradled for more than ten seconds, when its ring shattered the silence.

'Hello?'

'Need some company?' her friend Kate said.

'God, I'd love to see you. But I've got to go somewhere.'

'Oh – where?'

'You're not going to believe this,' Jill said. 'Out to Evelyn's mansion.'

He had fed Doris coffee and nicotine pills and then dragged her into the shower and run cold water on her for ten minutes. He tried not to notice her naked body. He had always dreamed of sleeping with his sister someday but had never been able to bring himself to it.

He thought of Rick Corday, the other man Adam had accused him of being.

He wished he were Rick Corday now.

He put Doris on the phone and made her call Jill, whispering orders to her as she obviously looked for some way to warn Jill away from coming out here.

Every few moments, Doris would look up at the face of this total stranger and shake her head. How could this be her brother? Hadn't her brother died in the electric chair?

He took her downstairs to the den.

She screamed when she saw her mother's head on its side over by the fireplace.

He slapped her and made her help carry away the bodies of both her mother and the maid.

Then they sat down and waited for Jill to come.

It would be so sweet after all these years, he thought. So sweet to pay that bitch back for what she'd done to him. First Evelyn and now Jill. At last.

Chapter Sixty-Three

Winter wonderland. That's how Mitch saw all the snow now. Yesterday, before he'd found Cini, Mitch looked at the eight inches of white stuff as a curse, something Midwesterners had to endure because of impure thoughts or because of constantly (and secretly) abusing themselves.

But now, with the socialite case solved, and with Cini – he felt certain – agreeing to cooperate and clear Jill . . . well, it was a winter wonderland.

Whistling, he walked down the street to Cini's apartment house. Pretty co-eds all apple-cheeked and bundled-up passed him in twos and threes, their perfume lovely and wan and sexy on the night air. They probably figured he was on his way to pick up his date, he was so happy and all.

He winked at a snowman and bowed to a snow angel.

He picked up a tiny tricycle from the middle of a walk and carried it up on the porch; and he took a big chunk of icy snow and set it back in place on the snow fort from which it had fallen.

And finally—

He got a running start and slid down the snow-packed sidewalk the way he had when he was a kid.

Damn near falling on his ass.

And breaking a couple of bones.

But he kept right on whistling, right on passing pretty girls, right on dreaming of holding his own pretty girl later on tonight.

There was a Domino's Pizza truck parked in a NO PARKING zone several yards from Cini's.

Mitch went up the front steps just as the Domino's kid was coming down. The kid nodded. He was hurrying. This time of night was probably his optimum time of the evening.

The hallway was positively festive, several different kinds of music fighting each other for dominance, several different kinds of meals mixing into a not-unpleasant odor of heat and sweetness.

He went up to Cini's door and knocked.

Hard to tell if anybody was inside because of all the noise in the hallway.

He knocked again, louder.

The door opened behind him.

A kid with acne and a sarcastic grin was shrugging into a Navy P-coat as he pulled his apartment door closed behind him.

'You know Cini?'

'Sure,' the kid said.

'You see her this afternoon or this evening?'

'You her dad or something?'

'Or something,' Mitch said, showing him the badge.

'Wow,' the kid said. 'What's going on?'

'I'm just looking for Cini.'

'She in trouble?'

'Not at all.'

'I always thought of her as pretty uncool, actually,

way too uncool to get into any kind of trouble.'

'Uncool in what way?'

'Well, you know, she never comes over to my place when I ask her.'

Yeah, Mitch thought, that makes her uncool all right.

The kid pulled a dark stocking cap down over his ears. 'Cops. Cool.'

Mitch did some more useless knocking.

During a lull in the various symphonies, he pressed his ear to the door. Heard nothing.

He touched his hand to the doorknob.

Gave it a turn.

Unlocked.

He thought of how cautious she'd been when he'd appeared here earlier. Very suspicious. Two big imposing chains to keep him on the far side of the door.

Now it was unlocked.

Not like Cini at all.

He turned the knob. Pushed open the door.

The smell was high and sweet and he identified it immediately. Not something you mistake once its put into your personal computer.

Somebody had fouled themselves at the point of dying.

He was afraid he knew who.

From his jacket, he took a pair of gloves.

Had to be very, very careful now.

He found a wall switch and flipped it on.

She was sprawled across the couch, facing him, arms flung wide. Her head was tilted far back. Her throat had been cut. The front of her was a mess. Dried blood everywhere.

He checked out the apartment for anything else of note.

He wasn't whistling now.

Why had he ever been such a dumb sonofabitch as to whistle in the first place?

He went to the phone, even with gloves careful of touching the receiver, and called for the crime lab.

The gates had been left open.

The gates were never left open.

Jill's headlights shone on the darkness beyond the parted gates, the darkness that led up the winding drive to the even greater darkness of the great dark mansion.

She wanted to turn back. She wanted to be safe in the cozy warmth of her home.

But she had to talk to Doris, had to find out what Doris knew about Eric's murder.

She put the car in gear and started up the curving drive.

As the mansion came into view, she was struck, as she always had been, by how closed and obstinate it appeared, like an angry face. Only once, on Evelyn's fifty-fifth birthday, had the doors ever been flung wide and guests invited in. Japanese lanterns of green and gold and orange had lit the night like giant electric bugs. A small dance orchestra had played. Peter and Doris had acted like perfectly normal people living in a perfectly normal household. Even Evelyn had been kind that night, her smile, for once, seeming almost sincere.

But now the mansion was itself again; closed, hostile, impregnable as it towered against the racing clouds of the quarter moon.

She pulled up in front of the sweeping front steps and shut off lights and engine.

She took her flashlight from the seat, grasping it tightly. It could also be used as a weapon.

She got out of the car. The sub-zero weather attacked her like a hungry beast.

She crunched through the snow up to the steps, clipped on her flashlight, played it across the front of the vast house.

The massive arched front door stood open.

Once again her impulse was to flee, to run back to the safety of her own place.

She tried to convince herself that the girl Cini would tell the police the truth. But what if Cini refused? Then who would Jill turn to?

She needed to go into the house.

She angled the flashlight beam through the open door and walked up the steps.

When she reached the door, she paused, listening.

No lights anywhere inside. No sound.

Moonbeams highlighted the winding staircase that cut through the center of the house.

She walked inside, her footsteps loud and hollow on the parquet floor. She found a light switch, tried it. The electricity was off.

'Doris? Doris?'

But silence was the only response.

She walked deeper into the house, memories returning as she did so. The great stone fireplace; the short hall leading to the servants' small apartment; the den—

She stopped, looked in.

At one point, the den had been her only retreat. Peter and Evelyn both displeased that she'd started working again, Jill had shut herself up here, watching the highly improbable romantic adventures of Sandra Dee and Troy Donahue or Frankie Avalon and Annette Funicello on the late show. A prisoner is what she'd been; a prisoner.

The den had been changed, the style of furnishings more modern now. To double-check herself, she turned the lamp switch to On. No lights came. The power really was out. She lifted the receiver of the telephone to her ear. Somebody had also cut off the phone.

The smell came to her, then.

She knew instinctively what the odor was, but consciously wanted to deny it.

She stepped over to the desk and trained her light on the floor.

Puddles and splotches and puddings of dark fresh blood covered the Persian rug.

She raised the beam of the light and followed the trail of blood behind the desk, back of the couch, along the built-in bookcase and right up to the closet.

The brass doorknob of the closet was smeared with blood.

She played the light along the bottom of the closet door. A small river of dark blood was flowing from inside.

She had never heard her heart pound so loud.

Once more, her impulse was to flee.

But now she had to know – had to see for herself – what lay inside the closet.

She put her finger on the blood-sticky doorknob and started to turn.

'You really don't want to see what's in there. Take my word for it, Toots.'

Peter. He'd always called her Toots.

She froze there for a long and disbelieving moment. She couldn't mistake the voice of the man she'd loved for so many years – Peter. She was afraid to turn around and see who had spoken.

But how could it be Peter?

He was dead, executed in the electric chair.

This had to be some kind of memory trick. Being in the mansion again had made her think that the man was—

She turned slowly around.

The man with the white hair and the James Coburn face stood in the den's doorway, looking at her.

He walked out of the shadow and into the moonlight. He wore a light gray expensive suit. The jacket was soaked with dark spots. His hands were bright red. She didn't have to wonder what it was.

'You look a little shocked, Toots. Like you're surprised I'm alive or something.'

He kept coming, slowly, closer, closer.

'If you're worried about Doris, she's fine. I just sort of tied her up so she couldn't call anybody.' He gave her a little-boy mock frown. 'I guess she wasn't very happy about what I did to poor old Mom. I thought she might be grateful. You know, given what that bitch did to us all our lives.'

He was close enough to put his hand on the flashlight and try to tug it away from her.

She held on tight.

He slapped her.

Very fast and so hard that her eyes teared and for a moment everything went dark.

'One thing you'll have to get used to now, Jill. I'm not the nice old easy-going Peter I used to be. Now when I tell you to do something, I expect you to do it. You understand?'

She didn't say anything.

He slapped her again, so hard that he rocked her back on her heels.

'You understand?'

'Yes,' she whispered.

'Good. Very good.'

He turned her gently around so that she was facing the closet.

'You never did like my mother, did you?' He laughed.

'Now don't lie. We're too old to lie to each other anymore. You couldn't stand her and she couldn't stand you. Well – maybe you'll be a little more appreciative than Doris was.'

He opened the closet door and shone the light on Evelyn's head, which he had set on the shelf above the hangers.

The rest of her body, blood-soaked, was propped up against the base of the wall.

Jill tried very hard not to scream. Very hard.

Mitch decided to tell Jill in person about the girl named Cini. He wanted to be able to hold her, comfort her, after she'd heard such bad news.

Traffic was a bitch, many of the people over-cautious on the snow and ice, many others completely reckless.

In the course of his forty-five-minute drive, two drivers honked at him, one gave him the finger and one made a face at him. These kind of road conditions brought out the worst in people; they got uptight and took their uptightness out on everybody else.

He passed through a dour working-class neighborhood before seeing the relative glitz of Jill's neighborhood, everything refurbished and shiny clean and upwardly mobile.

He had to park a block away.

He smiled at the Christmas music coming from a CD store. Not Thanksgiving yet and already merchants were trying to put people in a buying mood. Mitch was glad that people honored Christ's birthday so irreverently. If Christ were alive today, that's just what He'd be doing, hawking CDs.

He knocked first and then, getting no response, rang Jill's bell.

He kept looking at the passersby. He liked people in their winter clothes. It made them more vulnerable, more human. In summer you saw all the hard human angles and the sweat, and picked up on all the smells. It was nice, every once in a while, to see people who resembled big dumb friendly bears.

He rang the bell twice more before thinking: She isn't home.

On the phone, in the bathroom, maybe working in the darkroom – by now Mitch had eliminated all the likely things that would have kept Jill from bounding down the stairs the way she did when she suspected it was him.

No bounding now.

Just a cold dark front stoop. And a cold dark front door.

And an unanswered bell.

He thought: Where the hell is she?

He wasn't sure why exactly, but his cop instinct told him that something was wrong here. She should be home. Because of the way the press traipsed after her these days, she almost never went out at night.

But now she was gone.

Again that quirky but urgent sense of something wrong. Where the hell was she, anyway?

'So you're taking me with you?'

'That's the plan, Toots.'

'How far?'

'I'm not sure yet. Probably Vegas or someplace like that. Then I catch a plane. Right now, the cops'll be looking for me around here. They'll be watching the airport.' He smiled over at her. 'Meanwhile, I'll be whizzing down the Interstate with a nice new hostage.'

When they'd left the mansion, he'd steered her to his car but when she saw the bloody head of Adam Morrow in the backseat, she went into momentary shock and would not get in. First Evelyn and the maid and now this man's head in the backseat . . .

Now they were in her car and she was driving. This time of night, this area of the city, traffic had thinned. Buried beneath snow, and tinted by mercury vapor lights, all the working-class houses looked small and shabby and sad.

Peter held a gun on her. He looked quite comfortable and quite content doing so. Every few minutes, she'd glance at his face, at the mask plastic surgery had put there, and think: No, this isn't Peter. This isn't possible. Peter died in the electric chair. But then he'd speak and she'd know it was Peter for sure.

He had given her directions a few minutes ago. She said, 'Where are we going?'

'A storage garage. I need to pick up a suitcase. Got my traveling money in there. A quarter million.'

'I won't be able to drive all night, if that's what you're thinking. I'm drained, Peter, and I'm trembling. My whole body is trembling.'

'Soon as we get my stuff at the garage, I'll buy us something to eat.'

She almost smiled. 'Something to eat? You think that's going to do it for me?'

'It'd better, Toots. Because you are going to be driving all night. Up here, hang a left.'

She turned left.

'Six, seven blocks straight down,' he said.

They passed a block that held three different taverns. On the sidewalk of the second one, an old man was throwing up, his vomit a lurid green from the tint of the neon sign in the window.

Peter said, 'I'll bet he'd go out with you.'

That was one of Peter's old gags. He'd see somebody notably ugly and say, 'Bet he'd go out with you.'

She said, 'Don't you feel anything for what you just did?'

'You mean killing my mother?'

'Yes.'

'That's kind of funny, coming from you.' He genuinely laughed. 'I mean, all those years when you wanted to kill her yourself.'

'No, I didn't. I just wanted to leave.'

'Well, bitch, that's just what you did, didn't you?'

The cold anger. The old Peter. She knew better than to push him past this point.

Even the streetlights in this neighborhood were dim and dirty. Tiny ethnic houses cowered against the night like children trying to fend off a blow. The cars parked along the curbs were ancient rusty beasts.

'You're going to kill me, aren't you?' she said after a time.

'I have to admit the thought *has* crossed my mind.'

'Will you make it fast? And do it with a gun?'

The smile. 'Still making demands, eh, Jill?'

'Just don't— The axe. You know.'

'Not to worry, Toots. I left the axe lying at the front of the family manse. And anyway, you don't have to worry about dying until we hit Vegas. Up here, pull in.'

She pulled in.

At the far end of the alley she could see cyclone fencing and powerful thief lights. The storage facility.

She drove toward the light.

She was still trembling badly and trying hard not to.

Mitch called the station and asked the dispatcher to put

Jill's license number out. If anybody spotted it, they should call in, but not stop the car. He didn't want to embarrass Jill if she'd just gone for a ride or something.

Chapter Sixty-Four

It didn't take Peter long to empty out the little garage and pile everything in the trunk of Jill's car. He locked up behind him, making sure he'd left no traces of himself behind. All the time, he kept glancing over his shoulder to see what Jill was up to. He had the car keys in his pocket. She wasn't going anywhere.

He was starting back to the car when they came seemingly out of nowhere, the same two punks he'd run into before, one of whom he'd beaten up.

The black one put a gun, and a damned big one, to Peter's back and said, 'Slide all the way over, man. I'm doin' the drivin' tonight.'

The white boy was just now opening the back door and getting in.

Peter got in. He looked at Jill who started to say something but didn't.

In the backseat, the white kid said, 'I got a gun, too, man. So don't try anything, you dig?'

This was just crazy as hell, Jill thought.

Just crazy as hell.

Mitch sat in his car, punching numbers on his cellular phone. He called Jill's friend Kate. She didn't sound unduly happy about hearing from him, not after the way he'd dumped Jill that time.

'So you haven't talked to her tonight?'

'You really sound upset, Mitch. Is something wrong? Is there something you're not telling me?'

'No. Everything's fine.'

'It doesn't sound fine, Mitch.'

'I'll talk to you later – and thanks.'

They took Peter Tappley down a couple of blocks to a garage in which he could hear growling and barking.

Peter could hear the sounds from the garage even above the cold night winds soughing in the bare trees. Jill, sensing something terrible about to happen, found herself defending Peter.

'He's not a well man. He didn't mean to hurt anybody.'

'Hey, bitch, I don't remember askin' you to talk, you dig?' the black kid said.

They parked and dragged Peter out of the car. The white one hit Peter first, hard enough to drive him to his knees. Then the black one kicked him.

Jill screamed.

The white one reached in the car, grabbed her by the hair and pulled her out into the snow. 'Now I'm gonna make you watch, bitch.' He pushed her up to the side of the garage.

A patrol car spotted a car matching the make, year and color Mitch had described, eighteen minutes after he put out the call. The patrol car pulled closer to check out the license plate.

This was the one they were looking for, all right.

* * *

The garage reeked of old, damp newspapers, garbage long left to mold, and wood reeking with decades of rain and rot.

The middle of the floor was empty. Jill wondered where the growling and barking had come from. She'd assumed in here. Now she knew that there was some kind of kennel nearby.

'You gonna travel, man?' the white punk said.

'Travel?'

'Yeah, you know, goin' somewhere.'

'Yeah, I guess so.'

'And you're tryin' to tell us,' the white one said, 'that the only money you got is what we found in your billfold.'

'I'm sorry, boys, that's all I've got.'

The black one kicked him again.

Peter knew he had at least one rib broken now.

'This here's our special place, man,' the white one said. 'Guys like you try'n hold out on us, we start bringin' the dogs in. One at a time.'

Peter thought of the quarter million he had stashed in the false bottom of his suitcase.

No way was he going to tell them about that.

No way.

They put on little shows for the neighborhood kids, they explained.

The little kids loved it.

They sure did.

Peter, they said, he was going to be tonight's entertainment.

They pitched him face down on the floor and then the white kid went and got the first dog.

Mitch got the call from dispatch just as he decided to go

back to Jill's place and check it over. Maybe she was inside, injured or—

'We located the car you were looking for.' The dispatcher then gave Jill's license-plate number and the location where the car had been seen.

Mitch broke several traffic laws getting there.

What the hell was she doing in that kind of neighborhood, anyway?

Jill stood at the front of the garage and watched as the dog – some variant on a Doberman – stalked Peter, backing him up against the walls, teasing him, tripping him, sniping and growling but not yet biting.

The punks loved it. They giggled a lot.

This was better than any horror show on HBO.

And every once in a while, one of them would say, as the dog seemed about to spring, 'Hey, man, you wanna tell us where you're keepin' the rest of your money?'

'Please,' Jill said. 'Please call the dog off.'

But they were losing their patience and their humor. They screamed at Peter, 'Where's your money, man?'

The dog jumped then, slamming Peter into the wall and then knocking him to the ground. He was all hunger and hatred, the dog, ripping, rending Peter in long bloody slashes.

'It's in his suitcase somewhere!' Jill screamed. 'Now pull the dog off!'

The black one went to get the suitcase. The white one stood with Jill, smiling. 'Too late, bitch. I couldn't pull him off now if I wanted to.'

'Peter! Peter!' she shouted.

But by now little human was left of his face – the flesh stripped away, one of his eyeballs torn free of its socket. The dog was now concentrating on Peter's throat. Peter used fingers, forearms, elbows to keep the animal's teeth from finding his Adam's apple. He rolled left, he rolled right, he kept his chin to his chest as much as possible, but in the end the dog was too fast and too strong.

He found Peter's throat and began the process of tearing it from his neck.

Instinctively, Jill started to lunge for the animal – she couldn't just watch Peter die – but as she took a step forward, a pistol shot could be heard even above the dog's slavering frenzy. At first the dog showed no effects from the shot, but then it abruptly stopped and collapsed onto Peter.

Mitch came in, the black kid in handcuffs trailing behind.

Mitch took care of the white one next, and let Jill go to Peter Tappley.

He wore a mask of blood, only one blue eye visible now, a flayed imitation of a man.

She knelt next to him, seeing both the man and monster in the bloody and now disfigured face. She tried to think of him at his best – when they'd first met so many years ago, when she'd been naïve and desperate for love – just as he'd been then. But then he'd become . . . something else.

She took his trembling hand – his entire body was shaking – and listened as he cried, 'Mother! Mother!' through the blood that was filling his mouth.

And then he was silent.

And still.

And after a time, there in the raw blood-spattered garage, the winter winds sounding like the ghosts of forlorn old men, Peter Tappley died.

Chapter Sixty-Five

After the gawkers arrived to see what had happened, eager for the sight of blood, and then the squad cars came and the ambulance and then the crime lab van, Jill went over and sat in Mitch's car.

She wanted to be happy. On their way over to the garage, Peter had explained how Evelyn had set up Eric's murder so that Jill would be blamed. Doris learned of the plot afterward and would testify about it to the police.

Jill was free again.

And should right now be feeling very good about things.

Mitch got in the car, smelling of the cold night against the warm air of the heater.

'Hey,' he said. 'You're crying.'

'Yes, I guess I am.'

'You going to get mad if I ask you why?'

She smiled. 'Uh-huh.'

'OK. How come you're crying?'

She started to say something and then realized there was nothing she could say – nothing at all.

He took her to him, held her with great gentle strength. A few gawkers, temporarily distracted from the juicy spectacle of a man ripped apart by a dog, watched them.

'How about if I say I love you?' he said. 'Would that make you feel any better?'

She laughed. 'Well, you could try, I guess.'

'I love you. There, did that work?'

'Well, it certainly didn't hurt anyway.'

'Then I'll do it every five minutes until we start to see some definite improvement.' He set his wristwatch. 'Got one of those teeny-tiny alarms. Every five minutes it'll remind me to tell you I love you.'

'Could we leave now?' She wanted to respond to his playfulness – she knew how hard he was working to make her feel better – but she couldn't.

'I was thinking the same thing. About leaving.'

The alley was so crowded with cars and sightseers that it took awhile to get to the street.

They rode a long time in silence.

Jill stared out the window at the night but really didn't say anything.

'How you doing?' he said.

'Pretty good.'

'You look beautiful.'

She smiled. 'Yeah, I'll bet.'

Then his alarm went off.

'Well, guess what time it is?'

'Why don't I say it this time?' She was getting in the spirit of his little game and it felt good. 'We'll alternate. Every other five minutes, I'll tell you that I love *you*.'

'Hey, that's not a bad idea.'

'All right,' she said. 'I love you.'

When they reached a red stoplight, she leaned over and gave him a long and passionate kiss.

'Hey,' he said, 'this is just like being a teenager again.'

Later that night, in bed, they both decided they were

too tired to do anything so they tried to sleep but couldn't. Then they decided they might as well do something because there wasn't anything else to do anyway.

So they did something and they had a great time doing it and then they finally got to sleep there in the dawning light, wrapped round each other in true, tender and groggy love.

There was a Christmas Eve party at Jill's a month later. Kate was there, and Mitch of course, and Marcy (having recuperated from the terrible cold she'd caught from being tied up naked in the basement all those hours) and Doris, too, looking drawn and pale but seeming determined to have a good time for herself. She said her plans were to sell the mansion and move to the family ranch in Montana.

They mentioned only briefly the events of the past few weeks – the suicide of Arthur K. Halliwell, for instance, and the indictment of the three prominent citizens who had helped Peter fake his execution.

They exchanged gifts, and Marcy got pleasantly potted on the rhubarb wine she was drinking (Kate had picked her up because they lived in the same neighborhood) and Doris sang some medieval Christmas carols, Jill not having exaggerated how well Doris sang and played the guitar.

And after it was all over, after the guests were gone, after Mitch had helped with the dishes and Jill helped Mitch get the cherry cobbler stain out of his best white shirt . . . after that, they went to bed and held each other fast, feeling a dizzying assortment of things – love and lust and friendship and admiration among them.

And then Jill said, 'Just a minute.'

And went out and put on her very favorite record, her

Perry Como Christmas Album record, the one she'd loved since she was six years old.

And with Christmas music filling the entire house, they made long and wonderful love.